THE ASTONISHING WORLDS OF PIERS ANTHONY

THE [...]

His newest adventures—i[...] worlds face love and dang[...]

"Fresh, imaginative!" —**Publishers Weekly**

THE APPRENTICE ADEPT SERIES

The incredible story of one world inhabited by two spheres—the technology of Proton and the magic of Phaze.

"It's fun-and-games time again with the Gamemaster himself, Piers Anthony!" —**Rave Reviews**

BIO OF AN OGRE

Piers Anthony's enthralling life story.

"Incredibly honest . . . entertaining . . . fascinating!" —**OtherRealms**

MERCYCLE

The ingredients include one boy, one underwater bicycle, and a mermaid or two—instant adventure, just add water!

"Piers Anthony [is] always entertaining!" —**Rave Reviews**

THE BOOKS OF TAROT

On the planet Tarot, dreams can come true—as well as nightmares.

"Anthony is as facile as he is prolific." —**Cincinnati Post**

**Turn to the back of this book
for a special excerpt from Piers Anthony's
exciting new novel, KILLOBYTE . . .
available from G. P. Putnam's Sons.**

HARD SELL

PIERS ANTHONY

ACE BOOKS, NEW YORK

Portions of this book originally appeared
in slightly different form in the following magazines:
Chapter 1 (originally titled "Hard Sell") in *If* magazine, August 1972
Chapter 2 (originally titled "Black Baby") in *If* magazine, September 1972
Chapter 3 (originally titled "Hurdle") in *If* magazine, December 1972
Chapter 5 (originally titled "Life") in *Twilight Zone* magazine, December 1987

This Ace Book contains the complete text of the original hardcover edition. It has been completely reset in a typeface designed for easy reading, and was printed from new film.

HARD SELL

An Ace Book / published by arrangement with
the author

PRINTING HISTORY
Tafford Publishing edition published 1990
Ace edition / May 1993

All rights reserved.
Copyright © 1990 by Piers Anthony.
Material excerpted from *Killobyte* by Piers Anthony
copyright © 1993 by Piers Anthony.
Cover art by Romas.
This book may not be reproduced in whole or in part, by
mimeograph or any other means, without permission.
For information address:
The Berkley Publishing Group,
200 Madison Avenue, New York, New York 10016.

ISBN: 0-441-31748-0

Ace Books are published by The Berkley Publishing Group,
200 Madison Avenue, New York, NY 10016.
The name "ACE" and the "A" logo
are trademarks belonging to Charter Communications, Inc.

PRINTED IN THE UNITED STATES OF AMERICA

10 9 8 7 6 5 4 3 2 1

CHAPTER

—◀1▶—

"Interplanetary call for Mr. Fisk Centers," the cute operator said.

Fisk almost dropped his sandwich. "There must be some mistake! I don't know anybody offplanet!"

The girl looked at him with polite annoyance, as though nobody should be startled by such an event. "Are you Mr. Fisk Centers?"

"Yes, of course," he said. "But—"

Her face sifted out, smiling professionally. The screen bleeped, went blank, and finally produced a man. He had handsome gray hair and wore the traditional Mars-resident uniform: a cross between a spacesuit and a tuxedo. He was seated behind a large plastifoam desk, and a tremendous color map of classical Mars covered the wall beyond.

"Welcome to Mars, Mr. Centers!" the man said, putting on a contagious grin. "I am Bondman, of

Mars Ltd." Somehow he managed to pronounce "Ltd." the way it looked.

Fisk was fifty and had been around, but he had never been treated to an interplanetary call before. It wasn't just the expense, though he knew that was extraordinary. He just happened to be one of the several billion who had never had occasion to deal offplanet. Probably Mars Ltd. was economizing by using OVTS—Open Volume Telephone Service— but it was still impressive. "Are you sure—?"

"Now, Mr. Centers, let's not let modesty interfere with business," Bondman said, frowning briefly. "You're far too sensible a man for that. That's why you're one of the privileged few to be selected as eligible for this project."

"Project? I don't—"

The Marsman's brow wrinkled elegantly. "Naturally it isn't available to the common run. Mars is too fine a planet to ruin by indiscriminate development, don't you agree?"

Fisk found himself nodding to the persuasive tone before the meaning registered. "Development? I thought Mars was uninhabitable! Not enough water, air—"

"Most astute, Mr. Centers," Bondman said, bathing him with a glance of honest admiration. "Indeed there is *not* enough water or air. Not for every person who might want to settle. Selectivity is the key—the vital key—for what can be a very good life indeed. Mars, you see, has space—but what is space without air?"

"Right. There's no good life in a spacesuit. I—"

"Of course not, Mr. Centers. The ignorant person believes that man must live on Mars in a cumbersome suit, and so he has a low regard for Mars realty. How fortunate that you and I know better!" And before Fisk could protest, he continued: "You and I know that the new static domes conserve air, water and heat, utilizing the greenhouse effect to make an otherwise barren land burst into splendor! Within that invisible protective hemisphere it is completely Earthlike! Not Earth as it is today, but as it was a century ago. Think of it, Mr. Centers—pure clean air, gentle sunshine, fresh running water! Horses and carriages—automobiles, guns, hallucinogenic drugs, and similar evils prohibited! A haven for retirement in absolute security and comfort!"

Something was bothering Fisk, but the smooth sales patter distracted him and compelled his half-reluctant attention. "But they don't have such domes on Mars! That technique was developed only a few months ago, and is still in the testing stage."

"Brilliant, Mr. Centers!" Bondman exclaimed sincerely. "You certainly keep abreast of the times! Of *course* there are no domes on Mars *now*, as you so astutely point out. Why, it will be years before they are set up—perhaps even as long as a decade! This is what makes it such a superlative investment *now*, before the news gets out. Provided we restrict it to intelligent men such as yourself. Now I'm sure—"

"Investment? Now hold on!" Fisk protested. "I'm not in the market for investment. I'm comfortably set up right now, and—"

"I quite understand. Naturally you're not

interested in a *mediocre* investment, Mr. Centers,"
Bondman said, frowning skillfully. "Do you think
I would insult your intelligence by wasting your
time? No, you have the discernment to identify
the superior value when you encounter it, unlike
the common—"

"*What* investment?" Fisk demanded, annoyed
by the too-heavy flattery. The intrigue of the
interplanetary call was wearing thin, and the
objection he couldn't quite formulate still nagged—
and he wanted to finish his sandwich before it got
stale.

The man leaned forward to whisper
confidentially. "*Marsland!*" he breathed, as
though it were the secret of the ages. His
voice was so charged with excitement and rapture
that Fisk had to struggle to maintain his emotional
equilibrium. Could there be something in it?

After a pregnant pause, Bondman resumed. "I
see you understand. I was sure you would! You
comprehend the phenomenal potential in Marsland
realty, the incredible opportunity—"

"I *don't* comprehend it!" Fisk snapped, gesturing
with his neglected sandwich. "I have no use for
land on Mars, and I'd consider it an extremely
risky investment. That dome technique is still in
the prototype stage; it may not even work on Mars!
So if that's what you're—"

"Yes, of *course* you want to see the brochure,"
the salesman agreed irrelevantly. "And you shall
have it, Mr. Centers! I will put it in the slot for you
immediately, first class. I'm sure you will examine
it most—"

Suddenly, facilitated by some devious mental process, Fisk's nagging question came into focus. "You aren't on Mars!" he cried angrily. "Mars orbit is fifty million miles outside Earth's even when Mars is closest, it should take a good ten minutes to get an answer by phone."

"Congratulations," Bondman cried jubilantly. "You have just qualified for our exclusive genius-intellect bonus certificate! Of *course* I'm not calling from that Mars you see in the sky! I'm here at the Mars Ltd. promotion office. Mr. Centers, I'm so glad you were sharp enough to solve our little riddle within the time limit! You're the very kind of investor we prefer! I'll insert the certificate right now! And I'll be seeing you again soon. Bye-bye!"

And while Fisk was marveling at the peculiarly childish "bye-bye," the image faded.

He lifted his sandwich, a fine torula-steak on soyrye with enriched onion sauce, but found he was no longer hungry. He was sure this was a sales gimmick for something worthless, but Bondman's contagious excitement had gotten to him. Maybe there *was* a good investment on Mars!

Well, no harm in looking at the literature. He certainly didn't have to buy!

He didn't have long to wait, either. His mail receiver was already chiming with an arrival.

He picked up the bulky printing and spread it out. It was a first-class presentation, all right, with color photographs and glossy surfacing that must have cost dearly to transmit. If he hadn't been present when it arrived, he would have suspected a physical delivery rather than the normal mailfax.

Mars Ltd. must have oiled the right palms in the post office.

Well, he had to admit it: he was intrigued. He probably would not buy, but he would enjoy looking.

First there was the bonus certificate, entitling him to a twenty percent reduction. Fair enough—but hardly sufficient to induce him to buy without knowing the actual price. Then a spread on Mars: its discovery in prehistoric times, its variable distance from Earth (35-235 million miles), its long year (687 days) (Earth days or Mars days, he wondered . . . or were they the same?), low surface gravity (one third of Earth's), pretty moons (ten mile diameter Phobos, six mile Deimos), scenic craters, legendary canals—all familiar material, but calculated to whet the appetite for investment and retirement.

Then down to pay dirt: the proposed colony, "Elysium Acres," located on a map dramatically colored and named. An electrostatic dome a hundred miles in diameter, almost fifty miles high, enclosing a greenhouse atmosphere at Earth-normal pressure and temperature. Suitable for homesites, with carefully laid out horse trails and a delightful crater lake. Guaranteed weather, pollutant-free.

Fisk was middle aged and cynical, but this gripped him. Earth was such a sweatbox now. He hated having to take weekly shots to protect his system against environmental contamination, and the constantly increasing restrictions invoked in the name of the growing pressure on worldly resources made him rage at times like an imprisoned tiger. (What other kind of tiger *was* there, today?) Perhaps if he had married, found someone to share his—but that was another entire dimension of frustration, hardly relevant now.

This Marsdome pitch catered to these very frustrations, he realized. There must be millions like himself: well enough to do, intelligent, and sick of uselessness. What a beacon it was: an escape to an unspoiled planet . . . in comfort!

But of course he was old enough to control his foolish fancies. He knew intellectually that no such development existed on Mars—and probably never would exist. The sheer expense would be prohibitive! All that technology, all that shipment from Earth . . . why, passenger fare for one person one way would amount to two hundred thousand dollars or more, assuming emigration could even be arranged. And for him it was completely out of the question.

Yet he couldn't help studying it. Elysium Acres— such suggestion of bliss! Could it possibly be true— by the time he turned sixty? Why not, if they were able to finance it?

There was the real rub. Money. How much to establish the dome, stock it with good atmosphere, import vegetation, calculate and maintain a closed-system ecological balance, construct access highways, lakes, houses, service facilities? There would have to be hospitals,

libraries, administrative buildings, emergency
staffs—all the accoutrements of civilization, in
short. Billions of dollars to maintain; perhaps
trillions to construct. Naturally the brochure did
not provide the price list.

But if it *were* affordable, and if it *were* possible
for him to go—what a temptation!

He punched his personal info number for his
net worth, just checking. The totals flashed on
the screen after he had provided his identification
code: liquid assets just over five hundred thousand
dollars sterling; investments at current quotations
just under two million; miscellaneous properties
and options six to eight hundred thousand, pending
urgency of sale. Grand total: a generous three
million.

Enough, with proper management, to tide him
through the twenty-five years until his retirement
annuities matured. He was hardly fool enough to
jeopardize any of it by investing in pie-on-Mars!
But it had been fun dreaming.

The dream lingered next morning, a welcome
guest staying beyond courteous hours. Fisk show-
ered in the sonic booth, depilitated, and dressed.
As he arranged and set his graying locks
he wondered irrelevantly whether the salesman
Bondman used the same brand of hair tint he
did. He studied his face in the mirror, picturing
himself as a hard-sell agent, lifting his brow artfully to augment a pregnant pause. Yes, he did
look the part; perhaps he would be good at
it.

But then, subjectively, he saw the signs of what he knew was there: the circulatory malady that bound him to Earth for life. His quarterly medication kept it under control—but a trip to Mars, with the necessary accelerations and drugstates, was out of the question. That was why Mars would never be more than a dream for Fisk Centers, no matter how conducive the sales pitch. He would always be a portly, subdued Earthman.

So it was time to end it. He filed the Mars Ltd. literature in the recycle bin and watched it disintegrate. Then he punched breakfast. He felt lonely.

The phone lighted. "Yes?" he said automatically.

"Interplanetary call for Mr. Fisk Centers," the cute operator said. She had changed her hairdo, but it was the same one who had placed the call yesterday.

"Come off it, girl!" he snapped, aware that there was nothing more useless than taking out a personal peeve on an impersonal employee. "It is *not* interplanetary!"

Bondman of Mars phased into view. "Of *course* it is, Mr. Centers," he said genially. "The Mars Ltd. office is legally Mars soil, you know. An enclave. We have to undergo quarantine before reporting for work, ha-ha! Now I trust you have studied our brochure—"

"Yes. I'm not buying."

Bondman looked hurt. "But you haven't even heard our price, Mr. Centers. I know a man as fair-minded as you—"

"I'll never go to Mars."

"Remember, you get a special bonus price, because of your intelligence and judgment. I'm sure you'll recognize—"

"I have a circulatory disorder. Inoperable. Sorry."

Bondman laughed with a finely crafted lack of affectation. "You don't have to go to Mars, Mr. Centers! We're talking about *investment!*"

"I told you I wasn't looking for—"

"You've studied the plans for Elysium Acres? The phenomenal hundred mile dome, the luxurious facilities, the nineteenth century atmosphere— literally!—the scenic lots? Of *course* you have! Mr. Centers, you know the value of things. What do you figure it will cost? I mean the entire setup on Mars, gross?"

"Ten trillion dollars," Fisk said, believing it. "Plus upkeep of billions per year."

"Would you believe *thirty* trillion? But you're remarkably close, Mr. Centers! You certainly comprehend investment! You merely underestimated the importance of this development to us—and to the world. We're putting everything into it, Mr. Centers! Another developer might do it for ten trillion, but we put quality first! Thirty trillion! But we know we'll make a profit in the end—and of *course* we have to consider profit, Mr. Centers! We're businessmen, like you!—because believe me, sir, there is a demand! Earth is crowded, and in ten years Earth will be a veritable nightmare! Elysium Acres will be an incredible bargain *at any price!*" Bondman held up a hand to forestall Fisk's possible objection. "Now I'm not forgetting that you can't go, Mr.

Centers. I'm merely pointing out what an attractive
investment this is going to be. Some will have the
incalculable privilege of retiring in Elysium Acres;
others will merely make a fortune from it." And here
he dropped to his supercharged confidential tone. "I
hope to do both!" He paused just long enough for
that affirmation of faith to penetrate, but not long
enough for Fisk to generate an interjection. "Now
we're subdividing E.A. into lots of one hundred feet
square, give or take a foot, ha-ha! Enough for a
comfortable cottage and garden. Twenty million
of them—yes, that's correct, Mr. Centers! That
dome is a hundred miles across, and there'll be
eight thousand square miles inside, and two and
a half thousand lots per mile—but I don't need to
do elementary mathematics for you, Mr. Centers.
Twenty million lots for thirty trillion dollars.
That comes to one million five hundred thousand
dollars per lot. A bit high for Earth, considering
they're undeveloped—*but this is Mars!* Those lots
are priceless, Mr. Centers, priceless—yet they will
be put on the market at a price any successful man
can afford." He held up his hand again, though
Fisk had made no motion to interrupt. "But Mars
Ltd. needs operating capital, Mr. Centers, and we
need it *now*. So we are offering, for a limited time
only, a very, *very* special investment opportunity.
You can buy these lots as investment real estate
today for a tiny fraction of their actual value. So
although you may never have the privilege of going
to Mars yourself—and please accept my heartfelt
condolences, Mr. Centers, for I know how much
you would have liked to retire in Elysium Acres—

you can still benefit while advancing a noble cause through your investment."

Fisk was more impressed by the emotive delivery than by the content. Salesmanship really was an art! "How much?"

"Mr. Centers, we are offering these lots at—now listen carefully, because this is hard to believe— at *one quarter price!* Three hundred and sev-en-ty thou-sand dollars for a property worth one mil-lion five hun-dred thou-sand dollars." Bondman spaced out the syllables to make the figures absolutely clear and emphatic.

"That's my bonus for nabbing your 'interplanetary call' gimmick?"

Bondman rolled his eyes expressively but did not take exception to the description. "Of *course* not, Mr. Centers! That's the one-time special-offer bargain price. For you alone we provide the *bonus* price." Here he paused to make that dramatic conspiratorial lowering of voice. "Don't tell anyone else, because if word got out that *anyone* beat the bargain price there would be resentment. Even. . . ." and a great rippling shrug bespeaking consequences so vast that it would be foolhardy to invoke them by name.

But he did not speak that mind-shattering figure. Instead he fed it into his mailfax. The full contract emerged from Fisk's slot. He rifled through it while Bondman waited expectantly, anticipating the client's amazed pleasure.

Three hundred thousand dollars. In other words, the straight twenty percent reduction the certificate had promised.

It did seem like a good buy. Still, Fisk had some experience in such matters. He skimmed through until he found the "small print"—actually regular type buried in an otherwise innocuous paragraph.

Ownership remained with Mars Ltd. until the stipulated amount had been paid in full. In the event of default, the property reverted to Mars Ltd. without refund. The risk of capital was all with the purchaser, unless he bought outright for cash. Very interesting.

"Now you see the bargain we are offering you, Mr. Centers," Bondman said gravely. "Frankly you are one of the very last to receive the three-hundred seventy-thousand figure, let alone the bonus deal. Demand has been even greater than we anticipated, with many people buying multiple lots. Blocks of four, or even more. There will have to be a price increase. After all, Mars Ltd. needs capital; it is ridiculous for us to sell so low when our own clients are turning around and selling their lots for more! Why only last week a man sold five for two million flat—and he'd only bought them last month! He made a one hundred and twenty thousand profit on a three-week investment—and that's only the one we know about. Others—" here his shoulders rose in another eloquent shrug. "Where, Mr. Centers, is the limit?"

"Why didn't the second buyer come to you first?" Fisk inquired. Actually the described profit was only about six percent, and normal fluctuation of the market could readily account for it. But it did seem to augur well for Mars Ltd.'s growth prospects.

"Apparently he didn't realize our price was as low as it was," Bondman said sadly. "He thought he had information. The biggest sucker is the one who thinks he knows it all, right, Mr. Centers? If he had only checked with us . . . but of course our price *won't* be lower, after this week. So he has a good investment anyway—though not as good as it could have been. You understand?"

Yes. Fisk was certainly interested now. Buy for three hundred, sell for four . . . but he knew better than to appear eager. "I might take a lot or two," he said. "But it's a lot of money. I'd have to liquidate my other investments, and that would take time."

"I understand perfectly," Bondman agreed instantly. "I had to do the same when I invested in my own first Mars lot. It was well worth it, of course. Fortunately we have a time payment plan exactly suited to your situation. Ten-year term, so that it will be paid up when Elysium Acres opens and the real gold rush begins. Irrevocable six percent interest. Just three thousand two hundred and fifty dollars a month covers all, Mr. Centers—we absorb the cover charge! How does that suit you?"

Fisk checked the figures quickly in his head. They were fair: six percent on a decreasing principal. No funny business there, no usury. And he would be able to liquidate his investments profitably within a year and pay off the rest, saving the interest. Some contracts had penalty clauses for early payment, but this one didn't, fortunately. "Sounds good," he admitted.

"Good? *Good?*" Bondman demanded rhetorically. "Mr. Centers, how would you like to buy a cyclotron

at the sheet metal price? *That's* how good it is!
But that isn't all! What we are talking about
is three-two-fifty a month, one hundred dollars
a day to control a genuine Marsland property
now selling for—" here he broke off, nodding
significantly toward the contract with the secret
figure. "And with values quadrupling—or more!—
in the period of agreement! Mr. Centers, you
are actually investing a paltry three-two-fifty a
month—for a return of at least *one million five
hundred thousand* in a bare decade!"

Fisk knew. Three hundred thousand dollars, plus
ninety thousand dollars accumulated interest for
the ten year span. For one-million-five. A net profit
of one million eleven hundred thousand, or over
one hundred and ten thousand per year—*per lot*.
With just three lots he could triple his fortune!
"Still, it's a sizable amount. Are you sure it's safe?
I mean, suppose something happens and the dome
doesn't get built. The lots would become almost
worthless."

"Mr. Centers, it certainly is a pleasure to do
business with you!" Bondman exclaimed. "You don't
miss a trick! Of *course* there is a nominal element
of risk! Life itself is the biggest risk of all! But by
buying on time you can eliminate even that one-
in-a-thousand chance. Just consider: if something
should happen to abort Elysium Acres tomorrow—
and I assure you nothing short of World War Four
could squelch our plans—and then where would you
be anyway, ha-ha!—if it ended tomorrow, and you
had bought today and paid your deposit premium—
what would you have lost? *Three thousand two*

hundred and fifty dollars! Why Mr. Centers—you must blow more than that on one good suit!"

Extremely sharp observation. Fisk *had* paid more than that for his dress suit.

Bondman followed up his advantage, knowing he had scored. "Considering the one million five hundred thousand value—just what do you risk? ONE SUIT!"

"But suppose something happens in two years? Or nine? I can't afford to lose a suit every month!"

"Mr. Centers," Bondman said sternly. "I'm a busy man and this call is expensive. Don't waste my time and yours with inconsequentials! If you don't trust the stability of a fine new developer like Mars Ltd., *don't invest.* Or if you believe it will fail in two years, *sell in one year.* Your property will have increased in value at least ten percent—in fact, considering the coming price rise, twenty percent may be a more accurate estimate. But just to keep it simple, let's call it ten percent. That's between thirty and forty thousand dollars, right? And how much are you paying per year?"

"Between thirty and forty thousand dollars," Fisk said with a smile.

"So if you sell then, your return on your actual investment will be just about one hundred percent. This is leverage, Mr. Centers: taking a small amount of money to control a large amount of money. And the profit is yours even if, as you say, Mars Ltd. fails in two years. Or nine. Ha-ha." He leaned forward again, speaking intensely. "The dome may fail, Mr. Centers, but *you* won't!"

Fisk laughed. "Very well, Mr. Bondman. You've sold me. Just give me a little time to check around. . . ." This was a key ploy. If the salesman were out to take him, he would do anything to prevent a fair investigation of the facts. And of course Fisk wouldn't buy *without* checking. That was the big advantage in being an experienced fifty. He couldn't be stampeded.

"Certainly, Mr. Centers. In fact I insist on it! If we were looking for foolish investors we never would have called *you*. I'll be happy to provide the government property report—"

"Thanks, no. I just want a few days to make some calls." He was hardly going to use Mars Ltd. data to check out Mars Ltd.!

"By all means! I wouldn't have it otherwise." Then Bondman paused as though remembering something. "Of course, I can't guarantee your price, Mr. Centers. That increase is going to come through any day now—perhaps tomorrow. They never let us salesmen know in advance, of course, because some might, uh, profiteer at the expense of the customer. But I know it's soon. Your bonus will still apply, naturally, but fifty or sixty thousand per lot is a pretty hefty penalty for a day's time. Uh—do you think you could make it by this afternoon? Say, four o'clock? I don't want to rush you, and of course it might be as late as next week before the rise—but I'd feel terrible if—"

He'd feel terrible if he lost his commission because an irate customer balked at the higher price, Fisk thought. "I think I can make it by four." That would give him six hours: time enough.

"Excellent! I'll see you then! Bye-bye!" and the screen faded.

Fisk hadn't been bluffing. The Marslot investment seemed attractive, indeed, but he never made snap decisions about money. It wasn't just a matter of checking; it was appraising his own motives and inclinations. The best buy in the world—on Mars!—was pointless if it failed to relate to his basic preferences and needs.

He punched an early lunch and ate it slowly. Then he began his calls.

First the library informational service for a summary of Mars Ltd. operations. While that was being processed for faxing to him, he read the sample contract carefully and completely. It was tight: he would not actually own the lot until it was completely paid for, and he couldn't sell it until he owned it. Leverage? Ha!

But apart from that trap, it was straight. He could defang it by purchasing it outright. Not to mention the interest he would save.

The rundown on Mars Ltd. arrived. He settled down to his real homework.

Interesting—there was a cautionary note about "Ltd." That stood for Limited, and meant that the developer's liability was limited to its investments on Earthsoil—of which it had none. Its only Earthly enclave was, as Bondman had claimed, legally *Marssoil*. A nice device for impressive "interplanetary" calls to clients—but perhaps even nicer as a defense against lawsuit. An irate party might obtain a judgment for a million dollars—but unless he sued on Mars, there was nothing for him to collect. What a beautiful foil against crackpots and opportunists!

The company was legitimate. In fact it was the largest of its kind, having sold billions of dollars worth of Marsland to speculators in the past few years. The Elysium Acres project was listed too. A note said SEE GOVERNMENT PROPERTY REPORT. Fisk sighed and punched for it, as it hadn't been attached to the main commentary. He had a lot of dull reading to do!

The phone lighted. It was four already! He had meant to make some other checks—well, they hardly mattered. He had verified that Mars Ltd. was no fly-by-night outfit.

"Did you come to a decision, Mr. Centers?" Bondman inquired, sounding like an old friend.

Fisk had—but a certain innate and cussed caution still restrained him. The deal seemed too good to be true, and that was a suspicious sign. But aside from the "leverage" hoax he could find no fault in it. He decided not to query the salesman about the time payment trap; that would only bring a glib explanation and more superfluous compliments on his intelligence. Better to let Bondman think he was fooling the client.

"I might be interested in more than one lot," Fisk said.

"Absolutely no problem, Mr. Centers!" Fisk was sure the salesman's warmth was genuine this time. "Simply enter the number of lots you are buying on the line on page three where it says 'quantity,' write your name on the line below, and make out a check to Mars Ltd. for your first payment. That's all there is to it, since I have already countersigned. Fax a copy back to us and—"

Fisk's mail-chime sounded. "Oh—the property report," he said. "Do you mind if I just glance at it first? A formality, of course."

"Oh, I thought you'd already read that! Didn't I send you one? By all means—"

Then a buzzer on Bondman's desk interrupted him. "I'm in conference," he snapped into his other phone. "Can't it wait?" Then his expression changed. "Oh, very well!" He turned to Fisk. "I beg your pardon—a priority call has just signaled on my other line and—well, it's from my superior. Can't say no to *him,* ha-ha, even if it is bad form to interrupt a sales conference. If you don't mind waiting a moment—"

"Not at all. I'll read the property report."

"Excellent! I'll wrap this up in a moment, I'm sure." Bondman faded, to be replaced by a dramatic artist's conception of Elysium Acres, buttressed by sweet music. The connection remained; this was merely Mars Ltd.'s privacy shunt.

Then there was a snap! as of a shifting connection, and Bondman's voice was superimposed on the music. " . . . tell you I'm closing a sale for several lots. I can't just pull the rug out—he's signing the contract right now!" A pause, as he listened to the response that Fisk couldn't hear. Then: "To five hundred thousand! As of *this morning?* Why didn't you call me before?"

Fisk realized that Bondman's privacy switch hadn't locked properly. It wouldn't be ethical to

listen, and he did want to skim that property report.
But the voice wrested his attention away from the
printed material.

"Look, boss—I just can't *do* it! I quoted him the
three hundred grand bonus . . . no, I *can't* withdraw
it! He's sharp, *and he's got the contract!* He'd make a
good Mars Ltd. exec . . . no, terms, I think . . . yes, if
we could get him to default on the payments, so the
reversion clause . . . hate to bilk him like that—I
like him . . . no, I'm sure he wouldn't go for the
new price. Not with the cancellation of the bonus
and all. That's a two hundred grand jump just
when he's about to sign . . . okay, okay, I'll try it—
but listen, boss, you torp me in midsale again like
this and I'm signing with Venus Ltd. before you
finish the call . . . I *know* they're a gyp outfit! But I
promised this client the bonus price and now you're
making a liar out of me and cheating him out of the
finest investment of the century on a time payment
technicality! If I have to operate *that* way, I might
as well go whole Venus hog. . . ."

There was a long pause. Fisk smiled, thinking of
the tongue lashing Bondman must be getting for
putting integrity ahead of business.

Fisk knew it was unfair for him to take advantage
of a slipped switch and private information—but
he *had* been promised the bonus price, and now
someone was trying to wipe it out. If Mars Ltd.
were trying to con him out of his investment, he
had a similar right to con himself back *in*!

" . . . all right," Bondman's voice came again.
"That's best. I'll try to talk him out of it so nobody
loses. But get those new quotations in the slot

right away. Couple other clients I have to call—they're going to be furious about that increase, but at least they were warned about delaying . . . yes . . . yes . . . okay. Sorry I blew up. Bye-bye."

The music faded, the picture vanished, and Bondman reappeared, looking unsettled. "Sorry to keep you waiting so long, Mr. Centers," he said. "Bad news. The offer I was describing to you—well, I'm afraid we'll have to call it off."

"But I just signed the contract!" Fisk protested innocently. "Are you telling me to tear it up already?"

Bondman's eyelids hardly flickered. "What I meant to say is that the conditions have changed. New government restrictions have forced up construction costs, and the whole Elysium Acres project is in jeopardy. In fact, Mr. Centers, we now have no guarantee that there will even *be* a dome on Mars. Under the circumstances I don't see how I can recommend—"

So that was the pitch! "We all have to take chances, as you pointed out," Fisk said briskly. "I should think that if your expenses go up, your prices would follow to compensate. So I should buy *now.*"

"Er . . . yes," Bondman admitted. "Still, it looks bad. I wouldn't want you to be left holding title to a worthless lot, Mr. Centers. Until this thing settles down—"

"My *lot?*" Fisk interjected with mock dismay. "*Lots.* I signed up for ten."

For a moment even the super salesman was at a loss for words. "T-ten?"

"Why not, for such a good investment. Leverage, you know."

"Leverage! Let me tell you something—" But then Bondman caught himself. He sighed. He put on a smile of rueful admiration. "You certainly know your business, Mr. Centers. I only hope you aren't taking a terrible chance with a great deal of money. Are you *sure*—?" But, observing Fisk's expression, he capitulated. "Well, then, just make out your first monthly payment for thirty-two thousand five hundred dollars, and we'll—"

"Thanks, no. I'm paying cash."

Bondman looked so woebegone that Fisk felt sorry for him, though he knew the salesman would still receive a handsome commission along with his reprimand for letting so many underpriced lots go. "Cash? The entire amount?"

"Yes. Here is my check for three million dollars, certified against the escrow liquidation of my total holdings. That saves you the annoyance of time payments and gives you a good chunk of the working capital you need. Your boss should be well pleased, considering your rising expenses."

"Uh, yes," Bondman agreed faintly as Fisk faxed check and contract back to him. The originals remained with him for his records, but the faxes were legal too. The deal was closed. He owned the lots outright, and could not lose them by payment default. If he needed working capital himself, he could sell one at the five-hundred thousand dollar price tomorrow.

Bondman stared bleakly at the documents, then pulled himself together. "It has been a real pleasure doing business with you, Mr. Centers," he said with a brave smile. "I'm sure you'll never regret your purchase. Uh, bye-bye."

"Bye-bye!" Fisk returned cheerily as the connection broke.

But something about the salesman's expression just as the picture faded bothered him. It reminded him of what Bondman had said during the morning call: "The biggest sucker is the one who thinks he knows it all. . . ."

The library information on Mars Ltd. was general and of course bland. Any negative remarks would have made it vulnerable for a libel suit, regardless of the truth. It had provided him with essentially the Mars Ltd. publicity release, but added the cautionary note SEE GOVERNMENT PROPERTY REPORT.

Fisk had been about to look at that report when Bondman's boss had interrupted . . . and the privacy switch had coincidentally malfunctioned. Very interesting timing.

After the price-increase call Bondman had been nervous and stuttery, hardly a super salesman. His facade had disintegrated—yet he had *known* the word was coming. Any salesman of that caliber should be able to cover better than *that*. Unless the whole thing was an act . . . to puff the confidence of a sucker who thought he knew it all. . . .

Fisk's hand shook as he lifted the property report, for now he knew what he would find.

Plainly printed in red ink: "This property is not adaptable for terraforming purposes. The lots are unimproved, unsurveyed, and without roads,

landing facilities or other improvements. Access is
extremely poor. Site is subject to frequent ground
tremors prohibiting construction of permanent
buildings or erection of static-dome generators.
Approximate value per lot is $300.00."

CHAPTER

~⟨2⟩~

Fisk Centers sank wearily into his foamer. He reached out of the froth to dial a cold drink while his suit dissolved from his sweaty torso.

No drink came. Then he remembered: his credit balance was down, and half his apartment appliances were out of service until he made repair—of his financial situation.

"I'm too old to be destitute!" he lamented, still hardly believing it. But he hadn't been too old to be bilked out of his fortune by a hard-sell outfit.

Frustrated, he stepped out, letting the spume drain away. He punched for a new suit, knowing that a brave new exterior would refresh his spirit.

The suiter did not produce.

Fisk stood naked, slowly coming to grips with his condition. He had never before suffered from malnutrition of credit, and he had hardly gotten

27

the feel of it yet. There was no clothing in his apartment. Why should there be, when the day's attire was always conveniently recycled after use? *He had nothing to wear.*

He was no lean bronzed muscular youth who could trot outside in Adamic splendor and stare down anyone who blinked. When properly suited, Fisk was portly; bare, he was unconscionably avoirdupois. More bluntly: fat. Of course he wouldn't be that way long if he didn't find some way to renew his dietary credit.

He had been politely inquiring about situations for a gentleman with his qualifications—and receiving tacit demurrals. Hunger would very shortly put an end to that. It was past time to hustle out and *get a job.* If he could only figure out *how.*

He punched for the newsfax want ads, and was relieved to see the paper slide into the hopper. So long as he could communicate, he could function.

Quickly he eliminated the ads obviously intended for women, for youths, and for specialists. The economy was in one of its periodic recessions that always seemed to come when the opposite party was in control, so there were few promising entry-level positions for the untrained. The main field available to him was—sales.

Fisk winced. He had been taken by a salesman. But that was certainly a kind of experience. Why couldn't he sell a legitimate product himself?

But as he read more closely he discovered that here, too, the demand was for special types. He could not afford even the nominal six week hiatus for insurance training; he needed a credit balance *now*. He could hardly peddle household machinery, when the first requirement was to purchase the demonstrator models. He couldn't even go for a preliminary interview—not in this dishabille. And he absolutely refused to go into illicit land sales.

The remaining offerings were scant, and not particularly enticing. *Artificial Manure, no exp. req.* That stank! *Artistic Photography, Special Interest, 50% comm.* No, he wasn't ready to peddle pornography! *Intangible, must travel.* No doubt that salesman *had* to travel, when his intangible turned out to have intangible *value*, too.

In this morass one item snagged his wandering eye and hauled it back. *Call Collect.* No product, no requirement, just the number.

Well, whoever ran that one understood Fisk's desperation. He could apply there even if his phone credit stalled. So he punched the number, collect.

To his slight surprise, the call was accepted. A nervous-looking middle-aged woman appeared on the screen. She looked at him sharply. "Yes?"

"My name is Fisk Centers. I'm interested in employment. Your ad—"

"I know what the ad says!" she snapped. "If this is your idea of a joke at our expense—"

Fisk belatedly remembered that he was unclothed. He had been so preoccupied by his predicament that . . . well, too late now. Honesty was always the best and only policy. "I'm—broke. My suiter's been interdicted. I need a credit balance in a hurry—as you can see. I shall be happy to provide my identity code, if you wish to verify—"

She smiled fleetingly. "I *see*. The position is open. Expenses and commission. If you qualify."

"I have to tell you I'm fifty and untrained in sales. I suffered a business loss—"

"Oh? What kind? If you were rolled—"

"I bought into Mars Inc. Ltd., I mean. Mars Ltd. Ten lots in Elysium Acres. Cash."

She whistled. "They say one's born every minute, but *your* kind comes only once a week! You lost—"

"The shirt off my back," Fisk finished, trying to smile.

"At *least*," she said, eyeing him again. "When can you report?"

"I beg your pardon?"

"You want a job, don't you?"

"Oh!" Fisk had been so well braced against another turndown that he was hardly prepared. "As soon as I get dressed. Uh—"

"We'll call it a business expense," she said. "Have a suit on us, Mr. Centers." And the OPERATIVE light flashed on the suiter.

"But I don't even know your business!" he protested feebly as he hastened to the unit.

"Mr. Johns will explain all that at the office." She paused. "You can work with nonwhites?"

"I pride myself on my inflexible nonbigotry."

"But you understand that a certain discretion may be necessary. . . ."

"I can keep my mouth shut." He was familiar enough with middle class values to realize that this constituted a pretty compelling agreement. He could take the job or reject it, but he could not talk about it elsewhere.

She smiled again, this time with genuine warmth. "Mr. Centers, I think you'll do very well with our organization!"

Fisk was met at the office by a hard-looking young man. "I'm Chic Johns, procurement. You'll be on sales, of course. Know anything about the adoption racket?" the youth demanded.

"Nothing. I—"

"Good. We'll tell you all you need to know. We sell babies."

"I don't think I understand—"

Johns appraised him cynically. "Right. You look like a businessman and you talk like one. We like that. Just remember: we don't gab about business matters to third parties. You take the client's order and deliver the body and collect the cash. We do the rest. All in strict privacy. Right?"

"But I understood it was against the law to assign a monetary value to—"

"It's like this, Centers. The state agencies charge for costs, always inflated, which is really the same thing as selling for a profit. Thousand dollars minimum for a live body. They make their bundle, never you fear. But they're choosy as hell. No black on white or yellow on black, know what I mean? If the client balks, they find him 'unqualified' and he's on the blacklist and he can die childless for all they care, he's *out*. Lots of good potential parents hung up that way. So it's up to us private concerns to fill the vacuum. We don't ask questions, we don't have restrictions. Client tells us what he wants, we get it for a price, just like any other business."

Fisk found this hard to assimilate. "But these are *human beings!* Surely you wouldn't place an innocent baby with unfit parents!"

Johns shrugged. "*I* wouldn't—but my end is procurement, not placement. *You're* the one who decides. But remember, we don't have the staff to do a damn security check on every family that wants a child. And who's to say who's 'fit' or 'unfit'? Some pretty rough people are mighty good to their kids—and some pillars of society, the kind the state agencies like, are raising speed demons, not to mention the *real* addicts. Our record is at least as good as the state's, when you consider the family, not the class—and we deliver much faster. So we just charge enough to discourage anybody who's in it for laughs. Would *you* pay thirty, forty grand for a piddling black baby if you didn't mean to take care of it?"

"No, of course not. But—"

"Sokay. Here's the procedure book. Take it home, study it today. Tomorrow's your first ass."

"Ass?"

"Assignment. Tomorrow maybe you'll place a poor black baby in a rich white home, Centers. Twenty percent commission on the gross. Maybe eight thousand dollars for a day's work. Like the notion?"

"I'll, er, try my best," Fisk said uncertainly. It was a job. . . .

The book was far more sophisticated in language than Chic Johns had been, providing elegant explanations and justifications for the private enterprise adoption procedures. But the man's callous summary seemed essentially correct. State regulations were so complex and picayune, and state agency staffs so overworked, that many worthy prospective parents were unfairly denied adoptive children. At the same time, many innocent babies were forced to grow up in impersonal institutions where they soon became so backward as to be unadoptable. Even a bad family appeared, on balance, to be a better environment for a child than a good state orphanage. *A child needed parents*.

But Fisk, double-wary after the bilking Mars Ltd. had accomplished with its plausible sales pitch, checked carefully for the pitfalls. This manual could be biased, deliberately distorting the state agency picture in order to justify the need for private enterprise.

He phoned the library information service and verified that state institutions were run according to strict and basically fair precepts, so that orphans were not actually deprived—but adoption into families was still preferable. He learned that no adoption was legal unless court-approved, so that if this seeming detail were omitted a child could be taken away at any time, even from the most loving and competent parents. This was the main complaint lodged against black market outfits: their frequent failure to nail down adoptions in court.

The procedure book Chic Johns had given him was supposed to contain all he needed to know about placing a child for adoption. Yet it made no reference to the court requirement.

Fisk reviewed the library material carefully. Theoretically it was impossible for a baby to be adopted without court sanctions—i.e., via black market. But now that he had a notion which lines to read between, he saw that there were avenues. The problem was not placement, for many more people wanted children than the supply could accommodate. The problem was the acquisition. Some few babies might be born unrecorded—but the overwhelming majority arrived in hospitals or with sanctioned medical supervision, and all of these were duly recorded. Once recorded, they were in the computerized system; the state *knew* the whereabouts of every recorded human entity. But some few officials were susceptible to corruption, and supervisory agencies were chronically overworked, so there was a practical loophole for continuing siphoning of babies theoretically destined for legitimate placement. If no one complained, and no one checked to make certain a given baby had arrived, the computer's entry was in fact fictitious . . . sometimes.

But it would be premature to assume that he had landed in such a black market enterprise, Fisk told himself. He had gotten in trouble before by jumping to conclusions—and he needed the job. The court would make its own investigation at the time of the adoption, and if anything was wrong, the transaction would be voided. It was the ethical responsibility of the placement agent—himself— to make arrangements for such legal blessing. So long as he saw to that, he was only providing a necessary introductory and advisory service, and being paid *for* that service, not for human flesh.

A little something nagged at him subliminally, but the thought of an eight-thousand dollar commission for one day's work refuted such doubts. His best course was to try the job, honestly, before judging it. He could always quit once he had verified the facts, if that was the way it went.

The woman was back on duty in the morning. "All set, Mr. Centers?" she inquired over her mounded paperwork.

"Ready to try," he said. "There's a lot more I'll need to know, but I should be able to work it out as I go along."

"Good. Here's your first lead. Find out what they want and report back here. Don't talk business over the phone; we never do that. Remember, make no promises; just say you'll try."

That simple! Fisk took the card she proffered and read it: Michael Ormand, with an address in one of the newer apartment complexes.

But why no business over the phone? An order was a fairly straightforward thing.

Ormand was a genial muscular man of about thirty, with a scalped-looking crewcut and the inset metal contacts of a spaceman. Fisk tried not to stare. He knew about the brain-to-machine synapses used by interplanetary crewmen, but had never seen the implants this close before.

"Mars shuttle?" Fisk inquired, feeling a twinge for another reason. It was foolish to resent everything connected to Mars, but that wound still pained.

"Venus," Ormand answered. "But I'm through with all that. No more shuttling. Going to retire now that I've made my pile. Want a family."

"That's what I'm here to discuss!" Fisk said with what he hoped was the proper note of professional encouragement. This was easy enough, so far. "May I ask what you plan to do now?"

"It's none of your business, but I'll tell you. I'll grow mugwumps."

"I beg your pardon?"

"Mugwumps. Venusian pseudo-plants. Very pretty, use no water or sunlight, smell like a lemon. Big demand here on Earth, but I'm not doing it for the money. Made my pile already, I said. Challenge, you know. Never been cultivated before."

Fisk made a mental note to look up mugwumps, as he had not heard of the name in this connection before. "I see. What kind of child were you thinking of adopting? You understand we are a private, fee-charging agency. We do our best, but we can't make promises—except that we don't collect until we deliver."

"Sure. No red tape, that's what I like. I figure a little girl, nine or ten. Healthy, you know?"

"Nine or ten months," Fisk repeated, writing it down.

"Months? *Years!* What would I want with a squalling baby?"

"Oh," Fisk said, nonplussed. "Sorry. I thought— uh, how long have you been married?"

"Married? Spacemen don't marry! What would I want with a gold-digging wife?"

Fisk choked. "Mr. Ormand! If you want to adopt—"

"That's *why* I want to adopt. A nice, sweet little girl. Catch her before she gets bitchy, train her right, you know? Older women are unmanageable."

"But—!"

"*You're* single, aren't you? *You* know what women are like!"

"But you can't adopt when you're single!"

Ormand glanced at him in surprise. "I can't?"

"Of course not! Only married couples can—"

The man smiled. "Oh, that's the agency pitch. Sure. That's why I called *you*. To cut out that bilge. Look, you don't need to beat up the price on me. I told you I'm loaded. Don't worry about it. Find me what I want and I'll pay. Within reason. I know what the range is for this sort of thing. And I'll give you a little bonus on the side for prompt service. Fair enough?"

Fisk was afraid of what would come out if he opened his mouth, so he kept it closed. Somehow he made his exit in good order.

"Ten-year-old girl? Sure, we can get," Johns said at the office. "That kind's a glut on the market. And he won't quibble on color or price! Good show, Centers! I can see you've got the knack."

This was not the response Fisk had anticipated. He had supposed the sale doomed. "But he's single!"

"So?"

"What about the law?"

Johns made a face as though he had heard a bad word. "What about it? Didn't you read the book?

Singles can adopt, if they have the means to make a good home. And this guy does. He'll bite for fifty grand, wait and see. Grand for you, grand for me, and grand for business!"

Fisk felt vaguely nauseous, but didn't want to imperil his income by raising uninformed objections. Ten thousand dollars could go a long way in reconstituting his life-style. "Do you *have* a ten-year-old girl? Uh, in stock?"

"You think I keep that kind packed in desk drawers? I'll *find* one," Johns said confidently. "Just a matter of making the connection, and a little quiet negotiation. Two days, maybe. Don't you worry about that. My end of the business, procurement. Just you go out on your next ass and see if you can land another order to match the first."

Fisk retained strong personal reservations about this business, but he went. As it happened, the leads fizzled. Some people merely wanted information and others backed off when it came to the point of actually ordering a baby. One lady seemed to be more interested in finding a husband, and Fisk barely escaped intact. Ormand was right: some older women did get predatory. Meanwhile, however much he might look the part, he was not a high pressure salesman.

On the third day Johns barged into the office hauling along a screaming tantrum of a spitfire. "Got her!" he exclaimed breathlessly, shoving the creature into the center of the room and leaning against the door. Blood dripped from a scratch on his cheek and his suit was torn in a couple of places, but he was smiling. "What a job!"

Abruptly the commotion ceased. A young girl stood there, of indeterminate color and culture. "Hi," she said to Fisk, nodding her short black tangle of hair pertly. "You the sucker?"

Fisk turned to Johns, dismayed. "Surely this isn't—?"

"Sure this *is*! Take her to your client and get the money. Real bargain for him! See those classic facial lines? That animal vigor? That instant self-control? You know the price."

Fisk found the moral ramifications too vast to contemplate on the spot, so he shelved them in favor of details. "He—he wants a—a nice, sweet little girl."

"*I'm* nice and sweet," the girl snarled. "When I want to be."

"Would you want to be sweet for a man who'll shell out fifty grand for you?" Johns asked her with a half-smile.

"Fifty grand!" she exclaimed, delighted. "Am I worth all that?"

"If you behave. At least until the deal's complete. After that, who cares? You're *in*."

"Yeah, who cares!" she echoed, with momentary mischief. Despite their manner of entry, Johns and the girl appeared to have a certain mutual appreciation of each other's motives.

Fisk had been concerned for the welfare of the child, but now he suspected that the client was the sucker she had implied. Should he proceed with this transaction?

What would he eat if he didn't? He had made no other sales (placed no other children, he corrected himself), and so his commission was zero. The office petty cash fund wouldn't carry him much longer. Sheer need was bruising his scruples.

"Sokay, Centers—take her away," Johns said briskly. "Clean her up and feed her first, so she doesn't snatch. Here's a couple tokens. Play it cool. But don't turn her over until you get his payment."

Fisk took her away, with a stop at a refresher booth to get her cleaned and dressed for presentation. He wished he could do the same for himself; his home foamer had quit the day before, and this was his fourth day on a one-day suit. Only extreme care kept him from looking seedy.

Of course he could always sell one of his Mars lots. But those were worth only one percent of what he had paid, and he couldn't bring himself to convert that 99% paper loss to cash. Marsland *might* eventually improve. . . .

"What's your name?" he asked belatedly as she foamed.

"Yola. Hey, I've never been in a public booth before. Neat!" Her voice emerged from a speaker beside the entrance. There was no vision screen, of course.

"How did Johns get you?" Fisk couldn't bring himself to use the term "procure" in this connection.

"The usual. I was doing time in solitary 'cause I—aw, never mind. The cage was glad to unload me, and not for any fifty grand, either!"

"The orphanage *sold* you?"

"They don't call it that. Order came through the Juvenile Parole Agency, which is a legit division of Youth Services. But somewhere along the way I got shunted, and here I am!"

"You mean you were abducted from your lawful guardian?"

"You don't know much, do you! It was just in the paperwork. Same thing, I guess. The usual, I said."

The usual . . .

"But how could you be transferred from a state institution to a—to here?"

"If I knew, I'd know enough not to talk about it," she said uncomfortably. Then she changed the subject. "Is it a nice family?"

"It's a single man. Spacer."

She didn't respond right away, and Fisk hardly needed to inquire why. Children learned early about life in institutions, and spacers were notorious for their planetfall orgies. This was a far cry from the philanthropic service he had half-anticipated.

"Well, let's go," she said, emerging. Fisk had feared she would punch some outrageous replacement outfit, but she was tastefully dressed for her age: eleven. She was small, as though undernourished, and not, despite Johns's remarks, black skinned. But she obviously derived from mixed ancestry. She looked well-tanned on the body, and had a certain Negroid cast about her features, but this was not obvious at a casual glance. No doubt neither pure black nor pure white had wanted her as a baby, as neither considered brown beautiful. So she was here. . . .

"So watcha gaping at?" she demanded.

He guided her to the fooder and inserted the second token. "Punch what you want, and make sure you have enough to fill up," he advised, hoping she would order too much, so that he would get to abate his sudden hunger on the surplus. He had been scrimping on meals too, necessarily.

She looked at him sidelong, and punched a supersoda and a miniature dog biscuit. "For you," she said, proffering the latter.

Fisk was too hungry to be properly furious. He chewed on the biscuit while she slurped the fragrant giant confection noisily. An unlimited one-sitting fooder order gone to waste!

But his conscience hung on. "Are you sure you want to go through with this, Yola? A single man—"

"A single *loaded* man. Think I'm dumb? Better'n solitary, for sure. I'll get to see shows, sleep late, and eat anything I want—"

"Then why were you fighting so hard when Johns brought you in?"

"I don't like being told what to do."

"Do you always throw a tantrum when—"

"Always. Matter of principle."

"That could get you into trouble."

She contemplated him obliquely as the soda drained to the vociferous dregs. "My middle name, grandad."

"Don't call me grandad!" he said sharply.

"Don't tell me what to call you!" she screamed, not stinting on the volume. It was amazing how far a soprano voice carried! People stopped in the street to look, and Fisk fought to keep the flush off his face. Then, sweetly: " . . . Grandad."

Fisk decided to ignore it. "We have an appointment, Yola."

"Right, Centers," she agreed with continued insolence. But he was determined not to let her have the satisfaction of his reaction.

Mike Ormand was pleased. "Very nice," he said, studying Yola with more critical intensity than Fisk thought appropriate for such an interview. He half hoped the child would pull an instant tantrum and void the placement, but for the moment she was every inch the demure pre-teen. "Here's your check, sir. Fifty grand, certified."

"Just a minute!" Fisk protested. "You can't just—"

"Why not, Mr. Centers?" Yola asked innocently. She turned to Ormand. "May I call you Dad?"

"Sure, kid. Go punch yourself a soda," he said amiably. "No hard stuff, now!" Then, to Fisk: "Don't worry. I didn't forget yours. I know how it goes. I made it out separately. So your office wouldn't know. Five thousand." He handed over the second check, winking.

"Not that!" Fisk cried, his moral anguish tempered by the greed of desperation. Five thousand would fuel his finances for a couple of weeks! "You—you two—don't even know each other!"

"What's to know, Mr. Centers?" Yola inquired prettily over her soda. This one didn't slurp, for she sipped with delicacy. "Dad's got a nice layout here, a real home. He's a nice guy."

"Yeah," Ormand agreed. "I've got what she wants, she's what I want, you've got your money. So it's done, we're all happy, and thank you. Now toddle off, Centers. You're interfering in family business."

"Yeah," Yola echoed almost inaudibly.

They were both reasonably satisfied, neither being quite the bargain the other supposed, and he did have the money. Why should he object? He had performed his function. He had a ten thousand dollar commission coming for this transaction! Yet he balked, feeling like a pimp. "We have to complete the contract and make arrangements for the formal adoption. There'll have to be a court hearing, and—"

"A *what*?" Ormand demanded incredulously. Then he caught himself. "Oh, sure. I'll take care of that. You don't need to bother."

"I *do* need to bother," Fisk said, his stubborn streak coming into play. "Somebody could take her away from you at any time, no matter how long—"

"Oh, that's it!" Ormand said, seeming relieved. "That's okay. Nothing's going to happen inside of ten days, is it?"

"Not that I know of. But there is no expiration on a counterclaim of this nature. Suppose a natural parent showed up in five years—"

Ormand laughed. "Fat chance. They'd never follow where we're going!"

"Where *are* we going, Dad?" Yola inquired.

"To Venus, of course. Got my one way passes for the next liftoff, just ten days off."

Yola spat out a mouthful of soda. "Venus!"

"Sure, kid. To farm mugwump. It only grows on Venus, you know."

"But there aren't any shows on Venus!" Yola shrieked as though mortally wounded. "No foamers, no fooders, no autobeds. It's just a perpetual sandstorm!"

"Right. Real challenge. Ideal for mugwumps, and no neighbors to butt in, 'cept for the shuttle every four months. Great life!"

"In a *spacesuit*!" she wailed, her anguish intensifying. "All day! And the trip there takes six months, cooped up in an old tin can with nothing but nasty ol' vacuum trying to get in!"

"The vacuum doesn't come *in*," Ormand said. "The air goes *out*. If there's a leak. And the trip takes longer, right now. And it's getting worse, because of the phase. That's why I have to make a tight schedule. The free-fall gets to you if you stay in space too long, specially if you're not used to it."

"Free-fall!" she repeated faintly. "I get sick just in the downshaft!"

"I don't understand," Fisk said. "If you're settling on Venus, why are you adopting a girl?"

"Why do you *think* he wants a girl, grandad!" Yola exclaimed tearfully.

"Well, it's a long trip out, and a rough, lonely life," Ormand said reasonably. "What grown woman would sign up for it?"

"A desperate one," Fisk said. "No other."

"Just count me out, Ormand!" Yola cried. "I'm no Lolita!"

Fisk couldn't resist needling her, though he was privately relieved about her change of heart. "You didn't object before, Yola."

"He wasn't going to Venus before!"

"Sure I was," Ormand said. "That's why I—"

"You stay out of this, child-buyer!" she screamed at him.

"Watch who you're sassing, kid," he snapped back. His temper was about as quick as hers.

She threw the soda cup at him. "I'll sass anybody I please, you—oh!"

For Ormand had grabbed her in mid-sentence and was hauling her over his knee. He flipped her short skirt up over her back. "No daughter of mine is going to sass her elders!" he said as his hand came down resoundingly on her little posterior.

Yola screeched incoherently. Fisk had some sympathy with each party, so didn't interfere. Yola certainly had no reason to like Venus, but Ormand was taking the kind of firm disciplinary action Fisk envied. They were working it out.

Then Yola jackknifed and bit the man on the ankle. It was Ormand's turn to exclaim with pain and rage. By the time he recovered his bearings, Yola had scooted across the room.

Fisk had been pleasantly bemused by the suddenness and violence of these proceedings, but now he stepped between them. "I'm afraid this isn't going to work. Here are your checks back, Mr. Ormand. I'll return this girl to the—"

"Uh-*uh!*" Yola said.

"Oh no you don't, Centers!" Ormand rapped, simultaneously slapping the checks to the floor. "I don't have time to get another girl. This one'll be fine once I get her broken in."

"Go break in your fat *head!*" Yola cried, casting about for something else to throw.

Fisk caught her by the wrist and hustled her out of the apartment, and this time she didn't object to being directed. Ormand charged after them, but Yola ducked back and tripped him with professional dispatch so that he sprawled ignominiously. Fisk wondered just what sort of education children obtained in state orphanages, for spacers were normally sure on their feet. They ran to the exit chute and jumped in.

She did look a little queasy in that brief free-fall, though there were other factors to account for that.

The house alarm was already sounding as they boarded the transport for the office. Ormand must have called the police! But they were on their way, and by the time the police net tightened . . .

"Let him rant," Fisk said angrily as the capsule popped into its vacuum tunnel and accelerated. "The adoption was never consummated. He has no call on you."

"Good," she said. "Where're we headed now?"

"To the office. Then Johns will return you to the orphanage, or wherever you came from."

"Not me!" she said. "I hate that place."

"But you agreed to go back! I heard you, in the apartment."

"I said uh-*uh*, not uh-*huh*, grandad!"

"You don't want to go to Venus, do you?"

"No. But I'm not going back in local solitary, either," she said dangerously.

"I don't see what choice you have, unless another client happens to be looking for a girl your age. And frankly, your spot tantrums don't make you very easy—"

"What do you want to do with these?" she asked, interrupting him. "They're made out to you, you know."

"I'll just explain the situation at the office—" He stopped, seeing what she held. "What are you doing with—"

"Ormand's checks?" she said innocently. "I figured we might need the money, so I scooped them up while—"

"His checks! Yola, that represents either stealing or acceptance-of-payment. It gives him a theoretical basis to—"

"To sue?" she inquired with mock astonishment. "Gee, *you* could get in bad trouble, Centers!"

"ALL VEHICLES HALT IN PLACE!" the capsule loudspeaker said. "STAND BY FOR INSPECTION."

"No wonder he's mad!" Fisk said as he punched the HALT button. "I didn't realize we'd taken his money."

"Mistake, huh?" she said, looking at the checks. Sometimes she was unbearable, but this time she seemed genuinely contrite. "Bad mistake."

"OPEN VENT." The police had connected a pressurized tube; the capsule could not be opened in the tunnel vacuum.

Reluctantly, Fisk pressed the OPEN stud.

"You dope!" Yola cried, slapping the CANCEL button before the machinery functioned. "They'll hang you!" She hit the EMERGENCY ACCELERATION next.

"What are you doing!" he exclaimed as the vehicle shot forward with the force possible only in vacuum, ripping away the police tube.

"Making your getaway, grandad," she said. "No sense having you in the hole for theft."

"But I was going to return the checks and explain—"

"And let *me* hang!" she accused him angrily.

"You have an unduly suspicious mind. Once the mistake is clarified, nobody will—"

"Uh-*uh*. Get that *uh* this time, Centers! You aren't going to return that money and void the sale. I told you I'm not going back to the pen. Not for anything."

"Do you mean you are willing to let me be charged with resisting-the-police—just to stay out of a legitimate orphanage! I can't believe that!"

"You can't, huh?" She considered for a moment. "Well, would you believe kidnapping?"

"Yola! Of all the ridiculous—"

"Or maybe child-molestation? My word against yours, Centers. Want to see my act?"

"SUSPECT RUNNING. CUT POWER IN TUNNEL."

Fisk knew how guilty that sudden flight made him seem. Why *would* he take Ormand's money (or *seem* to!), then break out of a routine police net? With a screaming eleven-year-old girl! Yola

really could hang him! And she was brat enough
to do it.

He had once supposed this job would benefit his
fellow man and make people happy. . . .

"You're pretty much of a sucker, aren't you,"
Yola said as the capsule drifted to a lifeless stop.
"What're you doing in a racket like this?"

"Because I *am* a sucker," Fisk admitted,
demoralized. "A Marsland salesman took me,
and I'm broke."

She looked at him as though sorry for a broken-
winged bird. "Well, we're caught anyway. It's
nothing personal, Centers. Maybe I'd better go
back to Ormand. He's the kind of bastard I don't
mind scr—"

"Yola!"

"Oh come off it, grandad! You have a dirty mind.
I mean I can always run away before he goes to
Venus. So he's got what he deserves: nothing."

Her spark of charity was as awkward as her
ruthlessness! "But that's dishonest! If you don't
intend to—"

"All right, sucker. It was only a silly notion to get
you off the hook, 'cause you're a decent sort under
all that quaint naivete." She began tearing up her
recently machined hairdo. "By the time they get
this kidnap/molestation rap untangled, Ormand'll
be on Venus, you'll be in the clink for trial, and I'll
be a ward of the court, where maybe I can finagle
a better deal for number one. Will that make you
feel better?"

Fisk saw that it was futile to attempt to reason
with this gutter child. The police were already

applying another pressure-exit to the capsule. He'd
just have to present his case and hope the police
considered all the aspects of the situation before
doing anything irrevocable. Certainly he wasn't
going to capitulate to this attempted extortion!

"You're so cubical, you're a tesseract!" she
exclaimed. "Look, grandad, you're a nonsurvival
type. If you'll just shut up and let me handle it,
I can—"

The capsule opened. "Crawl out in a hurry—
you're blocking traffic!" a police voice yelled down
the tube.

Fisk's mind was still on Yola's offer to complicate
things yet further. "Never!" he cried to her.

Naturally the police misunderstood. A sleepdart
buzzed along the tube like a vengeful fly and pinked
Fisk on the sweaty forehead . . . and he found
himself standing insecurely before a tall desk in the
police station. Yola was beside him, and Ormand
had a chair nearby. The Law could be devastatingly
efficient when it snared the innocent.

"Serious charge. Kidnapping a minor from
a private apartment," the Lieutenant behind
the desk said as the dart nullifier took effect.
"You understand you have the right to consult
counsel before making your statement, et cetera,
et cetera?"

"I'm sure I can explain everything without the
necessity of counsel," Fisk said hastily, knowing
that the police preferred dispatch. "This girl—"

"What he means is," Yola interjected, "we were
just going to the court to arrange for the
adoption."

"You *were?*" Ormand said, surprised and, oddly, not particularly pleased. "I thought—"

"We were *not!*" Fisk said. "I was taking her back to—"

Yola kicked him. "To fetch the adoption papers," she said.

The Lieutenant turned to Ormand. "What's this about adoption? You told us your daughter had been kidnapped."

Ormand hesitated. "I, er, maybe there was a misunderstanding. I'll just take her home now." He came up and grabbed Yola's arm.

"Get your filthy paw off me!" she screamed automatically. "You can't tell me what to do, you child beater!"

The lieutenant made a note. "Child beating."

Fisk had a certain grudging sympathy for the other man. Ormand still thought a simple spanking or two would bring Yola into line, but he would learn—

The desk phone lighted. "For you," the Lieutenant said to Fisk, turning the screen to face him.

It was Johns. "What's this about you being arrested?" Johns demanded. "We run a respectable outfit here. You're fired, Centers!"

"But I've still got the child! The adoption can't—"

Johns screwed up his face in perplexity. "Child? Adoption? I don't know what you're talking about! Have you been messing around with something on the side?"

Fisk began to see what sort of a bag he was to be left holding. Naturally Johns wouldn't admit to dealing in black market babies, here in the hearing of the police! "But—"

"Just get our 80% to us pronto and we'll forget the embezzlement charge, however," Johns finished, clicking off.

The policeman made another note. "Embezzlement." He looked up. "Are you *sure* you don't need an attorney?"

"This is all a misunderstanding!" Fisk cried despairingly. But it looked hopeless. If he returned the checks, Johns would charge him with embezzlement of company funds; if he kept them, Ormand had him on kidnapping. Both were ruthless enough to hang the intermediary. And Yola hadn't even started on her child-molestation act yet.

"There's funny business somewhere," the Lieutenant said thoughtfully. "Damn funny!" He pronounced the improper word without the vowel, legitimizing it. He turned to Ormand. "This is a nonwhite child, and you're a white spacer. She can't be your natural issue."

"Sure I could," Yola said, keeping her option open. "My mother's black, and I won't say what business she's in, but it's near the spaceport. She—"

"Yeah," Ormand agreed, manifestly not pleased but riding with the inevitable. "You know how it is."

"How old are you, Ormand?" the Lieutenant snapped.

"Twenty-nine. That's why I'm retiring. You have to, after thirty."

"And you?" he said to Yola.

"Eleven."

The Lieutenant turned back to Ormand. "And how old is the minimum for a space license?"

"Twenty-one." Then Ormand saw the trap. "Well, maybe *before* I—"

"Looks like a black market operation to me," the Lieutenant said. "Five to two you're an ineligible parent. Single, with no permanent home, and you can't take an underage child offplanet—"

"No, no!" Ormand cried, turning pale even for a spacer.

"So you paid a fat check to a shyster outfit to sneak through a black baby—I know damn well you weren't going to any court for adoption, whatever you told the child!"

Ormand fell back, whipped.

Without seeming to take a breath, the Lieutenant pounced on Fisk, who had just started to relax. "And you, Centers. You *represent* that black market racket, squeezing human blood out of both ends. You're selling an innocent ward of the state to an ineligible child-beater, and embezzling on the side, and maybe kidnapping too—"

"Yeah," Yola said, enjoying this. "Don't forget child moles—"

"And to top it off the brat's a little bitch nobody can handle without a whip in one hand and a prayer-book in the other!"

"Yeah," Fisk and Ormand agreed together. Yola glared.

The Lieutenant smiled knowledgeably. "In short, three fine fat fish on the line, suckers all, tugging the hooks into each other. As if I didn't have *important* cases to handle in my off-days! Now are you three going to work out your own squabble, or shall I do it for you?"

Yola and Ormand both quailed, but Fisk had an inspiration. "Lieutenant, if you will please permit us a moment to confer privately—"

"Sure, I'll wait," the officer said generously. "Thirty seconds."

"Here—*now!*" Fisk snapped at the other two, pulling them into a huddle. He had never before attempted to manage people so boldly, but desperation gave him genius. "Ormand, if I get you off the hook and find you an age-of-consent girl who's willing—"

"Yeah, yeah!" Ormand agreed eagerly. "Keep the money. Just—"

"Yola, if I arrange a legitimate adoption, court-approved, so you'll never have to go back to—"

"Yeah, yeah!" she echoed fervently.

"Time!" the Lieutenant called.

Fisk stepped up to the desk. "As I was saying," he said so smoothly he surprised himself, "it was all a misunderstanding. Mr. Ormand was looking for a wife to take to Venus—he's going to be cultivating exotic Venus plants for export to Earth, you know— and the agency thought he meant the phrase 'little girl' literally, not knowing the way spacers talk. When the two were introduced, the error was quickly apparent. He was naturally upset, and so was the girl, as you can readily understand. In their confusion they exchanged some unkind words—"

"Yeah, yeah!" the two whispered.

"So Mr. Ormand may have said 'kidnapped' when he meant 'defrauded.' A natural error in the circumstances. Actually I was taking the child back to—" Here Yola opened her mouth, but he elbowed her warningly. "To assist me in locating the *correct* subject. One of the sixteen-year-old girls just graduating from the orphanage, eager for the security of marriage. Young enough to be, uh, malleable. Who likes to travel—even as far as Venus, where there would be no female competition for attention."

"Yeah . . ." Ormand said, his face lighting. "Sixteen, love-starved . . ."

The lieutenant nodded. "You're pretty smooth, when put on your mettle," he admitted approvingly. "But what about Miss Tantrums, here? You have to shut her up before she says something I might have to jail you for."

Fisk could have done without such candor. "Once we have clarified Mr. Ormand's situation satisfactorily, I will—" Here he paused to gird himself for the sacrifice. "I will take Yola to the court to—to adopt her myself. I am, I believe, an eligible parent."

Yola's mouth fell open. "Gee—*really?*" she breathed ecstatically.

"Yes, really," Fisk said, hoping he wouldn't regret this decision of expediency for the rest of his life. "I'm young enough to be your father, you know, and I've, er, always wanted a black baby."

CHAPTER
⟨3⟩

"**U**p, Fisk!" Yola said. "Earn your daily Bonus and Commission or else."

Fisk Centers rolled over groggily. "Else *what?*"

"Else *this!*" An avalanche of icy foam descended on his head.

He struggled upward, gasping for breath, suddenly wide awake. "What was that for?"

"Well, I did warn you," she said contritely. "You look like a walrus surfacing."

"Nonsense. I don't have tusks."

"A *toothless* walrus, then. Fat, wet, stupid—"

"*You're* about to look like a spanked brat!"

"No time," she said. "Bolt your food, Fisky. Today you go to work for your living."

"What makes you so certain I'll have any better luck today than I have all week, pesky?"

"Because *you* handled the week; *I* set up today. While you snored."

"I should have stayed single," Fisk muttered as he stumbled to the suiter and let it dry and dress him. "Or at least gotten married. The last thing any sane man would do is become an adoptive father to a pre-teen hellion."

"Right," she agreed. "Especially when he has to live off her money."

"That's *my* money! Twenty percent commission for—"

"For selling an innocent child on the black mar—"

"Shut up!" He stepped out of the suiter, resplendent in blue jeans, checkered shirt and goggles. "What did you do to the setting?" he roared.

"Well, for your job," she said. "Hurry up."

He tore off the goggles. "My job—doing *what?*"

"Selling cars, of course."

"Cars! I'm no mechanic!"

"That's all you know, Dad. Salesman don't have to know anything about the workings. Just believe in your product and sell, sell, sell!"

Fisk punched a soyomelet. "Believe in my product, she says. I haven't even *driven* a car for five years! Now I have to sell—" He took a bite, but paused before masticating it. "*What* car?"

"Fusion. They've got a real nice commission deal—"

The mouthful of omelet sprayed over the table. "The atomic racer? The radioactive juggernaut that makes the obituary headlines every other week? The—"

"The same. They're making a play for the middle

class market, and they need middle class salesmen. Hot chance for you."

"Hot is an ironic understatement! Listen, Yola—do you realize that my annuities don't mature for another twenty-five years, and are voided in the event of deliberate suicide? If I die tomorrow in a Fusion, you inherit nothing!"

"Term life insurance," she answered. "That's their bonus. Life and Comm. You live off the comm., of course; but if you die—"

"Enough, child! The longer I listen to you the worse I feel. I'm not going near any—"

"Suit yourself," she said. "We'll run out of money tomorrow."

"Tomorrow! There's enough for at least another week!"

"You forget you have a family to support. Two don't live as cheaply as one, you know." She paused, serious and for the moment rather pretty in her brown-faced way. "Fisk, it's a good chance for you. I thought you'd really go for a decent income—"

Fisk sighed. "I'll talk to the man. But it'd better be strictly salesroom. If I have to go near a living Fusion, I'll resign on the spot."

"Sure," she said in a way that hinted more mischief. "Come on—you're due to report in twenty minutes."

"Fisk Centers? Right!" the executive at Fusion Motors said briskly as Fisk introduced himself. "Your daughter here set it up. Glad to have a man of your experience with us!"

"Experience? I haven't—"

Yola tromped his toe, and Fisk realized that she had invented suitable qualifications for him. "Time to set that straight right now!" He took a breath.

"You're in the weekly Hurdle, starting at ten today," the man said.

Fisk's breath whooshed out. "I beg your—"

The man guided him out of the service exit. They stepped into a massive garage fraught with menacing machinery. "Bill, he's here!"

Fisk tried again. "Look, I don't know what she told you, but I'm not—"

"Here's your co-pilot, Bill. Bill, this is Fisk. Used to be with Ferrari before the antipolluters closed down their commercial branch. Drove in the Antarctic cross-country a couple times, maybe twenty years ago. Going to sell for us. I want him to get a real feel for the Fusion, but you'll have to carry the burden this time."

"Great!" Bill said, shaking Fisk's hand with a grip of steel and rubber. "Come on, Fisk. We've got just thirty-five minutes till blastoff, and you'll need briefing."

"But I—"

"Don't get me wrong," Bill said, hustling him along while Yola trotted excitedly behind. "I'm not denigrating your experience. But there's been a lot of development in the past two decades, and most of it has been led by Fusion, and the Hurdle is a real workout. If anything happens to me, you'll have to take over, because the finish line's the only safe exit. Ever drive over 500 before?"

"Well, I—" Then it occurred to Fisk that Bill wasn't talking about distance, and certainly not about regular highway travel. Stunned, he fumbled for a suitable way to set things straight immediately.

Yola caught up. She smiled sweetly at Bill. "Can I come too? I love racing!"

Bill looked at her with leathery compassion. "Sorry, kid. No juniors allowed. This is a rough course, and it changes every week. You'll have to watch it on the customer screen. Mine's the purple Eight."

"Oh." She looked dangerously sullen, but she fell back.

"Bill, there's been a misunderstanding," Fisk said, already out of breath because of the pace Bill was setting through the monstrous garage. "I can't—I never—"

"Here she is," Bill said proudly, pulling up at a tremendous sculptured vehicle with eight massive wheels. "Hop in. We'll get strapped while the tug takes her there, and I'll brief you while we're moving." And he gave Fisk a powerful boost into the open cockpit.

The tug started moving the moment they landed in the firm molded seats, hauling the car bargelike out of its niche and down a ramp. Bill saw to Fisk's complex protective harness before attending to his own.

"But I'm only supposed to be a salesman!" Fisk cried. "I can't get involved in a race! I have absolutely no—"

"No problem. Boss always breaks in the new men like this. Idea is you don't need to know every detail about the car, you just have to believe in it absolutely, and the details will take care of themselves. So we don't load you down with statistics and all that junk; we just show you. Once you've raced the Fusion special, you're a believer."

"But I'm trying to tell you! I don't know the first thing about—"

"Sure, the boss explained. You've never touched the Fusion before. And twenty years is a long, long time, in racing. We'd have let you sit it out this week, but my regular co-pilot isn't out of the hospital yet. But I know you've got the stuff. I used to watch that Antarctic cross-country race when I was a kid. Those glaciers, those ice crevasses—" He shook his head. "No, the Hurdle isn't rougher than *that*. But it *is* different, and you've got to ride it several times before you get the feel. So, I'll drive, and you just handle the map, okay? Nobody tackles a new race in a new car, cold!"

Appalled, Fisk could only nod. At this point it almost seemed better to take the horrible ride and keep his mouth shut. At least his driver was competent, and it would be a one time only experience.

"Actually, that map is important," Bill said consolingly. "I can't take my eyes off the track when I'm at speed. They do it that way to make sure it's fair. New track each run, nobody knows the specific layout until the race starts, and then he has to figure out his strategy from the map. So it's a necessary job, and don't you doubt it for a moment. One misreading and you're dead."

Fisk came to an abrupt decision: he would blurt out the truth and get released from this race right now. "Bill, I—"

"I wouldn't drive without a mapman. My co-pilot tried that a couple weeks ago, when I was out at the last minute with the one-day intestinal grippe. You know—bathroom every ten minutes, ready or not. Didn't dare drive. So he took it alone, 'cause you can't get a 'co' in the last moment and we didn't want our entry scratched. That's why he cracked up, trying to read the map before he got out of the Tunnel. . . ." Bill shook his head. "Fifteen hours in surgery, and he'll have to drive next time with a prosthetic hand and a plate in his skull. Ran way over the insurance, and he's got a family to support. That's why I have to run a good race this time. Got to help him out."

Fisk realized that if he spoke out now, Bill would have no co-pilot. Then he would have either to take it alone, risking the same fate that had wiped out his partner, or drop out of the race entirely. Then his friend's medical bills would ruin his family.

Fisk well understood the problems of financial ruin. He had been a moderately wealthy man not so long ago. It was not a fate he would wish on anyone.

". . . true dual-purpose car," Bill was saying. He evidently liked to talk, but his topics became him. "Motor's always at full power, of course, so the clutch guides it. Not the kind of clutch you knew, eh? No gearing, just engage for the percentage of power you want. Depress gently, and you've got a gentle touring car; goose it, and you've got a real racer! I use a model just like this for city traffic. . . ."

What could he do but stick with it? Racing terrified him, and not just because of his health—but there were more things riding on this than his preferences.

". . . duplicate controls, but yours will be inactive. Except for the indicators; you need to watch them in case of emergency. Regular steering wheel, you see; nothing complicated. Fusion's designed for the simpleminded—that's why I like it! And over here . . ."

Now the tug was maneuvering the car into the starting stall. A giant chronometer above was ticking off the last seconds before the start. Fisk squirmed within his harness, feeling cold sweat on palms, face and underarms. He hoped that the term insurance was for a large amount.

"The map will fall into the fax hopper there as the gun goes off," Bill said. "Grab it and—"

There was a faint pop! through the armored hull. Paper dropped. And the car ground forward with such authority that it was all Fisk could do to breathe. There was very little noise; pollution-control had really clamped down on loud sports, and both the hydrogen/helium fusion engine and the mercury vapor working fluid were almost silent. Also, it seemed, the cockpit was soundproof.

He had to admit it: this *was* a nice piece of machinery.

On either side the competing cars were shot out of their stalls. Blue, white, green, red, yellow;

internal combustion, steam, electric, jet, atomic and assorted hybrids. The industry had claimed that stiff antipollution standards would ruin it, but in fact it had led to a marvelous flowering of superior new types. The money that had once been wasted on planned obsolescence of style now went into improvement of mechanics. Drivers still had to buy a new car every three years to keep up with fashion—but now they obtained a superior product each time. And this was where that superiority was demonstrated: in professional competition, using the same cars sold in the showrooms. It was a drag race start: thirty bright vehicles straining forward on a ten mile straightaway. But no noise, no fumes.

Fisk sneaked a look at the speedometer. His duplicate was functioning, but it took him a moment to find the MPH scale amid the massed dials and digits. The main scales were feet per second and kilometers per hour, but he was pedestrian enough to orient on old-fashioned miles per hour. They were already doing 150, and accelerating rapidly! And the other cars were keeping pace or pulling ahead, so that their group velocity was deceptive.

"Look at the map!" Bill shouted. "What's the first hurdle?"

Fisk opened the map hastily and scanned it. Here he was daydreaming when his very life was at stake in an obstacle race at hundreds of miles per hour. Fortunately the map was simple and clear. "The Narrows," he said.

"The Narrows! That's a stiff location, but good for us. Hang on—we'll have to push it."

And, astonishingly, the acceleration increased. They began gaining on other cars.

"I thought you were flat-out before!" Fisk gasped.

"Hardly. This is the finest car ever made, overall. The Fusion's got more actual poop than any car on the market, and unlimited range. It's a little piece of the sun inside, you know—that's the heat of the conversion, four hydrogen atoms transforming into one helium atom in controlled fusion. Fuel's no problem—it's loaded when we make it, and it runs until the car is junked, on just that little bit of hydrogen. We have no top speed, really; car would shake apart before we ever reached max. Only limiting factor—oh, don't worry we *won't* shake apart! That'd take a bigger track than this!—only limiting factor in a race like this is the frictive surface: the tires. That's why we've got eight, and they're broad ones, too. But too much acceleration makes them skid a bit, and that's bad for control and worse for wear. Got to save the rubber or we'll have trouble finishing, even though the tires are solid. Guess you were still on pneumatics in Antarctica, eh?"

"I guess." Fisk realized that he had just received Lesson #1 in Fusion salesmanship. The car was so powerful that even solid composition (not rubber, of course; there were laws protecting the few wild rubber trees remaining) could wear out of round in the course of an hour.

But they were taking that risk now! They were overhauling car after car. The speedometer read— he looked again, astonished—390 MPH . . . 395 . . .

400 . . . and still rising! Air whistled by the little winglike vanes on the sides that were necessary for control at such velocity; even the soundproofing could not eliminate every vestige of that hurricane keening. 410 MPH . . . !

The boss was right. *Telling* him could not have been nearly as efficient as *showing* him, regardless of his presumed experience. When he got into the showroom and a customer asked him about power and speed, he would not need any artifice to describe the Fusion. He had seen it in action, seen the other racers falling behind at 430 . . . 435 . . .

"You haven't raced before," Bill observed mildly.

And it was out at last—too late. "I tried to tell you, but—"

Bill smiled. "But you're a sucker for a sob story."

Oh-oh. "You mean to say your co-pilot *didn't*—?"

"No, he did, all right. I do need that money, and that's why. But nine men out of ten would not risk their own necks in a grind like this to help out someone they'd never seen. You're too soft-hearted, and I'll bet you've been stepped on more than once, or you wouldn't be looking for a job at your age."

"Close enough."

"Don't worry about it, Fisk. Lot of people sneer because they haven't got the guts to be decent when the heat is on. I knew you weren't a racer the moment I saw you. You don't have racer's ways, and you're soft. But I wasn't going to embarrass the boss like that right before a race, and I *did* need a mapman."

"And you're a bit soft yourself," Fisk said.

"Helping your friend, sparing your boss, giving me a chance to get a job—"

Bill laughed easily. "Takes one to know one, doesn't it! Little girl set it up, right? Wanted her daddy to be a big man! Well, you *are* one, and not because of any fancy race. Got a child like that myself, wouldn't trade her! No, I'll cover for you Fisk. They can't hear us here; only contact is the radio, and that's one way: in. On the public band. So no driver can sneak in tactical info during the race. You're an honest man, and I like that, so I stopped you from making an ass of yourself, or seeming to. Man quits race at the start, the word spreads that he's chicken, no matter what the facts. After this you'll *be* a racer, officially, and nobody has to know the difference."

Fisk was beginning to find the man's solicitude a bit too confining. "But it isn't honest to—"

"It isn't right to make a scene right before a race, embarrassing the company and hurting the little girl's feelings. Got to choose your course in a hurry, even when the best one is ragged. That's racing. I figured more people would be better off this way, so that's the way I played it. Okay?"

What was there to say? "Okay," Fisk agreed reluctantly.

Then he saw the end of the track: slanting walls of concrete foam, narrowing the thirty car highway into twenty, ten, five lanes. Bill maneuvered the vehicle around the few remaining leaders with minute but expert turns of his steering wheel that nevertheless brought anguished squeals from the massive tires. At 500 MPH he passed the last and slammed into the Narrows.

"New leader and winner of the first heat, Fusion!" a voice announced. Fisk jumped, then realized that it was the car radio, that Bill had turned on. The race was being broadcast to the sports fans of the world.

"Sales: Fusion 24, Steamco 19, Duperjet 17. . . ."

"Hear that?" Bill cried happily. "The sales follow the performance, roughly. Usually the winner of a Hurdle is good for a hundred and fifty contracts or more right during the race. Much more, if something spectacular happens. We're ahead where it counts!"

Fisk was amazed. "You mean people are buying cars while they watch?"

"They sure do! When a car makes a good move, the sales-lines light up. Impulse buyers. Want to own a car with class. We're selling Fusions right now, Fisk—one percent commission on the gross goes to the driver. Five thousand dollars per unit, if they take the Special; less for the tamer models, though no Fusion is *very* tame! I figure each one for an average of $2500. If I run well this time and sell a hundred cars, that's two hundred fifty grand. Pretty good for a week's pay. Of course I don't always finish; then I get nothing. And most races I make less than one hundred grand when I *do* place. And I'd have to finish at least second or third just to cover my friend's medical expenses, if I wanted to do it in one race. But it's a living. I figure to retire after I make one really big killing— if it isn't myself I'm killing!"

"I see," Fisk said, chilled by the concept and by the rapidly narrowing walls of the Narrows. Five hundred miles per hour was an outrageous speed for a car, and now that there was something to measure it against outside . . .

"Oh, sorry—I didn't mean to rub it in, pal. You aren't a regular driver, so that commission doesn't apply to you. But I'll tell them you helped a lot, and if we do well the boss'll give you a nice starting bonus. Your commission will come from your showroom sales, mostly."

Fisk's concern had been about the danger, not the money, but he didn't push the matter.

Bill braked, using small parachutes that blossomed and dragged behind, rather than the pedal. They provided a steady reduction without slewing. Fisk was glad to have it. The Narrows, according to the map, was a one-lane chute with twelve-foot high barricades on either side. No one could pass there, so it would remain single file. It was a slow heat, as there were curves that would be disastrous at peak velocity.

But looking at the map was foolish: they were in the Narrows already! The crisscrossed timbers were invisible at this range, only a graying of view. Timbers of steel. Speed was less essential than control here. Any accident, and the Narrows would be blocked—and all cars behind would suffer. Bill had insured his own passage and placement by entering first.

There was a faint rattle. Bill cocked an ear alertly. "Check your gauges," he snapped to Fisk. "Probably that was an irregularity in the track; felt like it. But just in case—"

Fisk scanned the dials and lights. "All green and in 'normal' range."

"Right. Some of these buggies are more maneuverable at speed," Bill explained as he sweated the Fusion down and through. "They could leave us behind on a track like this—if they could only pass us. We're heavy, and prone to chassis stresses. Not the fault of the car—it's inherent in the mass, and much of that mass is shielding that we simply have to have. If any of those other cars carried our weight-penalty, they wouldn't have a chance in this race! But here in the Narrows we lose no ground. If anything's wrong, we can slow down and check it out. Next straightaway we'll show 'em dust! What's next on the map?"

"Hairpin."

"Say, we're really in luck! That's our worst time loser, except that now we've got first crack at it. The big ugly god of Hurdle racers must be smiling on us. We might even win this one, baby!"

Bill continued to slow, but even at 150 the huge racer skewed and tilted on the gentle curves, alarming Fisk uncomfortably. He was not, despite appearances, in perfect health, and this was not the healthiest type of stress for him.

Then they shot out of the Narrows—and there was Hairpin, brightly blazoned and barely a hundred yards distant.

They were at a comparative crawl of 120 MPH now—but in just two seconds Bill was slewing into

the approach, deliberately skidding the rear wheels
and braking. The next car was close behind: a jet.
Fisk watched it in the rearview screen, so as not
to have to watch the nightmare ahead. He knew
the jet's wheels were merely for support. The only
thing that stopped it from being a flyaway winner
on the straightaway was the pollution damping: the
jet with its flaming exhaust had to meet almost
prohibitive standards of emission control. And of
course it was chemically fueled, which meant it
couldn't go far compared to a car like the Fusion.

But such thoughts were merely irrelevant flashes
in passing. They were down to 90 now, whipping
around another killer bend of Hairpin while metal
groaned and dirt flew wide. Fisk thought he heard
another rattling, but realized that it was merely
the splay of pebbles thrown up against the bottom
of the vehicle. Outside each curve there was a six
foot drop-off onto an escape lane; the turn had to be
made tightly or there was no second chance. "Fusion
still leads," the radio announced. "Excellent tactics
in a slow second heat. Sales: Fusion 26, Duperjet
21. . . ."

"Not much pickup on the Narrows," Bill
explained in fragmentary fashion between the
body-smashing maneuvers. He was heel-and-toeing
it now, working accelerator, clutch and wheelbrake
almost simultaneously with his right foot while his
left controlled the movable wind vanes for additional
control. The parachute brakes had been jettisoned,
for they could not be turned on and off like this. Fisk
was amazed Bill still had concentration for chatter
while performing such heroic feats of motestry.

"Because I held up the line. Crowd likes action. But we're in good field position. Watch us go once we pass Hairpin!"

They braked again, down to 60, for the sharpest bend yet. It looked like the point of a knife. Fisk thought the turn impossible.

And someone ran out into the track.

Fisk became faint with impotent horror, but Bill's reaction time was like an old-time mousetrap. He swerved to miss the figure, throwing the car into a four-wheel or perhaps even a two wheel tilt, and careered off the bank to drop into the escape lane. The two men bounced like yo-yos in their harnesses as the great car landed, but they and it took the fall without physical damage. Good construction, good safeguards, good luck!

The jet following did likewise, landing more gently because it had only half Fusion's mass. Thus it was moving faster, and pulled up even.

There wasn't room for two. They jostled together and spun about. The side vane of the other car—Duperjet, Fisk realized—cut through the Fusion's bubble top, opening a neat incision in the shatterproof material. Then the lighter jet was ahead, reorienting in a fine display of equilibrium, and blasting back down the intercept lane to rejoin the race. Missing a turn did not, it seemed, disqualify a car; it merely delayed it. Delay of even a second could be extremely costly, of course, depending on the competition.

Already three other cars had navigated this fold of Hairpin, and more were coming. The dust was fluffing higher as the road eroded. The remaining entries would be taking the curve virtually blind—another disadvantage of trailing the leaders.

Bill guided the car to a safe slowdown, then slapped a hand to his head. "Get her moving!" he cried thickly. "The—" Fisk saw the blood.

"My controls don't—" Fisk began; but he paused as he saw Bill slump. How badly had the man been injured? The harness prevented him from looking more closely.

"New leader!" the radio cried. "Fusion and Duperjet spun out on Hairpin. Steamco first! Sales: Steamco 32, Fusion—one moment, the cancellations are still coming in—Fusion 21, Duperjet 15. . . ."

The car had finally stopped—but it was blocking the sole escape lane for this turn. Any car that missed this hairpin would shoot right this way at sixty or better, probably out of control. The ballooning dust guaranteed that the onrushing vehicle would not see the Fusion in time to stop, even if it were in condition to do so. This was a very bad location!

Something knocked on the bubble, and for a heartbeat he thought the collision had come already. But it was the figure who had started this disaster by materializing in the forbidden territory of the Hurdle Hairpin. He was going to have something to say to—

"Yola!" Fisk cried in dismay. He should have known!

She yelled something, but in the confusion he couldn't make it out. Then she pointed at Bill.

"Duperjet clipped him, thanks to you!" Fisk shouted back, trying to make himself heard through the bubble.

"Fisk, let me in!" Her voice came through the unnatural vent.

He found the canopy switch on Bill's side and jerked it. The bubbletop yanked itself up, its ripped portion catching, then springing loose. Yola jumped inside.

"Close up and get rolling!" she ordered, settling into Bill's inert lap. "First car that misses that pretzel—pow!"

An apt summation! "But I can't—my controls don't—"

"Don't give me that! You'll kill us all!" She looked back. *"Here comes one now!"*

Fisk's hand found the changeover switch as his foot came down on the accelerator clutch. The car lunged aimlessly, all eight wheels spinning in the dirt. He grabbed at the steering wheel, easing up enough on the clutch to let the wheels catch. "But there's nowhere to go!" he protested belatedly.

"Back on the main track, stupid! We've got to get this guy to a doctor. He's bleeding!"

And Fisk was somehow guiding the seeming behemoth down the track at rapidly increasing speed. His lightest pressure on the pedal elicited a surge of brute animation that was frightening in its vast strength. No car was behind; that had been a false alarm. But he knew they could not have remained in the escape lane. And she was right about Bill: the man was hurt, perhaps seriously, and every minute they delayed getting him to medical attention might reduce his chance of survival. There was no way out but on.

Then a car did appear in the escape lane, nosing out of the dust cloud as though from a brown tunnel, and Fisk involuntarily goosed the Fusion back onto the main track, his tires screaming as he turned. Fortunately for him, there were no further hairpin loops.

"What are we in for next?" he asked her, his hands sweating. He was moving the monster— but how long could he control it? Every time he pushed down on the pedal, the wheels destroyed themselves a little in their tigerish effort to accelerate the vehicle instantaneously. But it was either ride this tiger or be smashed flat by the one following.

Yola scrambled for the map, which had strewn itself across Fisk's feet. "The Elevated," she said. "Better get up speed."

"No thank you! I'm doing eighty now, and I know my limits. We're just going to limp out the safest way we can find, and—*what were you doing on the track, anyway?*"

"Have it your way," she said with affected nonchalance. "But I'm a race fan from way back, and I think you'd better get it up. Ever see the El on the newscreen?"

"Brilliant recovery by Duperjet!" the radio exclaimed. "Fusion is not out of the race, but trails the pack and is moving erratically. Sales: Duperjet 55, Steamco 49, Gasturb. . . ."

"Never watched sports." He looked around nervously. "Look, Yola—Bill's a nice guy, and it's your fault he's hurt. See if you can bandage him up, or something."

"What do I know about first aid?" she demanded rebelliously, as she always did when told to do something. But she began looking in the car pockets for the medicinal supplies that had to be there.

" . . . and Fusion 12—no, 10."

Then Fisk saw what lay ahead. *"That?"*

"What do you think? Watch those cars behind you."

Fisk was watching. They came up on him at an alarming clip as they navigated the last of Hairpin and accelerated. The track was widening here, but one slow vehicle could be disaster. Perforce, he speeded up.

Yola found a rolled bandage and began stretching it out. Fisk knew her hands were dirty—they always were—but kept his peace. Infection was the least of their present concerns! "We're taking a beating at the box office," she said. "But we're still in the race, and we're not last, either. Yet."

Still the cars came, showing no inclination to yield the right-of-way merely to avoid a possible crash. Fisk's adrenaline squirted. He stamped down hard—but not too hard—and the car surged forward as though its speed of a hundred miles per hour had been mere idling. It was a fine piece of machinery, and it could hardly perform like this had it suffered mechanical damage in the accident. There was, indeed, a certain exhilaration in managing a brute like this.

They were booming up the steep approach ramp of the Elevated. The combination of acceleration

and angle shoved the riders back into their seats,
hard. Yola balanced precariously and Fisk felt the
first twinge of nausea. He had a circulatory disorder
that could be aggravated by sustained physical
stress. Ordinarily it didn't bother him, since token
medication kept the symptoms suppressed—but
ordinarily he didn't tackle obstacle races in 500
MPH juggernauts.

He could have relaxed and let it pass until he
had the opportunity to punch his formula from
a roadside med dispenser—if he didn't happen to
be isolated on a private track, responsible for the
lives of three people. Not to mention a five hundred
thousand dollar racer.

"It's on his neck," Yola complained. "All icky with
hair and gore. I can't make the bandage stay!"

"Then hold it there with your hand!" Fisk rasped,
resenting the need to split his concentration and his
breath in a situation like this. "We've got to keep
him from bleeding too much. If Bill hadn't swerved
to avoid you—"

She uttered a monosyllable Fisk didn't recognize,
fortunately, as he was pretty sure it would have
earned her another week in solitary back at the
orphanage from whence she sprang. But somehow
she fixed the bandage in place.

Then they were up, with the other cars close
behind. Ahead stretched mind-numbing miles of
twisted ribbon, five hundred feet above the ground,
tapering into a thread in the distance though it
was four lanes wide. What engineering it must
have taken to assemble this race course in just
one week!

The two following cars charged past, and the whine of their tires was momentarily loud. The odor of oil and hot rubberoid swirled in through the rent in the bubble, and fine dust stung his face.

Yola sneezed. "There can't be many more behind us," she muttered, torn between hope and regret. She clung to the straps of Bill's harness as the incoming gusts swept her black hair across her brown face. "But don't stop now! You have to take the El at speed, or you fall off."

She was speaking literally. The paving contorted like a living tapeworm, given animation by his speed of—ouch!—170 MPH. In addition, the hole in the bubble interfered with the streamline contour and created a dangerous drag that Fisk seemed to feel all the way down to the sliding tires. But their forward momentum was not enough. The road tilted into a forty-five degree embankment girded by token guardrails. He would indeed fall off— unless he maintained speed sufficient to match the needs of the curve, countering the angle. Routine for racers, who required banked turns for stability; terrifying for pedestrian Fisk Centers.

"Yeah," Yola said, licking her lips. At eleven, with her deprived background, she was more enthusiastic than afraid. He hadn't really needed to ask why she had sneaked into the race grounds. Because it was forbidden. She had wanted a ride— and now she had it. Quite possibly her last. . . .

More wind blasted in as he accelerated. "Close up that hole!" Fisk snapped as another warning wave of dizziness came over him. Now the blood

circulation to his brain was being inhibited! But to
stop was to die. Already they were sliding toward
the nether perimeter, and the drag was making it
worse, and he had to keep turning the wheel and
bearing down on the pedal to counter the drift. But
if he accelerated too strongly and broke the wheels
free of the surface . . .

"Don't tell me what to do!" Yola flared.

Fisk twitched the wheel the other way. The
Fusion jerked toward the rail. The bright water
of a scenic lake spread below: a natural safety
net. But if it was deep, they could drown, for the
massive car would plummet to the bottom; if it was
shallow, the fall would flatten them.

"Okay! Okay!" she exclaimed with grace. "You're
the driver!" She dug out some harness strap and
additional bandage and wedged the mass into the
gap. It helped.

Now Fisk was able to gain the speed he needed.
200 . . . 250 . . . 280—and finally the drift abated,
and they were cruising in a kind of stasis. It was,
actually, rather pleasant in its way; the velocity
anesthetized his sense of proportion, and the
balancing forces lulled his circulatory incapacity.
What remained was a growing sense of well-being
and power. He was no longer Fisk, the hard-sell
sucker; he was Fisk the Supreme! "The Secret Life
of Fisk Centers . . ."

Then the curvature and banking reversed.

Fisk was driving for his life, and there was
suddenly no joy in it. He slewed across the strip
at 300 MPH without any exact knowledge where
he was going or how long he could last. His brain

tried to black out, but he wouldn't let consciousness depart and leave him in the lurch. He tilted his head back as far as he could, trying to let the blood in his system flow level to the gray region that needed it.

"Slow up! Speed down!" Yola screamed. "Watch the sky below—" Which was just about the way Fisk saw it.

"Duperjet still the leader," the radio announced. "Sales: Duperjet 78, Steamco 60, Electro 44. . . ."

Then the tilt decreased, and they were rolling down the steep exit slope at 350. Fisk knew there had been many miles of elevated ribbon, and that he had covered every twist at daredevil speed, but his memory had a short-term blank on the subject. That was fortunate for his equanimity, unfortunate for his security, since memory-lapse was another signal of his functional impairment. At six miles per minute, nothing but blind reflex had carried him through; but before long his reflexes would cut out too. After this—if there *were* an after!— he would carry spare medication on his person at all times.

Yola was silent and staring. Yes, it must have been good, to faze her like that.

" . . . Fusion 13. . . ."

At the foot of the ramp was an impenetrable bank of fog. The road led directly into it.

Fisk sighed. No way to avoid it. This was obviously part of the course. Another hurdle. He turned on the lights, and they were searing beams of brilliance that might well have been windowed from the solar conversion of the engine—but the

best they could do here was about two hundred feet.
No doubt some company specialized in producing
such nonpollutive pseudo-smog for just such hurdle
races! The car was moving at over 500 feet per
second, according to the relevant scale of the
speedometer. 360 MPH. How many seconds would
it take him to come to a stop?

He applied the brakes: both parachute and wheel.
The car slowed with neck-wrenching suddenness.
Bill groaned.

Good: it proved he was still alive. The smell of
burning rubberoid infiltrated from somewhere. It
could hardly be *his* tires—

"Keep moving!" Yola screamed. "Fogbank always
has stuff in it—"

A gap opened in the road. By the time Fisk
reacted, it was too late to react. The car hurtled the
twenty foot void with no more than a noisy jolt.

"Try *that* at half the speed!" Yola muttered
faintly.

Fisk had to agree with her. Undervelocity was
just as dangerous here as overvelocity. His
conservative course was to maintain middle-range
speed: say 200 MPH.

Then a wall appeared: stone and steel, by the
look.

Fisk swerved left, barely in time. In the fraction
of a second it took to get there, he found the
wall was oblique, cutting across the lane only
gradually, right to left. His instinct had been
accurate, and he had dodged the hurdle. Had he
swerved right . . .

"Try *that* at half speed!" he mimicked.

"Luck," Yola said despairingly, as though her own life were not part of the stakes.

Not all of the fog was outside. Fisk's arms were becoming leaden on the wheel and even his eyelids felt ponderous. His system had taken just about all it was going to. He was out of adrenaline. Wisps of cloud passed between his face and the instrument panel—or perhaps it was between his eyeball and his brain.

"Wake up!" Yola screamed. "THIS IS NO TIME FOR SLEEP!"

Fisk snapped alert, laughing—and, momentarily, that did it. He felt refreshed, ready to continue another couple of minutes. She thought he was so confident or foolhardy that he was deliberately relaxing! She didn't know about his disorder, since she had only been his daughter for two weeks. And why should he tell her now?

"Duperjet is out of the race!" the radio cried. "Crack-up in the Slalom—"

Fisk bounced over a devastating washboard trap and emerged from the fog. It hadn't actually been so bad. It would have been another matter in the press of the pack, however. Maneuvering invisibly to gain position, forced by other cars into that wall—had that been Duperjet's fate?

Or had Duperjet, too, suffered some injury in that Hairpin scrape, leading to eventual disaster? All because he hadn't anticipated his child's mischief? Was Duperjet's driver dead because of him?

But they were out of the fog and into a forest. Green concrete pseudotrees or pilings rose from the highway in a seemingly solid mass. They were cold:

ice had formed on them and snow coated the ground. Fisk was reminded of the Antarctic cross-country race he had supposedly driven in his youth, and he shivered.

"The Slalom!" Yola cried despairingly. "Doom!"

But, as with the wall in the fog, the pilings were less impenetrable than they seemed from a distance. In the seconds it took to reach the first, Fisk saw that they were spaced well apart. There was room to skid around them, if forward progress was not excessive. The tracks of many vehicles showed the routes other cars had taken.

But across the main trail were wheels themselves, and jagged pieces of metal: the debris of a recent accident strewn across the course. Duperjet, surely. This was dangerous territory—but it was nagging guilt he felt, not fear. Suppose one of Duperjet's wheels had been loosened at Hairpin. . . .

" . . . Fusion 19 . . . Duperjet 09. . . ."

The buyers certainly had little sympathy for a loser. Yet Duperjet was a fine car! It had led the pack after that spinout—no fault of its own!—but now that it had crashed, nobody wanted it. Fusion was recovering sales—but what a grisly way to succeed. It was as though he had killed a friend to obtain his commission. Far better to quit the race.

But he was already on the treacherous snow surface, and there was no way out but on, as the saying went. He was falling under the sway of stress fatigue again. Fisk willed his remaining strength into his hands and aimed the vehicle at the widest aperture between groups of pilings, following the common trail. Here and there the refrigerative grid showed, scraped temporarily bare by the passage of the pack, giving him slightly improved footing. He was still doing over 300 MPH, and he knew better than to attempt to change speed here.

Yola covered her eyes. "You drive like a zombie," her mouth said from under her hand.

The trail split. A piling lay dead ahead. Dead was the word! Fisk forced a message down along the resistive nerve tissue of his right arm, and the arm convulsed a bit, pulling the wheel around just that fraction necessary. The car slewed right, scraping paint against the piling on the left and almost dislodging Yola's hole-stuffing. At this point he hardly cared; it was as though car and racetrack were far away. Even his own extremities were almost beyond reach; his heart was laboring to the point of incipient collapse, but the life-sustaining blood was not getting through. He was numb and terribly tired all over. . . .

Yet somehow he would not let go entirely. He wasn't certain whether it was stubbornness or guilt, or what the object of either condition might be; but he hung on. A thin rivulet of animation trickled along the buried conduits of his pallid flesh, extending from corona to index finger. As the pilings loomed, his muscles twitched, and the car shaved by, never quite hitting, never quite sacrificing the traction so necessary to keep it from following Duperjet into destruction. Here Fusion's huge mass gave it traction when a lighter car might have skated. The impact of their passage howled about the myriad death traps of the Slalom, and if he were the lyrical type he might have immortalized the experience in poetry . . . and then they were out of it.

"We're alive!" Yola cried, amazed. "At least, *I* am. For a while I almost wished I was back at the orphanage!" She looked at Fisk. "You can stop here, zombie. We're out of the woods and nobody's behind anymore."

Fisk ignored her. Now there was straightaway, long and level and dry. Far ahead he could see several other cars. The Fusion had actually gained on them during this last hurdle. The race wasn't over yet—and as long as he was *in* it, why not *win* it?

It was madness, he knew—the futile delusion of grandeur of an oxygen-starved brain, its frontal lobes anesthetized. He didn't care. Bill needed a large sales-tally for his friend's medical bills—and perhaps for his own, coming up. Fisk was responsible for the Fusion's fall from first to last place in the Hurdle, and for Bill's injury, and perhaps for Duperjet's demise as well. What further harm could he do? There was power under his foot, if not in his body or brain. Why not invoke it, double or nothing?

"Daddy, what are you doing!" Yola whispered as the car accelerated.

"You willful little brat, you got me into this!" he snapped. "Now you're going to see it through." He *was* mad: insane, not angry. His brain had gone berserk and was running faster than the car! He had never suffered this effect of his malady before.

It was as though another personality had fought to the surface—a completely un-Fisk monster.

No, not true. It *was* him. His true personality, shackled by decades of civilized restraint, had at last emerged. And he *had* experienced this effect before: when under the multiple emotional stresses that had led to his acquisition of Yola. Then he had *talked* his way out of trouble; now he would *drive* out.

The girl was a tough refugee from a state institution. She didn't like having the patsy-Daddy submerge. "So it's like that, Centers," she muttered. "Well, want to know what's next? The Mountain!"

Fisk-normal quailed, but the demon aspect who had usurped control of his body said in fine detergent-opera fashion: "Yeah? You think I'm chicken? Watch this!" And his right foot crunched down harder.

The speedometer read 400 MPH. It climbed rapidly, as the tireless eight-tired machine obeyed the imperious command of a lunatic.

"Steamco 86, Electro 59, Gasturb 49 . . ." the radio said, and continued on through the entire list of twenty-six cars remaining in the race. Fusion was back up to 24, reflecting its slow recovery of position.

Slow? They were doing 500 now, and Fisk's foot was a marvel of unremitting ponderosity. This was a fair sized straightaway—the kind where power counted. Fusion's favorite track. The gap between him and the pack was closing. How much would this buggy do, flat-out? 570 . . . 580 . . . it was as though he heard the numbers as sales announcements instead of seeing them as miles per hour.

"This is suicide!" a little voice cried. At first he thought it was his civilized-self-conscience, but it turned out to be Yola.

Fisk's eyeballs seemed to be locked in their sockets, able to move only marginally to cover the contours of the road. He could not see her face or judge how Bill was doing. In fact, he was a machine himself, with his arms levering more or less together, sharing his drastically limited muscular power as though connected by an old fashioned limited-slip differential.

600!

Suddenly the straightaway was ending, and he was overhauling the pack at a phenomenal clip. *Great!* The demon exalted.

"You fool—it's the Mountain!" the Yola conscience screamed, afraid. But there was no meaning for Fisk except that beautiful passing of competitors on the fast track. So they had written Fusion off, eh? Fusion was going to win!

Then his foot came up involuntarily. Yola was down beside the pedal, prying it loose. And the pack moved ahead again and crammed like so much floating refuse into the drain-like access to the next hurdle.

"Fusion has merged with the pack," the radio said, surprised. "Looked for a moment there as if—but the driver was too smart to risk a pass on Mountain. We thought Fusion had mechanical trouble, but obviously not! Sales: Steamco 101, Electro 75, Gasturb 55, Vaporlock 44, Fusion 38. . . ."

"Wow!" Yola cried, forgetting her apprehensions of the moment before. "You may be crazy, but we're back in the sales money! What's your cut of the gross, Fisk?"

He didn't answer, knowing how little the money was compared to the lives and medical expenses depending on it. She had climbed back into Bill's lap, and Fisk's foot was free; but now the ascent was too steep to permit high velocity. He trailed the pack at a poor 380 MPH.

It was the Mountain Hurdle. The course wedged into a two lane thread along which cars were spaced like traveling ants. A cliff developed on the right, the dropoff becoming tall and sheer. Ahead, a car tried to pass another precipitously, about the way Fisk-demon had intended to pass the entire pack. But the banking of the road reversed, throwing it too far out, and the vehicle sailed into space at 350 to torpedo into the water-trap below. Water gouted as it struck.

"Coaldust slipped!" the radio cried, almost bloodthirstily. "Twenty-four remaining in the Hurdle at the two-thirds point."

The velocity-demon that now governed Fisk's ailing body took note. A lot of cars would not finish because they were too eager. He had to bide his time with a conservative strategy until he hit another straightaway or other suitable medium for all-out poop.

Meanwhile, Mountain was a terror. Visibility declined as the blind curves became sharper, and a small thunderstorm was anchored at the crest,

pelting the entries with rain and hailstones. He had
to slow to a crawl of 280, pacing himself by the car
ahead. In a nonrace situation the turns would have
been so gradual as to induce highway hypnosis; but
here they were enough to smash him from side to
side in his harness as he navigated each one. Yola
hung on somehow; she seemed to have her arms
under Bill's straps so that she could cling by the
elbows.

Through the blasting rain, the drops vaporizing
with the enormous impact, for his velocity converted them into bullet-hard pellets. Around a stalled
car, barely glimpsed in the spume. Then came
the descent, and Fisk accelerated down the glassy
slope.

"Steamco 129, Electro 114, Vaporlock 68,
Fusion 59...." They were moving up on sales
faster than on the pack, perhaps because the
spectators knew what would happen on the
next level heat, but it wasn't enough. The
demon would settle for nothing less than total
victory.

"Oh-oh!" Yola said. "Loop's next. Cool it,
leadfoot."

Bill groaned again. He was showing signs of
recovery, but Fisk didn't care. His eyes were on the
desertlike sandflat beyond. Gently rolling dunes
were artfully placed to alleviate the monotony
and impede progress; a straight-line route would
necessarily take in several of them. The alternative
was to waste time going around. He had no idea
what it was like to drive on sand. But if the other

cars could handle it, so could this fine Fusion—and this might be his last chance to pass the pack before the finish.

"Steamco still leads going into the Loop," the radio said. "Pack's pretty close and tight, though. There's likely to be some action. . . ."

Indeed there was. Now Fisk observed the Loop, nestled in the angle between the Mountain terminus and the Dunes plain. It seemed to be about three lanes wide—but the pack contained about fifteen cars, and few of them were giving way to let the procession become orderly. The Fusion was gaining, but would strike the Loop just after the pack did.

It didn't look as though there were any inherent limit on speed, here; the faster he went, the less likely he would be to fall off at the upside-down apex—provided he had the car under control. So long as nothing got in his way. But could his defective body take the sheer pseudogravitational strain? The Fusion was willing; the flesh was weak.

The first car hit the Loop. Up and over it went at some five hundred miles per hour, like a toy. Only car lengths behind it came the second, closing. Steamco and Electro, no doubt. Then, squeezing in two and three abreast, the pack, vying for position even as they encountered the vertical ascent. And the Fusion was bearing down at 550 MPH, still accelerating, still gaining.

Steamco shot from the corkscrew exit and landed on the fringe of the sandflat. Dust billowed up momentarily. Electro smacked into this and swerved, stirring up a greater cloud. Then the pack was tearing through like so many piranhas.

But Fisk was entering the Loop at 600 MPH. "Hang on!" he yelled, though Yola needed no warning. They smashed into the vertical curve and Fisk's breath left him. This was in effect a ten or fifteen G spaceship takeoff, he was sure, and his body was already weak from the prior strain and his existing disorder.

Yet he clutched a painful gray awareness, on and off.

" . . . spectacular crash!" the radio was crying avidly, and he realized he had failed, and could expect nothing but agony before he died. . . . "Pileup just beyond the Loop—"

Not him! But he was headed for it at 650 and up. *That* was the reality that kept him fighting: the climbing needle, signifying his conquest of—

"Stop!" Yola screamed thinly.

But it was too late to stop. They were upside-down, plummeting headfirst, level, taking off, upside-down, proceeding along the awful corkscrew of the Loop. Instead, Fisk shoved the pedal all the way to the floor, connecting engine to wheels without any bleeding of power, and rode the descent lane into ever increasing velocity.

670 . . . 685 . . . magic pictures on his retina. . . . 700 . . . 715. . . .

"Crazy. . . mad. . . deranged. . . berserk. . ." Yola gasped as the incredible markers passed. It was all she could summon breath for.

730 . . . and they were sailing off the skirt of the Loop.

740 . . . the wheels seemed hardly to touch the sand, and only the little vanes kept the car level. 742 . . . 744 . . . coming slower now. The great machine shuddered as though its stress limit had finally been met, and all that was left for Yola was a shaken moan. What power!

745. This was the ultimate glory!

" . . . fire prevents recovery of the bodies . . . total loss . . . worst disaster of the year . . . *look at Fusion!*"

Glory!

Dead ahead, half concealed by a low dune and a sinking dust cloud, was the roadblock. Licks of flame shot up, and smoke was piling into the sky. No chance to turn. A thousand feet away—and in less than one second they were upon it, traveling at 750 miles per hour, and his foot still savagely mashing the pedal. The Fusion was tearing itself apart, and eradication was a microsecond away, but Fisk would not even attempt to ease up. Already he was touching the vane-angle switch.

The low dune shoved the rubberoid and metal aloft in a single mighty convulsion. The great wheels barely touched the flaming corpse of the nearest car.

And they were airborne as the shaking became almost intolerable. Fumes siphoned in through the stuffed hole as the car was bathed in fire. The speedometer stood at 760.

"Great God," Yola screamed in a whisper. *"We've cracked the speed of sound!"*

"Fusion is past?" the radio gasped. *"Fusion hurdled the pileup!"*

They landed, and the sand swirled up behind in little tornadoes spawned by the vacuum of their sonic passage, but the mighty machine crunched on. The flames were far behind. Fisk's hands and arms were senseless and stiff in a kind of living rigor mortis, but straight ahead was all the car needed in the way of a directive. Now at last his foot began to creep up from the pedal.

"What? What?" a voice mumbled.

"Hey, he's coming to!" Yola cried as Bill stirred.

"Keep him quiet!" Fisk's voice rasped. "We're still doing 690 on sand!"

"Sales," the radio said. "Steamco 152, Fusion—one moment, it's still changing—that feat of piloting really stirred up the—never seen anything like it—*Fusion takes the lead in sales!* Fusion 173, Steamco 152—one moment—"

Bill lifted his head. "God, man, that's near my best! What—"

"I had to take over," Fisk said tersely. He was still fighting the rising tide of gray behind his eyes.

"Yeah. My head. But—"

"Revised sales," the radio said. "Fusion 208—folks, it's *still* changing! We can't get a fixed reading. The race isn't even finished . . . Fusion 249 . . . 261. . . ." There was an unexplained pause, then: "Folks, to recap: There has been a fifteen car collision on the Dunes just beyond the Loop, but the remaining cars are still running. Here's the replay. . . ." Another pause, as the screen viewers saw the film. "Steamco retains the lead on the track, but that's all, and Fusion is coming up fast. The others—seven cars, I believe—are picking their way around the wreckage, avoiding the flames. None of them will finish in the money. It's a two car race! Fusion, not known for its maneuverability, pulled such an extraordinary feat of—Fusion 319!—those orders are pouring in! Here's the replay on that hurdle of death: see, that's Fusion firing out of the Loop—look at that! IT CRACKED MACH ONE! We thought the car was out of the running, then this! The buyers are really impressed! Hell, *I'm* impressed, and I've been in this business for—most racers would have been smashed to pieces, busting sound like that, let alone doing it through flame! Fusion 370 . . . 401—folks we can't keep up! Unprecedented sales for an unfinished race! Looks like a record in the making, even if Fusion doesn't win the Hurdle! 452—I gotta buy one myself. . . ." The announcer panted into silence.

"That tells it! Bill exclaimed. "Sweetest music I ever! And I thought you couldn't drive!"

"I *can't*," Fisk said. "I'm sicker than you are."

Bill looked at him. "You're white as bare bones! You have a heart condition? I've lost some blood, but I've taken lumps before—better let me take over! Kid, get down on the floor or somewhere."

Yola scrambled down, finding a place to squat between the bucket seats. Bill clicked the switch, and Fisk's controls went dead. Now he could relax. These regular racing drivers were almost as tough as their cars!

"What's next?" Bill demanded, angling the car

gently around another dune.

"Tunnel," Yola said, wrestling with the map.

"Fusion 607. . . ."

"Get that!" Bill cried. "We match our sales! 607 MPH!"

Fisk just lay back and let himself slide back into whatever oblivion awaited. The drive-demon was gone, but the regular Fisk still needed his medicine. The race's end could not be far off, and it did look as though he were planning to survive.

"Fusion 726. . . ."

Bill shook his head. "Fisk, I don't know exactly how you did it while I was out, but you've just made us rich. Those sales are going to hit a thousand! It's a bandwagon now—everybody in the world wants a Fusion! We'll get two million five in commissions!"

"They'll come to their senses and begin cancelling after the excitement passes," Fisk pointed out. Now that he could afford to faint, he seemed to be recovering strength, perversely.

"Sure—but those'll be made up by the other buyers reading about it in the fax. That always happens, and they generally do balance out, close as makes no difference. Don't worry; we've got record winnings! And the credit's yours! So you took her through mach, did you! I never had the nerve."

"Terrific!" Yola cried, liking the idea of fame.

"Uh, better not," Fisk said, eyeing the tiny mouth of the approaching tunnel. Bill sounded normal, but Fisk didn't trust the man's condition. He had been unconscious for a fair period, and must have lost a significant quantity of blood—and an error in judgment of so much as six inches could be fatal, in that tight passage ahead.

"No, no, Fisk—you did it, and you'll get the commission. When I tell the boss how you pulled it out—"

"We'll be rich!" Yola exclaimed with innocent childish avarice.

Fisk hadn't been talking about money. His first concern was seeing them through the tunnel alive. Steamco had just entered it, and at the rate the Fusion was going there would be contact between them inside that darkness. Was Bill intending to vie for position, even now?

But it seemed money was a factor, because of the tremendous sales spurred by his mad exploit of moments ago. Yola's greed and Bill's misunderstanding sent a negative ripple through the weary convolutions of his brain. "When you tell your boss that, he'll fire you for allowing an unqualified driver to take over and play roulette with machinery and people's lives in the Hurdle. Because you *knew,* and he didn't. It was blind luck that got us through, as the tapes of the race will show."

Bill slid the car into the Tunnel as though he had done it all his life—as perhaps he had. "Maybe so," he said soberly. "Luck doesn't operate that way—not on the El or Mountain, and especially not by getting up speed to hurdle wreckage. There was driving genius in your hands and feet, like it or not. But you're right, it's bad business, and my boss would rather not know. Okay—we'll split

the take, half-half. It's right to share, because
I got hurt and you—"

As the Tunnel closed about them the rag and
strap plug popped out of the hole in the bubble,
urged by the suddenly compressing air within the
confined space. An almost solid blast of atmosphere
rammed in, striking Bill in the face and making
a stormlike turbulence within the bubble. The car
swerved, partly because Bill could barely see in
the gale, but mostly, Fisk knew, because of the
drag of the aperture itself. There was no room
to compensate, here; the stony walls were inches
close.

But Yola knew what to do, and since no one had
told her to do it, she did it. She crawled across
Bill's lap, probably kneeing him painfully in the
process, fetched in the tattered wad and jammed
it back into the hole. The storm subsided.

Fisk was able to speak again. "You got hurt
because *my daughter* ran out in front while you
were going through Hairpin! That almost killed us
all, and maybe Duperjet too."

"Take the money! Take the money!" Yola cried.

"You sure are one for making objections," Bill
said ruefully. "What *do* you want?"

This just stiffened Fisk's dubiously motivated
resistance. "I think we'd better just walk out of
your life when the race is over. A good—"

He had to pause, for they had caught up to
Steamco. The Tunnel was lighted, but irregularly;
the width varied from one to three lanes with curves
thrown in. Passing could be tricky—and Steamco

had no intention of *being* passed.

"A good sales-day is the least we can do to repay—"

But Fisk had to stop again as Bill swerved to pass on a subterranean straightaway and was quickly blocked off. Steamco had to know that there was no car to beat but Fusion, and the drivers would have been hearing the same reports about the sales. The only way the other car could recoup was by finishing ahead—or by putting Fusion out of the race entirely. That would shatter the dawning myth of invulnerability, and make Steamco the lone survivor and object for sales.

The passage narrowed, halting the maneuvering for a moment.

" . . . the trouble we have caused you," Fisk continued. "I'll find another job."

"Fisk, shut up!" Yola said. "You're throwing away two and a half million dollars."

"Fusion 981. . . ."

"Look, Fisk," Bill said earnestly as the dark walls rushed by and trickles of wind whined in through the stuffed hole. "I told you I'd cover for you about your lack of experience, laughable as that seems now. You've *had* experience, somewhere, somehow, even if you don't remember it. You're covering for *me,* really. And I'd never make trouble for your little girl. You don't have to sign over the money for *that.* I want you to have your share because you earned it. I wouldn't feel right letting you go away with nothing, after the way you—"

"I wouldn't feel right *taking* it," Fisk said firmly.

"You were right: any idiot can drive this car, and one just did. It was the *car* that pulled it out. It *is* the finest ever!"

"Fisk," Yola cried. "If you don't take that money—"

The dark track opened into a dual lane, then into a broad cavern spiked with stalagmites, casting their multiple and deceptive shadows. Many trails seemed to be open. Bill goosed the Fusion into a preemptive speed and angled for the far right opening. The Steamco moved over to block him, staying just ahead so that passing was impossible. It was more maneuverable, so could get away with this.

"I'll take the commission myself and make out a check for you," Bill said, as though nothing special were going on. "I'll take all the credit for the race, if that's the way you want it—but you've got to have your share of the commission. I can't take all the money for a race I didn't drive!"

"No."

Bill dodged the car again—which was impressive, at 400 MPH in the partially lighted cavern. But Steamco was ready, and stayed ahead. "You can't cover me forever, you bastard," he muttered. He was addressing the other car, Fisk decided after due reflection.

"Fusion 1038. . . ."

"I'll give it to your daughter, then. An irrevocable trust for her education, so she doesn't have to run onto any more racetracks."

"Yeah, yeah!" Yola agreed, but with less enthusiasm.

Fisk shook his head. "That money should go to your injured partner."

Another dangerous dodge that nearly put both cars into a post. "Twenty-five percent to your little girl, then." Bill looked grim. "A million will cover my friend's bill. You're making me settle for twice that. I don't like profiteering on something like this. I'm hurting in my conscience worse than on my head, and I can't dicker with you anymore. That's my final offer."

"Flip for it!" Yola said. "You go left next split, last moment. If Steamco goes right, you pass and Fisk takes the share."

"Okay!" Bill agreed.

Fisk was about to demur again, when the radio interrupted: "Folks, you'll be glad to know the drivers both survived Duperjet's crash. They blame themselves for misjudgment: too much speed in the Slalom, slipped on the ice. . . ."

Fisk felt a tremendous relief.

Bill accelerated again, almost nudging Steamco's persistent tail. As the post zoomed in on them, the first of a line of them, he nudged right, then cut sharply left. Steamco was caught on the right side, too late to compensate without cracking into the pylon.

"What's the *matter* with you?" Yola demanded as they stepped out of the tube at his apartment building. "We need money and you know it. Why wouldn't you take your share?"

Fisk hardly understood it himself. "What I did wasn't real. Some demon in me wanted the glory of winning the Hurdle, no matter what the cost. I was too sick to control it—"

"That's right!" she agreed. "You looked like a corpse! I thought sure you meant to kill us all!"

"But once the pressure was off, I regained control. By then it was too late to undo the damage—"

"But you brought it off!"

"The *demon* brought it off. But at least I didn't have to give that demon the satisfaction of making a profit from the episode. With no credit and no money—"

"Except that trust Bill's setting up for me that nobody can touch," she said. "Fisk, that money would have bought a lot of fun for both of us, and now all it's good for is *education*. Ugh!"

"Precisely. Education abolishes demons."

"I just don't get it!" she said crossly, putting her hand to the doorplate of their apartment.

"Neither do I," Fisk admitted. "I just knew that neither the racing credit nor the money was rightfully mine. I'll earn my fortune in my own way or not at all. That's my particular hurdle. Maybe it's a question of whether Dr. Jekyll or Mr. Hyde will govern."

"Who?"

He sighed. "Never mind. It's a devious point of characterization, and perhaps illusory. Every time I compromise my principles, disaster strikes. I tried to make an illicit profit in Marsland speculation and lost everything; I got involved in black market adoption and almost landed in jail. This time I very nearly killed us all. The demon offers material riches, but his real goal is misery."

She uttered the expletive he still didn't understand. "The first time you got a new exciting life. The second time you got me. This time you could've had—"

"At any rate, I'll never go near another racing car as long as I—"

"Hey, what's this?" she cried, lifting something out of the package slot.

Fisk looked at what she had found. It was a small square item with a gift tag.

Yola read it aloud. "You're a great sport. Sink Bill."

"That's 'Sinc.,' not 'sink,'" Fisk said. "For 'Sincerely.'" But she was already tearing open the wrapping with juvenile impatience.

Inside was a personalized ID ownership key for a new Fusion special.

CHAPTER

—◄ 4 ►—

"**M** r. Pontimer? I'm Fisk Centers of Perpetual Laser Memorial Gardens. I've come to give you the certificate to the free plot you have been awarded."

Pontimer's pale whiskered face was dubious. "Plot? What plot?"

His wife rushed up and pressed the door-release, admitting Fisk to the Pontimer's rather plain apartment. She was a thin, nervous woman whose manner suggested that she was used to putting up with abuse. "They called the other day, dear. It sounded so nice. A free space in the—the—" She stopped, grasping for an acceptable term.

"Memorial gardens," Fisk put in. Many people had deep neuroses about death, which was why the word was banned from his present vocabulary. He was not selling grave sites, he was doing memorial counseling. "We—"

"I'm no farmer!" Pontimer said indignantly. He was old and crotchety: the kind of man who required a meek wife.

"It's not a *garden,* dear," she said hastily. "It's— it's—"

Fisk saw that he would have to get more basic. "It's a cemetery."

"A graveyard!" Pontimer shrieked, shocked.

Sensitive subject, there! "Let's call it a place of interment," Fisk said, striving to eradicate the vulgar terminology and with it the vulgar notion that death was objectionable. This was the sort of education the profession did, necessarily. Once over this hump . . . "Actually, it's a very far shout from the conventional open cemetery you may have known in your youth. Population pressure has struck the memorial industry too, Mr. Pontimer! Today we have to make maximum possible utilization of land area. Our mausoleum—"

"Tea?" Mrs. Pontimer inquired, presenting an actual cup and pot.

Fisk was glad he was old enough to remember such niceties of the past. "Thank you," he said, accepting about four ounces of hot yellow liquid. "Our mausoleum is sixty stories high. But your plot is absolutely private! The dead have complete sanctity at—"

"*Dead?* I'm not dead yet! Who told you that?" Pontimer said with asperity. "I'm not going to die. My heart's as healthy as it ever was. More! I don't need any—"

"Oops!" Fisk, distracted by the awful tea,

had made the cardinal error of the novice. He had spoken the Forbidden Word. And now he was confronted with a living object lesson why that proscription was so stringently enforced. The client had spun into a morbid tizzy.

"*Pre*-need, Mr. Pontimer." Fisk forced a hearty laugh. "That means you pay now, die later." If he were lucky, that would defuse the word's connotations, making it possible to proceed with the presentation. Henceforth, though, he would keep a tighter rein on his vocabulary!

"Why should I pay now?" Pontimer realized with the cunning of the sick-minded that he had in some way put Fisk on the defensive. And the old man brightened visibly with aggressive importance. "Dying is bad enough, without you vultures coming around in advance to—"

"Dear!" Mrs. Pontimer exclaimed with rare courage.

But that was the question Fisk had been primed for. "I can answer that, Mr. Pontimer. It's a very good question and I'm glad you asked." He took a satisfying breath, having expended the standard ploy. *Compliment the dog that bites you.* "First, we live in inflationary times. Prices go up. You can't expire as cheaply as grandfather did, you know. Years from now it will cost still more. But you—"

"So pretty soon we can't afford to die at all!" Pontimer put in, cracking a smile.

And soon you'll have that dog licking your hand. "Right, Mr. Pontimer! But you can halt that trend by acting *now*. Invest today, and the price can never be raised for you."

"I thought the plot was free," Pontimer said sharply.

"Of course. I was speaking figuratively, merely explaining why it is to your advantage to make arrangements now. Quite apart from the fact that you can receive your plot absolutely without charge, no strings attached. This offer will not be repeated. But even if you *were* paying, it would pay you to act now."

"Oh. Maybe so," Pontimer said grudgingly.

"But more important, Mr. Pontimer," Fisk said, warming up nicely, "it is smart to make arrangements now, while you can specify exactly what you want. Do you know what usually happens when a person passes on without such preparation?"

"When you die, you die," Pontimer said. "What difference does anything make, once you're six feet under?"

A man with deep religious convictions would not have put it that way, Fisk thought, and made a mental note to avoid religious references. "It makes a difference to your widow," he said sternly. "Right at the moment of her grief, she has to make complex arrangements, not knowing your preferences. She may pay hundreds of dollars more than necessary, depleting your estate—all because you didn't care enough to plan ahead."

That got to him. "All right. I'll take your free plot."

"Excellent." Yes indeed—the bait had been taken. "Now you will want an adjacent plot for your wife, which we are offering at the special pre-need price of only fifty thousand dollars."

"Fifty thousand dollars!" Pontimer shouted before pausing for a coughing fit. "I bought this entire property for that! The lease to the land, I mean."

"How long ago?" Fisk inquired without hesitation, giving him the straight look the sales training course specified. The client's every reaction had been anticipated, and the winning responses were right there in the manual.

"Forty years." He pondered that, surprised. "Must be worth one million, today. Too bad it reverts to the state the moment we leave it."

Fisk pounced. "So your lease would cost twenty times as much today, still only for life tenure. But our plots, at fifty thousand, are no more expensive than equivalent accommodations twenty, thirty, and even forty years ago—*and your tenure is forever!* That's what modern technology and our pre-need reduction do for you. But such a bargain can hardly last long, obviously."

Fisk was afraid the client would spot the incongruity of using both inflation and the forty-year consistency of price as selling points. But Pontimer considered, then said: "Oh, all right. Fifty thousand for a plot—before it gets even more expensive."

Well. On with the manual. "Then you will need matching vaults, for only fifty thousand each, in order to use your plots."

"Coffins?"

Fisk almost winced at the crudity. "Vaults. To protect the caskets from the ravages of time and prevent settling of the ground, traditionally." That qualification was important.

"Oh—when the body decays," Mr. Pontimer said. "I've heard of that. But I thought they used metal now for the coffins, so the things can't break down."

"Caskets," Fisk corrected him. "Better yet, couches. No, the casket is not as stable over the years as you might suppose, Mr. Pontimer. Even the solid metal, hermetically sealed variety. And of course we don't handle that end; the funeral home provides the casket, so we can't be responsible. Every casket succumbs eventually, and then where are you? The vault will protect your remains from that unpleasantness."

But Pontimer had not lost sight of the money. "That's one hundred fifty thousand dollars! For a *free plot!*"

But the manual was way ahead of him. "Without our introductory gift of a plot and our pre-need discounts, the same thing would cost you double that amount at Perpetual Laser— and even more at competitive memorial gardens. But there is absolutely no obligation. You may accept your free plot and dispense with the remainder. I am merely trying to help you plan realistically."

Pontimer looked at him suspiciously. "Well, I'll just *do* that. Give me your free plot. I'll buy the damned vault somewhere else. A secondhand one,

or something. We'll see whether you mean it or
not."

Fool, Fisk thought. *You can't outsmart the
manual!* And who ever heard of a secondhand
burial vault? "I see you are an astute businessman.
Very well. You understand that this plot is non-
transferable. You have to use it yourself, or it
reverts to us. No re-selling. And you must use a
standard vault, wherever you obtain it."

"Oh." Evidently that no-sell stricture had just
punctured a dawning notion. Sell the free plot to
someone else for fifty thousand or less and make
a clean profit!

"Now we'll have to make an appointment for you
and your wife to tour the premises and select the
precise site," Fisk said, going into the next stage of
the sale. "We want to be absolutely certain you're
satisfied."

And while he negotiated the schedule, Fisk
mentally counted his winnings. Twenty percent
commission on what was shaping up to be at least
a one hundred fifty thousand dollar sale. Not bad
for an hour's work!

Of course, he did feel a bit of guilt about the
gimmick. The regular pre-need price of a plot at
Laser Mem. was forty thousand dollars, and it was
not the kind of lodging the average man preferred
once he saw it. By establishing an inflated "need"
price of sixty thousand dollars and offering one
"free" plot per family and requiring expensive
vaults, they were able to offer a "bargain"
package that cost just about the usual. $160,000
for $150,000. Many sales were made that way that

would not otherwise have materialized—and that was only the beginning.

Still, it was no worse than the norm for the industry. And it *did* represent a net saving over both the "need" and the "pre-need" prices. And everyone had to die sooner or later, so it was hardly a case of creating a market for a superfluous commodity. There were aspects of the sales spiel Fisk did not like—but he had discovered that there were aspects to *every* job. He had to compromise a little—or go into debt.

It *was* a necessary service, he reminded himself. People who did not plan for the inevitable were setting themselves up for much greater later grief than they deserved. Mr. Pontimer could not last long; his wife deserved the amelioration of the shock that this pre-planning would provide.

"And we provide an advisory service in funeral matters," Fisk finished aloud. "There is no obligation and no charge. You have only to ask— any time."

"How nice," Mrs. Pontimer said. She seemed genuinely relieved to have the matter settled. Not that it *was* settled, yet.

Yola knew, the moment he stepped into the apartment. "Fisky, you caught a sucker!" She flung her thin brown arms about his neck and kissed him.

"I made a sale," Fisk admitted, forceably disengaging. There were aspects of adoptive parenthood that disturbed him more than anything in the cemetery business. Such as an eleven-year-old daughter who insisted on vacillating between four-year-old tantrums and eighteen-year-old seductions. He was largely incompetent to deal with either stage, as well she knew. "I mean, I counseled a client about his memorial needs."

"How much loot?" she demanded eagerly.

He sighed as he stepped into the foamer. "It isn't settled, Yola. All they have agreed to so far is the free plot. If the normal course is followed, my commission would come to about thirty thousand dollars. More, if they respond well to tomorrow's tour."

"Yeah, I hear that tour's murder. Hey, when do *I* get to see the leaning tower? Must be weird in those stacks! All those dry bones—"

"It's a mausoleum. No visible bones—they're all sealed up in caskets and vaults. *And it doesn't lean!*"

She shrugged indifferently. "Multiple-layer berry patch. Betcha it stinks on hot days."

"It's air-conditioned—it doesn't smell. Yola, Perpetual Laser's plots are paying our bills— and we have plenty, the way you splurge on nonessentials. It's a profession, and you'd better give it due respect. The tower is entirely sanitary."

"A skyscraper full of corpses!"

"*Remains!*" But it was useless correcting her; it only brought him down to her level. "Punch us supper, will you?"

"Punch it yourself, cryptface!"

"Very well." Fisk reached for the fooder control. "Boiled seaweed and impurgated cod liver oil."

Yola ran around him and got her hands there first. "I'll do it! Chocolate cookies and ice cream Alamo."

"*a la mode.*" She could be managed, he saw. If only he had the ability to do it when he needed to!

The Pontimers arrived on the vacuum express. "Welcome to Perpetual Laser Memorial Gardens," Fisk said benignly. "As you can see, the mausoleum is completely enclosed by laser beams—our trademark. No intruder will ever penetrate these premises!"

"*We* just did," Pontimer observed, thinking he had scored another point.

"We are hardly intruders. The computer knows the difference, I assure you." Fisk showed them into the spacious ground floor and began the tour spiel. "The word 'mausoleum' derives from the tomb of Mausolus at Halicarnasssus, built in 352 B.C., one of the seven wonders of the ancient world. The Great Pyramid was another—the only wonder to survive until this day. Gradually the word 'mausoleum' came to apply to any large building containing the remains of an entire family—typically a royal family. The famous Taj Mahal is a mausoleum." Calculated to put things in their proper perspective, assuming the clients were educated enough to appreciate the references.

"They had lasers back in 352 B.C.?" Pontimer inquired.

Fisk ignored that. "Now the ground floor is devoted entirely to chapels. Every major religion is represented, and there is even a blank chamber for atheists, ha-ha. We are nondenominational, of course, but we honor every faith and scoff at none. Your own priest, pastor or rabbi knows he is welcome here. Many services are performed daily for your convenience." Fisk really liked this section; it was one of the better facets of the business. The clients evidently liked it too; they looked about and murmured appreciatively. No matter how small a part religion might play in their daily lives, most people liked to have a religious sanction for the important turning points: birth, marriage, death.

Of course this was really part of the sales pitch. Clients came for the tour thinking it was all settled—but the real push was just beginning.

Well, he thought uncomfortably, he didn't make policy. It was a living.

"Now your plots are on the fifth level," Fisk said guiding them to the elevator.

"How about making it the top floor?" Pontimer said. "Nearer to God, you know." He was more cheerful today; perhaps these elegant surroundings were abating his fear of the inevitable. It was Fisk's private theory that much of the abhorrence people had for death was its presumed loneliness, and the fancied discomforts of an exposed grave. Obviously there was plenty of company and comfort in this remarkable building.

"Sorry," Fisk said regretfully. "The upper floors are not yet in service. Occupation is from the bottom up. Each level is a complete self-contained memorial park. It will be half a century before every unit in the mausoleum is spoken for—and longer before complete occupation, naturally."

The elevator glided to a halt. Archaic devices of this nature were deliberately used here, to enhance the suggestion of ancient splendor. Also, they served as a better control on visitation. Timing was essential.

The door slid open noiselessly. Fisk waited for them to step out, knowing what would happen.

"Oh, it's beautiful!" Mrs. Pontimer exclaimed. Even grouchy Mr. P. assented.

That first impression was worth several thousand dollars to Perpetual Laser, for it predisposed the clients to buy at any price.

For the elevators debouched into the park section of the floor. White pebbled pathways curved around flowering bushes and led on to a central fountain that sparkled in subtly shifting pastel hues. The lighting was soft, as though dusk were verging: the twilight of a pleasant life, or the pre-dawn of a pleasant afterlife. The air was cool and delicately scented with pine and rose. Religious-seeming statuary was discreetly placed and illumined, but devoid of any specific connotations. The artistic nudes could be considered virgins or mermaids or random art, depending on the eye of the beholder; the avian representations might be doves of peace or hawks of war or even vague angels. The occasional granite snakes could be classed as refugees from Eden or as Ouroburos: resurrection. Living palms, violets, wheat, passion flowers, clover and ivy: each might be a symbol, but none *had* to be symbolic. Some of the abstracts resembled a crucifix from one angle, a Buddha from another, and something suggestive of Mohammedanism from a third—none being certain. Myriad live butterflies fluttered in the gentle breeze, of diverse and exotic species.

Fisk allowed them to take it in for the prescribed period, then showed them to an offshoot. An inconspicuous door in the park wall, rather like the opening to a moss-covered tomb, led into a somber hallway. The temperature was set at sixty degrees Fahrenheit. The Pontimers rubbed their arms unconsciously to fend off the sudden chill.

"Here you are," Fisk said. The acoustics here made his voice harsh.

"Here?" Pontimer was uncomprehending. "This is like a crypt!"

"It *is* a crypt," Fisk said. He grasped a bleak handle and hauled out a low drawer. "Refrigerated, of course. There is absolutely no decomposition. Guaranteed. A plot such as the kings of ancient times never possessed. How do you like it?"

There was a strained silence.

"I—I thought the park—" Mrs. Pontimer said hesitantly. "I saw some—"

"Some memorial markers," Fisk said. "Certainly. We do have a limited number of interments there. But location in the park proper is necessarily somewhat more of an investment. Naturally we have an excellent time-payment plan incorporating amount of balance insurance, that brings the park within anybody's reach—but I would not attempt to deceive you. It *is* more costly."

"Why?" Pontimer demanded, though he obviously knew that the trap was closing.

"Well, it *is* a rather special environment," Fisk said, feeling some sympathy for the fish as it wriggled on the hook. "Much less efficient, because of the vegetation and statuary, so it has to cost more." He was forgetting to stick to "investment" in lieu of "cost," but doubted that nicety mattered now. "But mainly it's because of special government regulations, sanitary and esthetic. The remains must either be cremated or sealed hermetically. A suitable memorial marker must be placed, so that the site can always be found despite changes in vegetation and layout. There is also an interment fee, as the ground there must literally be broken, refilled, and replanted. And the care of the site—clipping the grass, feeding the birds—yes, there are living birds here, too, but they tend to stay out of sight—watering, artificial sunlight—"

"You said we had to buy vaults," Pontimer exclaimed. "To go around the coffin, to stop the ground from settling. But here in this crypt *there is no ground!* So what's the vault for?"

Chomp! on the bait. Fisk had a momentary mental image of a fish in a mousetrap. A prospect was most vulnerable when he thought he had caught the salesman in an error. "State law, Mr. Pontimer. Everybody interred in a cemetery of any nature must be casketed and vaulted, regardless of the actual mode. Ridiculous, isn't it? But what can anyone do? The memorial industry has lobbied for simplification for years, without making any dent on the bureaucracy. It costs us more to accommodate full vaults in our freezers, but we must do it or forfeit our license to operate. Vaults are *necessary* when there is an actual ground burial, as in the parksite; but—"

"So, we have to pay for what we don't need," Pontimer said, shivering. Fisk was warmly dressed, but the clients were subject to the full ravage of the cold, by no accident. By this time the very notion of refrigeration after death was repulsive. Imagine shivering for eternity in a dark drawer.

"How—how much is it? In the park?" Mrs. Pontimer asked timidly.

"One hundred twenty thousand dollars a plot," Fisk said without hesitation. "Plus the vault, of course. And memorial plaque. Even with our fully insured easy-installment plan—well . . ."

Now at last he let them come out of the dismal hall. At the precise instant they emerged into the warm, wonderful scenic splendor of the park, he said: "We still allow for the free plot, however. Fifty thousand dollars credited toward the more elegant residence. And this week only we are waiving the interment fee on all park plots placed. But—" He gestured to encompass the marvelous beauty of it. "Such accommodation never does come cheaply. And with inflation—"

Mrs. Pontimer cracked first. She put her hand on her husband's arm. "Please, George—"

"It's a damn gimmick," Pontimer muttered, accurately enough. But he too had been shaken by the appalling contrast between park and crypt. He capitulated. "We can't take what little we have with us, and I don't care to leave it to our cheapskate third cousins. Might as well waste it on something nice."

Victory stared Fisk Centers in the face. And he escorted them to a pleasant alcove amid the lovely bushes where the fragrance of nature was especially serene, and there he counseled them into matching memorial sites for that exact location and two attractive vaults and a bronze Mr. & Mrs. plaque set flush with the ground so as not to obstruct the airy passage of the butterflies. All parties were well satisfied. And after that he rested.

Total investment: $350,000.

Commission: $70,000.

"Pontimer! Pontimer! Who sold Pontimer?" the supervisor called. The robosec was malfunctioning again, so that the records were not readily accessible.

"I did," Fisk said, looking up from his copy of CASKET AND SUNNYSIDE. This was a slow day, and several of the salesmen were doing phone duty, trying to develop new leads. This was mind deadening labor, so they did it in shifts. Fisk's turn was due in half an hour.

"Wife on phone. GS, for sure. Pick it up in the office and make it short. Ditch that magazine, will you? If a client saw *that* on the screen . . ."

"Right." Fisk didn't have to check his cardfile on that one; that sale had put him on the board as an effective salesman, and the initiative had brought him fairly regular success in the intervening month. "GS" meant grief stricken, so he knew what to expect.

Mrs. Pontimer's strained face was waiting on the screen. "Oh, Mr. Centers!" she exclaimed with relief. "Please, can you handle it?"

Evidently pre-need had abruptly become need. But he had to be sure. "Handle what, Mrs. Pontimer?"

"The—the—my husband—" She brought her handkerchief to her face.

"Mrs. Pontimer, I assure you that everything is in order here. The insurance will cover the remaining payments on your husband's plot and vault. We'll be glad to contact your funeral director and—"

"No, no!" she cried hysterically. "I couldn't bear to have a *stranger* doing it! Please, Mr. Centers—you said Per—Perpetual Laser would—you know about such things. I'm so—he never had heart trouble before—I don't know what to—"

The supervisor was back. "Go ahead," he muttered. "We're short on leads and it's good publicity. 'Laser Mem. assists GS widow.' Good experience for you, too."

This was not the kindest way to put it, but at least it bestowed the cemetery management's technical blessing. The woman obviously needed help. Perpetual Laser did advertise free advisory service, and now its bluff had been called. "Mrs. Pontimer, I'll be right over," Fisk said reassuringly.

"Oh, thank you, thank you!" she said. He cut the connection before she had the opportunity to break down completely.

Fisk took a priority highway and gunned his massive Fusion to two hundred, covering thirty miles in ten minutes. For him this was fast; for the car it was commuter's creep, as the machine

had the capability to crack the sonic barrier on
land, given running room. But it was handy, he
had to admit, having a car that was really a car.

Mrs. Pontimer was in a worse state than he
realized. She hadn't done a thing other than phone
him. Her husband lay on the floor where he had
fallen, half behind a heavy old table, a spilled
glass beside him. Fisk was able to reconstruct
what had happened fairly readily: the man had
been moving furniture at his wife's behest—it was
amazing what control even the meekest woman had
over the grouchiest man—working up a real sweat,
and had paused for a drink of cold water. And his
heart had stopped. Fisk had heard of it happening
that way: not during exertion, but just after.

Of course there was no excuse for it, since modern
medicine could abate virtually every heart ailment.
But Pontimer was the kind who didn't trust doctors.
Obviously he *had* heart trouble, because his wife
had immediately named that as the cause of
death.

It was obvious that Mrs. Pontimer had no
resources at all. She had been almost completely
dependent on her husband, and simply couldn't
cope with the disaster. Probably there were no
close relatives—he vaguely remembered a mention
of distant cousins—so she had called the one
person she thought could handle it: the cemetery
representative. Sensible enough, really.

The trouble was, Fisk knew very little about
the actual mechanism of the funereal end of it.
He had picked up the basics, of course, and a
number of tidbits from the mortuary magazines—

but that hardly prepared him for a fresh corpse and a distraught widow who wouldn't deal with strangers.

"Mrs. Pontimer," he said, keeping his voice calm. "Who is your family doctor?"

Her expression was answer enough. No help there.

"Perhaps you should lie down for a while," Fisk told her. "I'll take care of it."

"Yes. . . ." She meandered to an old couch.

Fisk called his own doctor. "I know this isn't your specialty, Al," he said apologetically. "But I'm in a spot and need a bit of advice myself, so I can *give* advice."

"Fisk, I'm really pretty busy this morning—hey! Is that in the background what—"

"Afraid so."

"You don't need advice, you need an attorney! Or didn't you do it?"

"You old fraud—I need a *doctor*. He had a heart attack. I think. Can you come?"

"Very well." Dr. Bickel was an old acquaintance. Fisk's circulatory condition had required a great deal of competent attention in the early days, and young Bickel of thirty years ago had handled it. Now Fisk's medication made the matter routine, but the friendship endured.

"Dead, certainly," Bickel said shortly later, checking the body. "You're lucky, Fisk. No question of foul play. Heart. He should never have tackled that table—not in the condition he was in."

"Lucky?" Fisk asked. "I'm just helping a client."

Bickel spoke in a voice too low for Mrs. Pontimer to overhear: "If it had been poison or a clout on the head, Fisk, *you* would have been implicated. Wife could have sworn you did it . . . these things happen, you know."

Ouch! "I'm—I'm in charge of arrangements," Fisk explained lamely. "I never thought—"

"That's why I cancelled my morning appointments and got the hell over here. I didn't save your circulation just to have it jinxed permanently by your soft brain. I'll make out a death certificate while you call an undertaker. He'll take it from there."

"Can't do, Al. She won't have a stranger doing it. And my company wants the publicity for making the arrangements."

The doctor looked at him. "Is Laser paying for it?"

"No. Except for the burial end. But she does need help. I don't think she has much money, and—"

Bickel shook his head as he let his breath out. "Fisk, how do you get into these scrapes? You have too soft a heart to deal with a professional mortician. It is essential to have an objective third party to handle such negotiations; that far you're on solid ground. But you do have to use an undertaker, Fisk—no way around that, in this state. Are you sure you have the gumption to do the necessary?"

"Morticians aren't *that* bad, Al! I've had some experience, after all—"

"No worse than cemeterians," Bickel muttered. "All right—leave her here with her husband while you go dicker with the mortician. When you phone

here you can introduce her to the funeral director,
so he's not a stranger. I'll stay here until they
arrive for the body."

"Thanks, Al," Fisk said gratefully. Dr. Bickel had
an excellent bedside manner; he would have Mrs.
Pontimer docile and reasonable within the hour.

"But first find out what she can afford—and no
matter what, *stay within it*. Understand?"

Fisk shook the doctor's hand. "I'll protect her
interests. Don't worry about that!"

But he had an education coming.

The presiding mortician of Deep Space Memorial
Chapel was most solicitous. He was dressed
conservatively and nothing about him could be
construed as offensive to any conceivable system of
belief—yet he carried about him the distinct aura of
afterlife. Fisk was reminded of the park statuary
of the mausoleum.

Mr. Black asked only essential questions, and
even these seemed to be largely formality.
Obviously the man had done spot research on
Mr. Pontimer via the population directory and knew
what he needed already. Almost too efficient.

Mr. Black conducted Fisk to the tastefully
carpeted selection room with such finesse that
Fisk made a note to emulate the technique for his
own tours through the mausoleum. The undertaker
was obviously master of a trade Fisk was only
learning.

The room was filled with elaborate display
coffins, each mounted at comfortable elevation for
inspection, each girt with dark cloth and with its

lid lifted. Some had bedsheets and pillows inside, and looked exceedingly comfortable.

"This is our Deep Space Trademark Platinum Memorial Couch," Mr. Black said softly. "Solid copper foundation with genuine platinum impregnation inside and out. You cannot obtain a more secure resting place at any price, Mr. Centers. Seamless exterior, unit construction, noiseless hinges, foam rubber interior. Available in Reclining Pink, Conservative Gray, and Forever Black."

Indeed, it resembled a padded treasure chest more than a coffin. Fisk had not realized that the dead rated such considerate repose. But he couldn't help asking: "Are you sure it's tight? The cemeteries require vaults—"

"The cemeteries are unnecessarily solicitous. This casket is so tight it can be sent to deep space without leakage. If we can interest you in our special Planetary Orbit Memorial—"

"*Orbit?*" Fisk hadn't heard of this.

"In the asteroid belt. Technically, the casket becomes a planet in its own right, circling the sun forever until the Judgment Day. The bereaved can observe it by telescope, drawing reassurance. A very fitting—"

"Uh, no thanks. Memorial arrangements have already been made."

"Very good." It was just as though the man had made no pitch to exclude the cemetery, but Fisk now had an insight into the competition. Burial in space! Perpetual Laser would have to keep on its corporate toes.

"About the cost—" Fisk hinted.

"By all means. This handsome couch is just eleven eighty-seven—a very reasonable investment considering its quality."

"Eleven hundred dollars?"

"Eleven thousand," Black said solicitously.

"Eleven thousand dollars?" Fisk's jaw dropped. "For one box?"

Black frowned as though embarrassed by the client's ignorant outburst. "For one superior casket, Mr. Centers, including the complete service, naturally."

"Oh." He should have remembered. The price of the entire funeral was predicated on the casket. Fisk began to wonder: Was he out of touch? Was the price in order? "Just what do we get with this cof—this casket?"

"Conveyance of the loved one, preparation, display in the slumber room, memorial service— all accomplished with tact and simple elegance by our experienced personnel. We take care of all legal details and records, of course."

"You mean there will be no additional charges at all?" Actually, it was no more than the cost of plot and vault at Perpetual Laser. . . .

"None by us, Mr. Centers. Unless you wish us to supervise the floral tribute, musician's honorarium, burial site and similar details."

It occurred to Fisk that Mr. Black had not done his homework quite thoroughly enough, and did not suspect that Fisk was a representative of the burial industry. This was the second time Black had smoothly attempted to usurp cemeterial prerogatives. "I suppose a few flowers would be nice—no, I think we'll omit them. Better to donate the money to charity. Put 'Please Omit' in the notice of service."

"I beg your pardon?"

"No flowers. They'll only wilt, and there'll be plenty of growing plants at Las—at the cemetery."

"But it is usual to have a floral tribute for the service itself," Black protested, evincing refined disapproval. "To facilitate a suitable Memory Picture."

Memory Picture: the mortician's term for a good looking corpse. Jokes were rife at the cemetery about such funeral foibles, and Fisk could not resist some gentle ribbing. "What are you talking about? This is a *funeral,* not a parade!"

"Mr. Centers, I see you do not properly appreciate our position. This is *not* just a funeral; it is grief therapy for the bereaved. The Loved One must be provided with the most favorable accouterments."

"Grief therapy? Who appointed you therapist? I'm just looking for a decent and inexpensive funeral for my client."

"Your client, Mr. Centers?"

Oh-oh. If Black found out now about the cemetery . . . "Mrs. Pontimer. I'm representing her interests, as a friend of the family. Figure of speech."

Black gazed at him for a moment, but made no issue of the matter. Fisk had to admire the man's aplomb as he showed the way to another casket.

"This is our Economy Plan, at a saving of four thousand dollars," Black said with a certain reserve.

Fisk felt a bit cheap, though he knew this was a merchandising strategy similar to what he employed in selling burial plots. Show an expensive one, then an obviously inferior one, then swing back to clinch the sale. The yo-yo technique: extremely effective against unsuspecting marks.

Cheap? This coffin was still almost eight thousand dollars! It was of simulated wood, with simulated knotholes. *Real* pine would cost several times as much, were it not illegal for such purposes. This was the kind of gaudy make-believe that was calculated to appeal to people of illiterate taste.

The mortician saw Fisk's expression. Without a word he showed the way to a third display. "Stellar Classic Memorial couch. Eighteen gauge lead-coated steel, counterbalanced top, innerspring mattress, contemporary styling, velvet lining—not elaborate from the outside, but quite well appointed inside. Available at a saving of two thousand dollars."

So now the "couch" nomenclature had dropped in price. Subtle, clever. "Cheaper than the last one?" Fisk asked hopefully.

"Than the first one. Nine eighty-seven, complete with service."

Fisk didn't like being managed. "Let's see your cheapest coffin. No trimmings, no grief therapy, no flowers."

"Really, Mr. Centers. You wouldn't want—"

"I might want to take my business elsewhere."

Black stiffened almost visibly at this unwarranted harassment. "Very well." He led the way brusquely through a door Fisk hadn't noticed before. The room beyond was gaunt. A lone deathbox squatted on the dusty floor, fashioned of unappealing fiberboard. It had no soft inner lining, no fancy coating, and even seemed slightly warped. Light showed through the cracks: it would be a leaky domicile. "Four eighty-seven."

"Still almost five thousand dollars—for this makeshift thing?"

"Including our minimum service, Mr. Centers," Black said with simple dignity. "We are unable to do it for less and remain fully compensated."

Fully compensated: the funeral trade's euphemism for charging what the market would bear. "Oh come off it, Black!" Fisk exclaimed, exasperated. "A human body can be transported and cremated for less than a thousand!"

"Mr. Centers: a human body can be thrown into the sewer for *nothing*."

Touché. Fisk had to bite his tongue to keep from laughing. What a sneer at crematoriums! Ashes were cheaper to handle and cheaper to bury, so neither morticians nor crematarians were particularly partial to remains.

Meanwhile, this pro could not be shaken loose. Fisk imagined what Mrs. Pontimer's reaction would be to seeing her husband lying in sad state in this cruel box. He sighed. She had barely fifteen thousand dollars in available funds, apart from a small widow's pension. That money would be

better spent on groceries and rentals: phone,
foamer, suiter and so on. But her grief would
never permit obvious cheapness in the disposition
of her husband.

Fisk raged inwardly, but he wound up with
the nine thousand eight hundred and seventy
dollar casket—which was, of course, the one the
funeral director had pegged him for at the outset.
He phoned Mrs. Pontimer and introduced Black,
who quickly made her feel at ease. Now Dr. Bickel
could go back to his practice, and the body could be
removed from the house.

Now for the lesser details. Disgruntled at his
own inefficiency as a bargainer, Fisk decided to cut
costs implacably on the remaining portions of the
ritual. Perpetual Laser had perfectly serviceable
chapel facilities that Mrs. Pontimer would certainly
approve, so the formal service could be held there.
And he would absolutely rule out nonessentials like
flowers. He might yet save a significant portion of
the widow's savings for the urgent needs of the
living.

Since the management of the funeral home
balked about preparing a notice of service excluding
flowers, Fisk decided to call Black's bluff by using
the mortician's phone to contact a leading florist
himself. Naturally the florist would insist that there
was nothing obligatory about flowers, and with that
leverage . . .

"Please omit—*what?*" the lady demanded,
shocked.

"Omit flowers," Fisk said patiently. "My friend's
estate is not large, so I knew you would understand

the necessity to economize. You would not want your product to be the one that dissipated the resources she needs for food and medicine—"

She appraised him carefully, with the briefest glance at Black, who was standing behind. Her voice softened persuasively. "We certainly do appreciate your position, sir. We of the floral industry are uniquely aware how very difficult it is to cope with this period of bereavement. Naturally you are concerned with the welfare of the survivors as well as that of your loved one. We certainly wish to do everything humanly possible to ease your suffering."

"Good," said Fisk, relieved. "Now if you'll just explain to the under—the funeral director, here—"

"However," she continued firmly, "have you considered the longer view? Sometimes an immediate saving may be had at the cost of a great deal of unnecessary suffering. You have the opportunity now—and never again, unfortunately!—to render meaningful tribute to your Loved One. Psychologists agree that funeral flowers comfort the bereaved as almost nothing else can. They provide an outlet for the expressions of sympathy for friends. They pay tribute to the life accomplishments of the deceased. Your experience and common sense must tell you that in this emotional moment the extra warmth and comfort of living flowers is essential to create a Memory Picture that will endure through the years."

Oh, no! Not the Memory Picture again! "Well yes, but—"

Her voice became stern. "But consider this, too: if you begin omitting flowers, what will be next? Minister? Music? All but the plainest casket? Memorial markers? Interment itself? When does a funeral service stop comforting the bereaved—and become merely a mechanical fulfillment of an obligation? Once you start subtracting warmth and human feeling, where do you end—and what do you have left?"

Fisk recognized a variant of the hard-sell pitch. But if he omitted the flowers now, he would seem to be vilifying human warmth itself! The florist had beaten him at his game. He couldn't risk cutting the flowers and having someone in the trade get through to Mrs. Pontimer to inflame her guilt through such aspersions.

"All right," he said. "We'll take a few flowers, and omit the 'please omit.'"

She was gracious in victory. "I was sure you would understand," she said with no trace of the smugness he knew she felt. "Now we have excellent Venusian mugwumps, the very latest and most elegant of floral tributes—"

"Hey, Fisky—whatcha doing at the body shop," a penetrating voice called.

Fisk whipped around. "Yola! What—?"

Then he saw her brown face on another phone. She must have called him at the cemetery office and been redirected here. She had the annoying habit of checking up on him possessively. He had to get off the line before she tore things up in her inimitable fashion.

"What happened, Fisk?" she demanded loudly. "You quit working at Boot Hill? Tenement tombstones get you down?"

Black eyed her critically, drawing the obvious inferences—and the florist was doing likewise from the other phone. "Memorials, not tombstones," Fisk said. "Yola, this is business. I've told you not to bother me at—"

"Hell, Daddy, the corpses don't care. You only croak once, you know!"

Wrong, he thought. He died every time Yola let fly in public.

"So you work for a cemetery," Black said coldly.

"What are you trying to do—cut us out?" the florist demanded, a sharp tone replacing her former persuasiveness. "Two can play that game! Burial isn't even required by law, you know, despite that expensive lobbying you folks are doing. A man has to die, but he doesn't have to wind up in a plot. Just remember—"

"You're jumping to conclusions!" Fisk cried desperately. "I was just—"

"What's bugging *them?*" Yola said, enjoying the consternation. "A carcass by any other name would rot as quick."

Black's composure broke at last, and the florist turned lily-white. All their labored euphemisms were being massacred!

But the mortician had a fighting heart. There was only a hint of a quaver in his voice. "If you want to spy on the profession, just examine your own skeletons first, Centers. What's your outfit?"

Yola burst into song. "Did you ever think as the hearse flew by, that you might be the next to die?"

"*Coach,* not hearse!" Black snapped involuntarily.

"PL," Fisk muttered, casting about for an inconspicuous exit.

"Perpetual Laser!" the florist said, pouncing like a hungry superhybrid pitcher plant. "Free plot gimmick. Freezing crypts. We deliver there all the time."

" . . . they wrap you up in a Plutofoam sheet—" Yola sang.

"*Shroud!*" Black cried. "*Robe,* I mean." He was certainly flustered now.

"Yola, this is no way to behave!" But Fisk knew remonstrance was useless. He could see her thumb jammed down hard on the OVERRIDE button, a precaution against termination of the connection from this end.

"Laser, eh?" Black said, swinging back to the attack. There could be no question of his courage under fire! "Hydroponic gardens, we call them. Artificial plantings on sixty stories. So-called non-profit corp."

"Non-profit corpse!" Yola screamed, delighted. "That's rich, ghoul!"

"Owned by a holding company who sells them space at inflated prices to make sure they *can't* make a profit. No taxes that way. But the real owners are reaping rich harvests from that dirt, let me tell you!"

"That land sold for five hundred thousand dollars per acre," the florist said. "So they charge five thousand for each six-by-three plot. Know what that comes to? Well over ten million dollars—*per level!*"

"The worms crawl in, the worms crawl out, the worms play Satellite on your snout!"

"And it's sixty levels high—not counting the cremain-urn mezzanines," Black said. "Talk of profiteering!"

Fisk spied a back door and made his escape while the trialogue sustained itself with increasing vehemence.

It was like coming in out of a hurricane. He found himself in a dark, rather cold passage reminiscent of the crypt tunnels of the mausoleum. He trotted along it, afraid Black would notice his absence before he cleared the building. Once he got home he would poke Yola's mouthy little head into the foamer and lock the machine on SCOUR!

The hall emptied into a chilly room containing several wheeled tables, each with powerstraps and shroudcloths. For the transport of corpses, obviously. The right side opened to a delivery platform for the hearsejets.

Fisk headed for the garage section, knowing that there would be a connection to the visitor's parking lot where his Fusion was docked.

He was mistaken. Every door was locked, and keyed to authorized personnel only. He couldn't get out.

He returned to the table-staging area, looking for another exit. Light suddenly showed at the far end of the entrance passage. Someone was coming after him!

Fisk jumped onto a table and pulled the shroud over himself. His action was irrational, since all he had to do was go back to face the moderate embarrassment lurking in the front office, apologize, and beat a humble retreat. He was not too proud for that. But his flight reflex refused to pay attention. It just wanted to get him away.

Clamps snapped about his ankles and wrists. Snakelike, a strap crawled over his abdomen and constricted snugly. Something like a helmet eased onto his head, holding it securely.

It was an automated operating table. Fisk opened his mouth to shout—and a jointed pincer jammed in a wad of absorbent gauze and taped it in place. To prevent noxious exhalations from the subject, probably, since dead bodies did not normally need to be gagged. Fisk struggled mightily, but only succeeded in shaking the shroud away from one eye, so that he could see the plain ceiling. The pincer had folded down into the table.

The table moved. Helpless, Fisk watched it bash through the swinging doors astride its track and cruise into a tiled and sterile-looking surgery room. *Oh no!* This was the undertaker's morgue!

Something else moved. It was an old fashioned multipurpose robot, the kind that knew any menial job when the appropriate occupation-spool was inserted. Semi-humanoid because the early manufacturers thought that was what the buying public wanted. The portion of the extremities Fisk could see by straining his eyeball almost crosswise in its socket had been fitted with a

scalpel, forceps, clamp and needles. Fisk had a
rough idea what these instruments were for. He
would have screamed if he could.

The dermasurgeon robot touched a switch. The
cart rolled forward a few feet, then abruptly tilted.
As his head swung up, Fisk saw that he was not
the first in line. Another corpse preceded him, and
his unit had just moved into the slanted on-deck
position. Assembly-line efficiency.

The other table was now tilted the other way:
head down. Fisk stared at it with burgeoning alarm
as the robot peeled back the shroud.

"Now, Mr. Pontimer," the robot said with morbid
mechanical cheer. "We shall set about making you
comfortable."

His eyes had not deceived him. It *was* Mr.
Pontimer, already here. The hearse must have
jetted out the instant the decision was made, and
brought the body back while Fisk was bargaining
about "Please omit." Appalling efficiency.

"Just one neat little painless incision in the
carotid artery of the neck," the surgeon said. Fisk
had forgotten that the spool-robots talked. But of
course it was just part of the prerecorded tape,
keyed in to the other job requirements. That way
the owner could verify the machine's programming
verbally. There was certainly no need to talk to the
dead—but also no need to turn off the sound.

"There, that didn't hurt a bit, did it? Oh blood
won't flow? Tut, tut; we'll just have to help it along
a little. One tiny prick of the needle—very good,
Mr. Pontimer, you didn't flinch at all!—and now
we'll start the nice sanitary Jupiter Mist Quality

embalming fluid gently coursing in. SAE 10-30 for all weather. Ha-ha, little joke there! It really is nothing more than the Balm-ex company's patented blend of formaldehyde, alcohol, glycerin, phenol, borax, water and Formula Q, that mystic ingredient derived from moon-lava and guaranteed to bring instant new softness and luster to you skin. Or your money back, Mr. Pontimer. Ha-ha. Now isn't that better? So cool, so smooth, so fragrant . . ."

Fisk became sick—but choked back his gorge, knowing that it would only complicate his situation. It was already hard enough to breathe with his mouth stuffed. He struggled with his bonds, but they had been made with rigor mortis in mind and were absolutely firm. Not uncomfortable, for bruised or battered corpses looked bad on display; but impossible to escape.

"And now, while the marvelous elixir of mortis, that sweet embalmer is replacing all the dark smelly old tired blood, let's just perform a smidgeon of decorative surgery on your face, Mr. Pontimer. Oh it is a nice face, for a human; please don't take umbrage! But there *are* just a few wee little tiny wrinkles here and there that make you look less healthy than you really are. Shall we apply a spot of Saturn Snow foundation creme? You'll look so nice they'll think you have a halo, or at least a ring, a Saturn Snow ring, ha-ha! Oh, your eyes, Mr. Pontimer; must close them! Clients are never supposed to witness the secrets of our excellent preparation room. Suppose we insert these dainty little Comet Everstick adhesive caps under the lids, so, and depress the skin ever so gently, so. Now you will sleep forever. Isn't that wonderful!"

Another cart sailed into the morgue—or, as the loquacious robot put it with the prescribed euphemism, the preparation room. This was a busy outfit. It was quite possible that one extra cadaver would not be noticed until after processing. . . .

"Ah, you are looking better already, Mr. Pontimer! I could have taken another twenty years off your life, had you come here for treatment twenty years ago! Embalming is most effective when commenced before death occurs. If only Mr. Black didn't require me to operate at such a disadvantage, waiting until *hours* after life is extinct! I really must go on strike for the right to embalm living people, don't you agree?"

That was some speech-tape the robot had, Fisk thought with a shudder. Had a sadist programmed it? Or a practical joker?

"But twenty years ago I would have had to use a needle and thread to sew your mouth together, with the stitches passing between your upper lip and your left nostril. Inside, where nothing shows, of course. Effective, but crude, you must admit. Today we are so much more civilized. We merely apply the Fang—beg pardon, the Nova Oral Pessary— to bring your teeth together and your lips *almost* together, just so. No, no, don't bite, Mr. Pontimer! It screws into your jaw automatically. It will hold itself in place until death do you part, ha-ha! Oh, does the screw hurt? I'm so sorry, I should have administered an anesthetic. We used to have you in stitches, and now we screw you. Oh, not funny? I apologize profusely! So thoughtless of me. But you see, robots don't think very much. Our bodies may be superior to yours, but our brains—well, can't cry over spilt oil! Now we'll just trim and tint your hair—oh, and we must do something about that ugly beard stubble, too. You really should have shaved before you died, Mr. Pontimer!"

There were sounds of trimming and tinting and shaving, as well as an indeterminate slosh and grind that had to be the Fang installing itself. Fisk's own jaw hurt.

"Now we'll simply seal the incision with invisible Future Age pseudoplastic tape, so, and it's done. Let's see your abdomen, Mr. Pontimer. Hm, none too healthy, I'm obliged to say. Suppose we just insert our little trocar in your navel and poke about your worn-out entrails—you really will not be needing them anymore, will you?—and suck them out through the tube. We'll find something so much better to fill your body cavity, Mr. Pontimer!"

The sound and smell destroyed what control remained to Fisk. His own gut heaved as though to evacuate itself without benefit of the robot's trocar. There was no stopping it.

And the pressure of the vomit blasted out the gag.

It took Fisk some time to recover, and longer to realize that he was now free to scream for help. But what good would screaming do, with no one to hear but this grotesquely preprogrammed machine?

In the interval the robot had completed the abdominal surgery, stuffed the hollow, and replaced the shroud over Mr. Pontimer. Apparently it was not going to do the remainder of the restoration immediately. No doubt the body had to "set" for a few hours for the embalmer to suffuse the outer tissues.

The tables moved again. Fisk found himself upended. The robot lifted away the shroud and leaned over Fisk's nether extremity: his head. It didn't seem to notice the vomit.

"Now Mr. Klondyke—so sorry to have kept you waiting, but we'll make up for that by treating you extra well. Shall we begin with the jugular vein? The scalpel moved toward his neck.

Desperation gave Fisk genius. This was not, could not be a taped machine! The dialogue was non-repetitive, and it was using proper names! This was a thinking robot, one who might respond to verbal commands.

"STOP!"

The knife paused. "Fine intellectual problem," the robot mused. "Mr. Black has put Mr. Klondyke on the schedule for this morning—but Mr. Klondyke wishes to countermand. Which directive takes precedence?"

"Mine, of course!" Fisk said, vastly relieved.

"No, I don't work for you," the machine said after pondering. "I work *on* you." The scalpel resumed travel.

"I'M NOT DEAD!" Fisk bawled.

Then he realized his mistake. "Splendid!" the surgeon said. "I can finally embalm a live subject! Oh, Mr. Klondyke, you have made my whole day!"

He would have to get an ambitious mechanical! Naturally the robot had no human sense of right and wrong. It cared only for the quality of its work—

and as it had explained to Mr. Pontimer, the fresher the client, the better.

But Fisk's life-gluttonous brain came through again. "I'm—I'm already done! I'm bursting with Jupiter Mist Quality SAE 10-30 with Formula Q! Marvelous lifelike job—your most brilliant exhibition of preparation skill! Just route me on to the display room without further retouching!"

The robot still hesitated. The scalpel wavered before Fisk's nervous jugular. Obviously the machine felt that something was not quite right.

"You're getting behind schedule!" Fisk said. "See, there's another cadaver on deck. Go on to the next. Every minute that passes makes embalming more difficult."

The robot looked. "Strange," it said. "There was no other client listed for this session. Just Mr. Smith and Mr. Pontimer and Mr. Klondyke. . . ."

"An emergency case came up! Mr.—Mr. Makeshift died of Neptunian Algae and has to be prepared immediately before he stagnates! Mr. Black says these remains take precedence!"

He had spoken the magic words. "Oh, well, if Mr. Black says . . ."

Fisk's table trollied onward, righting itself. The next specimen—the real Mr. Klondyke—tilted into place. "Now Mr. Makeshift, where would you like to be tapped? Mr. Black says you're to have priority treatment. . . ."

He had saved his blood and guts—but that was all. Fisk jolted to a stop beside Mr. Pontimer, and there he stayed, hopelessly bound. He was afraid to say anything more to the robot, lest the lure of a live body prove too great to resist after all.

Time trod on. Fisk grew hungry and thirsty, but had no relief. Worse, the strain of tension and confinement was aggravating his circulatory condition, making him feel faint. In due course he lost consciousness.

Motion woke him. Another robot was handling him, removing his clothing, washing his body. Fisk was too disorganized to realize that he was now free of the manacles. "I'm *done*! Pass me along!"

But he was weaker than he realized. He fainted again.

"And now you may view Mr. Klondyke," Black's unctuous voice said. "We regret that he will reside in the slumber room for only two hours, as the window for the launch is limited . . . you understand."

There was a subdued murmur of agreement.

A curtain parted dramatically. Light shone in, blinding Fisk so that his eyes closed automatically. He kept still, trying to fathom his situation.

"As you know, the final resting place for which Mr. Klondyke is destined is one of the most elegant conceivable to the mind of man," Black continued. By the sound of it he was standing nearby but facing away, addressing a small party of mourners.

Mourners . . .

He was in a casket, on display!

By fouling up the assembly line robots he had slipped into the slot intended for Mr. Klondyke. And the funeral director, so contemptuously confident of his apparatus, had never bothered to make a preliminary visual inspection.

" . . . whereupon the Ship of Shadows will follow that solemn trajectory unerringly to the very source of life itself, committing Mr. Klondyke to the ultimately purifying flame," Black continued. Fisk had to admit that the undertaker was good at this; his voice rang with impassioned sincerity. "Ladies and gentlemen of the Beloved Bereaved, I give you Solar Cremation!"

They were going to rocket him into the sun!

Now the Beloved Bereaved drew closer to the casket, eager for a solid glimpse of the recipient-to-be of this exotic terminus. Fisk kept his eyes tightly shut, afraid to do otherwise. Of course there was no equitable way out of this—but what was he to do?

Appreciative murmurs of the standard variety. "My, how lifelike!" "He's only sleeping!" "How *well* he looks!"

What were they—paid mourners? They should have spotted the imposition by this time! Fisk held his breath, waiting for the inevitable. In a moment they would realize that he was *not* their cadaver. . . .

Black had the finesse not to acknowledge the audible compliments on his restorative art. "Naturally he is only sleeping. His spirit survives forever! Now I shall leave you to your final farewell—"

"A-tisket, a-tasket, a green and yellow casket!" a girlish voice sang in the hall, coming nearer. The mourners hushed. "I wrote a letter, poison pen—" Then: "There you are, ghoul! What have you done with my father?"

It was Yola, bless her infuriating little heart. She had come to the rescue—in her fashion. Fisk slit one eye open.

No wonder the Beloved Bereaved had not yet recognized him. He was propped within a massive coffin that shadowed the better part of his face. A colored light shone down, not nearly as bright as it had seemed at first, no doubt tinting the highlights to bring out those lifelike tones while concealing the ravages of death. There were flowers everywhere, filling the room and the coffin itself and even encroaching on the body: him. And he wore some kind of tuxedo with a high collar to conceal the supposed scars on his neck. And there was a weight of makeup on his cheeks.

But fortunately he had been spared the eye and mouth fixers, not to mention embalming and evisceration. He had a right to look alive.

The mortician must have said something to soothe Yola, but any such attempt was foredoomed. Yola hated to be soothed, and now she had a legitimate grievance: the disappearance of her father. "Don't try to shush *me*, buzzard-beak! He was here this morning! I saw him on the phone, remember? Then you found out he was from the graveyard—and he disappeared. I'll bet he's in one of these meat-cans right here. You rubbed him out so he couldn't talk!"

Thank God for her vociferous loyalty! If anyone ever did 'rub him out' Yola would guarantee a miserable existence for the murderer. The entire crowd was staring at her and Black now, much to the undertaker's discomfort. *Die a little, funeral man!* Fisk thought sadistically.

Fisk sat up quietly. Flowers sprayed to the floor as he teetered dizzily, but no one noticed. Good— he was even equipped with fancy black shoes that fit. Nothing cheap about the Deep Space Memorial Chapel!

Yola continued to harangue the mortified mortician. "Fake outfit . . . damn taxidermist . . . slaughterhouse . . . stinking corpses . . . gyp deal . . ."

Fisk climbed out of the casket and clung to it, steadying himself. He needed a shot of his circulatory medication, but knew he had to hang on for a few minutes more. Once he got to the Fusion he could call Dr. Bickel. Right now he had to make the supreme effort.

He took a breath and cast loose. He wobbled, stumbled, and almost fell, brushing against a Bereaved. The man glanced at him, obviously taking him for another mourner, and made way. Fisk found a handkerchief tucked neatly in his breast pocket—a genuine nylon handkerchief!— and used it to mop his face as he barged through the group. He probably looked as much like a simultaneously bereaved and outraged relative as it was possible to be.

And he was out. He toyed for an irrational moment with the notion of finding a substitute for the coffin, either a dummy or another corpse, but fortunately realized that this was a delusion of his malfunctioning brain. He was lucky just getting away.

All the way out to the car he could hear Yola's shrill exclamations: mortuary pornography.

"Oh, Mr. Centers, it's so lovely!" Mrs. Pontimer said through her tears. "He looked just as if he were sleeping, and all those pretty flowers, and Mr. Black was *so* nice, and Dr. Bickel too—I know I could never have found such wonderful people without your help. And then the burial in your beautiful memorial gardens with the butterflies. I know ten thousand dollars is a lot to pay for a funeral, but it was worth it to—to—"

Fisk was glad she was in no condition to perceive his reaction. *Nice* Mr. Black! Ten thousand dollars? The insurance had covered the massive debt remaining on the burial facilities, of course, so that much was indeed a bargain. But the flowers had cost $5630 alone—what incredible lucre for "human warmth"! The musicians—Fisk couldn't remember at the moment where they had come in— had run another three thousand, union minimum. Plus other incidentals somehow not included in the all-inclusive main package. All told, the funeral come to just about twenty thousand dollars, despite Fisk's valiant efforts to hold costs down.

He had paid the difference himself, rather than see his client wiped out.

"So lovely!" Mrs. Pontimer repeated. Fisk new that it was the claim of the funeral trade that it was only delivering what the people wanted. It seemed that this was true, at least with respect to Mrs. Pontimer.

"Yes, lovely," Fisk agreed dutifully, thinking

of what Mr. Pontimer had gone through in the undertaker's morgue to achieve that grandeur for the display. Embalming, trocar, fang . . . but it *had* made him look better in death than he had in life. There did seem to be comfort in appearances, and the widow had indeed formed a therapeutic Memory Picture. Thus Black had delivered every part of the promised service.

Fisk shook his head. He wasn't sure he could distinguish right from wrong.

Yola had a message for him at home. "The ghoul wants you to call him back."

Fisk gestured her away. "Black has his money. I'm quitting the business. I'll sell candy corn on the street if I have to; I won't deal with the funeral trade anymore, any part of it. Just be thankful he didn't press charges against us, after you—"

"So call him up and tell him off," she said, punching the number. "Do I have to do *everything* for you?" Before Fisk could stop it, Black's face was on the screen.

The mortician gave him no chance to martial his sentiments. "I'll speak to the point, Mr. Centers," he said suavely. "I had thought you to be a typical cemetery salesman, but further information has enlightened me. I respect your motives and commend your success; you did economize substantially. But I must advise you that you are hopelessly naive about the profession. Had you been frank with me at the outset you would have discovered that our purposes are not antagonistic."

"Now look here, Black—" Fisk began angrily.

"Tell Mrs. Pontimer to join a memorial society. Her own disposition can be prepaid for less than five thousand dollars total, including a conservative floral tribute."

Fisk sat down suddenly. "You mean I could have saved—"

"And you yourself seem better suited to employment with the Death Insurance Agency, Mr. Centers. I have taken the liberty of recommending your name to their personnel office as a claims investigator. You do seem to have a talent for getting into the back rooms." He smiled briefly. "Good day." Black's face faded out.

"Death insurance?" Yola demanded. "What's he talking about?"

Fisk shook his head wearily. "I don't know either. But I have the sinking feeling that ghouls give good advice, when they give it at all. I do need a new job. I suppose this insurance outfit will contact me."

The phone lighted.

CHAPTER

5

Yola opened the phone line before Fisk could stop her, as she always did. Sometimes he was caught eating, and sometimes cleaning up in the foamer. This time, fortunately, he was fed and clothed, so for once avoided the embarrassment of a stranger's cynosure.

A fat man stared into the room. "Yola Centers?" he inquired.

"You mean it's for me?" she cried, girlishly flattered.

"For you and your father," the man said, smiling. "I'm Brown of the Death Insurance Agency. Mr. Black of Deep Space Memorial Chapel recommended you and your father as suitable prospects for our claim department."

"*Us?*" Yola exclaimed. "Not just *him*?"

Fisk, about to take over the dialogue, paused. He

had been anticipating the call from DIA without knowing what to expect, but he hadn't thought of expecting this. Maybe Yola would be able to get more pertinent information than he could. She was certainly more forward.

"What does it pay?" she asked.

"Twenty-five hundred dollars a week to start," Brown said. "No upper limit for really qualified personnel. But our standards of competence are stringent, and you may find it difficult to—"

"Well, okay," she said. "And how much for *him*?"

Fisk choked, but Brown wasn't fazed. "This is exactly the type of nerve we require. But in this case the figure is for the *team*. I know it isn't much—but we can't use you alone, unfortunately."

"I knew there was a catch," she muttered. "But there'd better be a raise pretty fast."

"Excellent," Brown said. "Here is the prospectus on your first assignment." And the mailfax issued a sheet.

Fisk made ready to formulate an objection, but his fifty-year-old brain couldn't marshal his thoughts rapidly enough.

"I hope you are successful," Brown said. "I shall transfer your first month's salary to your account. Sincerely—" and he faded.

"But I don't know anything about whatever it is!" Fisk cried belatedly.

"So hit their lit, silly," Yola said, heading for the fooder.

Fisk sighed and read it. Slowly he began to understand.

"Life" insurance was a death benefit payable to

the survivors of the insuree, so that they might exist despite the loss of income brought about by the person's demise. The insuree had to die to collect.

"Death" insurance was the opposite. In this age it was possible—and, indeed, commercially feasible— to reanimate the dead. The insuree was by this policy guaranteed the right to *stay dead*, in whole or in part, once his mortal term was over. The certainty of death had become one of humanity's most important rights. DIA would spare no expense, up to the face value of the policy, to see that no insuree lived again against his will.

"Morbid," Yola said appreciatively. "I'll work for 'em, but you'll never catch me taking out a policy on *my* death!"

"I don't know," Fisk said. "Consider the ghosts of the past. Human spirits who were not allowed to rest, and had to exist in misery after their decease. Their dearest wish was to be allowed to die completely. If I were in such a situation—"

"*Ghosts!*" she said witheringly. "Have you taken your anti-senility pill this month, Fisky?"

"The medication I take is for my circulatory condition—" he began, but gave it up. She was forever teasing him about his infirmities, chief of which was his age. Four and a half times hers. Next to that, she rebuked his slight obesity, that she claimed made him weigh four and a half times as much as she. She liked to imply that he was also stupid, and should have retired from active life two decades ago. She was, in short, a typical daughter, despite her recent adoption, and in his most secret heart he rather appreciated her little concerns.

"Have lunch," she said, shoving a hi-calorie, lo-vitamin strawberry splurge at him. "Fat old idiots don't need a balanced diet."

Fisk tooled the Fusion into the parking cavern of Exotic Disposals, Inc. "You know what to do?" he asked nervously.

"Fisky, after ten years at state institutions as a homeless waif, I'm a pro at sneakery," Yola said confidently. "Just do your part and it's quack soup."

"They'll make quack soup of *us* if they catch on," he warned her. "The business they're in—"

"Aw, they're clean," she said with less confidence. "You'll see."

"I sincerely hope so," he said with a shiver.

They got out and walked up the ramp to the entrance. "Now stand close behind me," Fisk murmured.

"You don't have to tell me! Think I'm as dumb as you are? Pull in your fat pos—"

"Sh!"

The screen came on as they stepped on the access plate. "Identity and mission," a voice demanded.

"Fisk Centers, salesman." He knew his image was being checked against city directory files.

"Product."

"Preparation Creme, miniaturization. Srinkfit brand."

There was a pause for verification. Fisk wasn't worried about that aspect; he was at this moment a legitimate agent of Srinkfit and was so registered, even though this was merely his cover identity.

The gate opened. Fisk stepped inside—with Yola in lockstep behind him, so that the electronic counter would pick up only one body. After the gate closed, Yola split away and hurried down a side passage while Fisk proceeded slowly toward the purchasing office. Stage one had been navigated successfully.

"All right, Srinkfit—strut your stuff," the purchaser said. He was a man of about Fisk's age and size, with a bald-wig concealing what was probably an unfashionably thick head of hair. There were hard lines around his eyes and mouth. The name on his identity plaque was Exunt—probably a business moniker.

"We offer a superior grade preparation creme that will match or exceed the tolerances on your present brand and provide better resolution," Fisk said, spieling off his memorized opening sentence. He had learned that, in the course of assorted efforts to sell sundry products: get that opening down pat, to break the ice and abate stage fright. The rest was better done extemporaneously, but not the start. "It costs more, of course—but the enhancement of quality in your end product more than justifies this."

"Document your claim," Exunt said cynically.

"That would take several hours, as you know," Fisk said. "I am prepared to leave a sample on speculation—"

"Uh-uh. We do top-grade work here, and use no products on spec. Unless Srinkfit posts a performance bond—"

Fisk put on the no-no expression, another sales

standby. "Not unless we oversee the operation."

The purchaser stood up, smiling. "Perhaps we can do business. Bring your sample to the lab."

"But I'm a salesman, not a chemist," Fisk protested, though this was exactly what he wanted.

Exunt punched a number on his phone. The SRINKFIT coat-of-arms appeared on the screen, replaced after a moment by the pretty answering-service girl.

"Will you accept Fisk Centers as overseer for a sample run of your preparation creme in Exotic Disposals accredited laboratory, five hundred thousand dollar performance bond?" Exunt inquired nonchalantly.

She did bat an eyelash, but only one. "One moment, please." She punched a coding on her own board. A green light came on. "Yes, your query was expected. We will."

Fisk stared. "You *will?*" He hoped he wasn't overdoing the surprise.

"You're new at this game, aren't you," Exunt said. "Most legitimate companies will go along with us. We run a clean shop here. The performance bond is merely to protect *our* clients." He showed the way to the lab.

Exotic Disposals did seem to be legitimate, Fisk thought, as he rode the hall belt. Exunt's every reaction was forthright. But Yola's report would be the one that counted. How was she doing now?

Yola ducked into the first available niche after she separated from Fisk. She touched the top

button on her dress. A faint pinging indicated
that she was not under electronic surveillance at
the moment.

She poked her head out and looked down the
passage. All clear. She stepped onto the near belt
just as though she belonged, proceeding toward the
cleaning depot. She had memorized the layout of
the building—a real chore, as it was large and
intricate—so knew where she was going. DIA
intelligence had ascertained the location of all
the electronic checkpoints as of the past month,
and her route was calculated to avoid these.

Except for one. There was screen-beam across
the entrance to the depot, and she could not pass
it without setting off an alarm. So she waited.

In a few minutes she heard a machine coming
down the hall behind her. All it needed to do was
ride the belt, but it was too stupid to turn off its
wheels, so it was riding *and* wheeling, thereby
making double time. She flattened herself against
the side and let it pass. It was a sweeper, its
brush-rollers drawn up, its dust-bags loaded like
the pollen-sacs of a honeybee.

Yola shook her head. No chance there. The
screen-beam would register the sweeper's precise
outline, and sound the alarm if anything were
added.

It looked as if this would not be a quick mission.
She hoped dear, dull Fisk was holding up his (fat)
end.

"Frank, this is Fisk Centers of Srinkfit," the
purchaser said. "Try this preparation creme on

your next client and let me know how it turns out. He'll remain for the duration, overseeing."

"Sure," Frank said. He was a freckle-faced youngster apparently in his teens. "Got two in the can now; want a control?"

"Excellent!" Exunt said. He departed.

Frank hauled on a long drawer. Within it was a naked frozen corpse of an old man, staring up. "Cancer," Frank said nonchalantly. "Allergic to anticarcinogens, by the look of him. Sad." He slid the body into a defrost chamber.

The second drawer had a younger man. "Traffic fatality. See, his rib cage is bashed in. Probably reached the hospital too late for complete revivification, and his relatives decided to write him off. Or maybe he had a death insurance policy; you'd be surprised how many kooks do." This one went into an adjacent melter while Fisk maintained a straight face. Did these people suspect his real identity? "Pick your subject and trot out our product; we'll have to work fast to keep them both percolating simultaneously."

Fisk swallowed and produced his jar of Srinkfit Creme. He doubted that he would ever become acclimatized to this particular business.

The melters were efficient. In a few minutes both corpses had been thawed and were ready for processing. Frank took Fisk's jar and opened it. "Which one?"

"The—older," Fisk said, hoping this was not going to be as gruesome as he feared. He had been well briefed, but . . .

Frank put one hand into a pocket suiter. The

machine hummed. Now he wore a skintight rubberoid glove. He transferred the jar and gloved his
other hand similarly. Then he scooped out a gob
of creme, rubbed it between his palms, and smeared
it over the body of the old man. He worked effi-
ciently, with marvelously quick yet gentle hands,
so that within a minute the entire corpse gleamed
damply. Fisk could see already that this unprepos-
sessing young man was master of his specialty.

Frank changed gloves and did the same with the
other subject, using his regular brand of lubricant.
"Okay, gentlemen—into the hopper with you both!"
He slid each corpse into an orifice of a large
machine, and closed the two doors.

Fisk let out his breath. He had been afraid he
would have to watch the evisceration, and he knew
his stomach would not hold still for that. "So you do
it mechanically," he said.

"Sure. In the old days they had to do it all by
hand, because no machine was delicate enough,
and it was pretty grim. Had to wear a wet-suit to
keep the gore off. But we've had the one deboner
for a couple of years, and liked it so well we bought
a second, just a couple of weeks ago. Cyborg, you
know—animate brain instead of a computer. Can
run rings around any true robot. You know what
they say: a machine doesn't *care*. A cyborg *does*."

"And these machines remove the—the contents—
without damage?"

"Sure. System is based on the old *tsanstsay*—the
Indian shrunken heads. You know how they cut off
the—"

"Yes," Fisk said quickly. He had read about that

process just yesterday, preparing for his mission, while Yola pored over her own homework for the same purpose. Today it was considered chic in some circles to have the entire body shrunk similarly and preserved for posterity. Thus the success of companies such as this one, catering to the current fashion. Fisk had absorbed a lot more than he cared to know about exotic modes of death and disposition, and understood that competition between specialist outfits was fierce. "What happens to the bones . . . and stuff?"

"Oh, let's see," Frank said, checking a list. "Old man gets cremated. Young one—fed into a converter to fission into electric power."

"What—blood and all?" Fisk asked with simulated surprise. What he really wanted was information on the specific disposition of the brain and nervous system. But such a question might alert Frank to Fisk's real mission. That was the very last thing he wanted. He had no desire to be shoved into the deboning machine.

"Everything. Strict regulations about that, and we honor them scrupulously. Those remains get packaged here and shipped to cremation and fission plants and we get a receipt. So there's no question."

It certainly seemed straightforward. More so than the anonymous tip that had made DIA suspicious of Exotic Disposals. Was this a false trail?

The two sinister machines with their animate brains completed their work and disgorged the products.

Fisk braced himself—but the change was so great that he could make no emotional connection between what he saw and what he knew it was. The bodies had been replaced by flat mannequins cut from soggy cardboard, in appearance. Human skins, emptied of bones, muscles and organs.

There was a noise as a disposal vat trundled up to accept those "contents" from the first deboner. Fisk averted his eyes as the stuff slurped from a side vent in the machine, down a chute, and splashed into the wheeled container. The smell was faint but unpleasantly suggestive. Frank put an identification tag on the collector, so there would be no mistake about the disposition of this particular mess, and let it go.

"Now for boiling," Frank said. "This is where the salve really counts." He slid the skins into a tank of fluid, sealed it, and turned up the heat. It was a pressure cooker. The gauge mounted to fifty pounds per square inch and stayed there.

"No need to separate 'em for this stage," Frank explained in response to Fisk's questioning glance. "The creme is absorbed into the skin by now, and no transfer occurs. But this'll take a while. Can't rush it. Let's eat."

Eat! Fisk wondered if he could.

Yola came to life at the sight of the third machine. It was a refuse collector. A large vat mounted on little wheels. She jumped toward it, lifted the lid, and climbed in, letting the cover down on top of her. Now she could pass the screen beam without distorting the outline of the machine.

It was dark inside, and cramped and uncomfortable, and the smell was ghastly. Her feet skidded on moist sticks, and something warm sloshed over her toes. She repressed her lively imagination, not caring to speculate what sort of garbage she perched on.

The machine trundled to a stop. Yola pushed up the lid and clambered out.

Just in time! The vat tilted, pouring its lumpy contents into a cavity in the floor. Bones, blood and tattered meat. Water sprayed from side vents, sloshing out the vat and washing the gory residue into the hole. Then a plastic cover passed over the floor-aperture, and the refuse machine backed out into the passage, intent on its next grisly collection.

The plastic rose out of the floor, manifesting as a complete sealed container. A tiny tug-robot pushed it to a stamping machine that burned a programmed address into the top, working from a tag left by the vat. Then the box went into a mailing chute.

Who would want a package like that, she wondered, her stomach churning. The fooder-machine supply company? She glanced at her feet and saw a thick red stain on both shoes' toes.

She kicked them off, peeled off her socks, and set the mess against the wall, a sodden pile. She would finish this mission barefoot.

Now to business. This room was the center of Exotic Disposals' cleanup network. The large cleaners and carryvats had to use the main halls, but there were many small service tunnels extending to every section of the building. Those were what she needed.

She opened her dress. Strapped to her skinny torso were twenty tiny machines, each the size of a mouse. She snapped loose the first, touched the activation button, and watched its miniature wheels buzz about. Just like a cleaning sweeper, only smaller. It was in working order.

She carried it to the nearest cleaner-tube and popped it inside. "Go, go, eegmouse!" she whispered. "Go make me a sensational recording!"

The mouse spun its wheels until they found purchase, then scooted upward along the curving tunnel. It knew what to do.

Yola snapped loose her other mice and fed them into all the tubes and passages she could find. *Now* the job was getting done.

Fisk was hardly hungry, but was happy to get away from the gruesome lab for a while. He hoped Yola had managed to stay out of trouble. By this time her eegmice should have made their recordings and returned to her. The information was in; all they had to do was get it out. She would have to watch for him, so as to rejoin him in lockstep as he stepped out through the exit screen. Then the several patterns would be compared to those on file at DIA headquarters, and the accuracy of the charge would be proven or disproven.

All simple enough in theory—provided Yola remained undetected. Unfortunately, she was a magnet for trouble.

He managed to consume a pseudolettuce sandwich and gulp down some milk. To his surprise, the food helped settle his stomach. They returned to the lab.

The cooking was done. The limp skin mockups had shrunk to barely a quarter of their prior size. They were rubbery and pale as Frank checked them and bundled them into the curing ovens.

This stage, too, was mercifully secluded. Fisk watched the dials that indicated temperature, humidity and abrasive application, and saw the items tumbling about within the ovens like so much old fashioned laundry, and wondered again how Yola was doing. Probably waiting impatiently for him.

At last the almost-finished hides emerged. Frank stretched them out on the mounting boards, inserted small stretcher frameworks, and closed off the openings. Two tiny hairless mannequins rather like unfinished dolls lay there.

"Now comes the acid test," Frank said, meaning it literally. Each figure was fogged with preparatory acid to bring out its surface qualities.

And the doll-sized old man looked more realistic than the doll-sized young man. "Have to confess," Frank said. "You *do* have a superior preparation creme. That's the best-looking shrink I've done this month!"

"Fine," Fisk said. "Notify Mr. Exunt, and you'll be able to use it from now on."

"Of course there's still some processing—got to insert eyebeads and teeth to scale, and put on some hair. But it sure looks good."

Fisk was glad this facet had worked out, for it
vindicated his pose as salesman. He would get a
real commission from Srinkfit on ED's order, too.

The shrunken figure would be touched up and
dressed up, the real skins wrapped around artificial
man-frames and returned to the grieving relatives
as tangible mementos. It was no more gruesome
than embalming or cremating, actually. Some
people kept a jar of human ashes—cremains—
on the mantel; others preferred a more evocative
reminder. Such as a shrink. Perhaps the
grandchildren got to play with it, Fisk thought,
saving the price of a doll. . . .

One by one the eegmice whizzed back. Yola
deactivated each and snapped it back into her
body harness. Ten were done; eleven, twelve.

There was a noise beyond the main screen-beam.
Another cleaner was coming in, no doubt. She
picked up two more mice, unconcerned. Quack
soup!

"I'll take those," a harsh human voice said.

Yola jumped and ran—but there was nowhere
to go. She had gotten careless—and now she was
trapped. She tried to hide the two eegmice, but
the Exotic Disposals' security officer obviously
recognized them.

Fisk entered the purchaser's office to complete
his sale. Two men were there—and Yola, strangely
quiet, in bare feet.

Fisk kept his face straight, knowing that
something had gone awry. She was supposed to

have avoided detection, once he siphoned her past the perimeter.

"No, we haven't touched her," Exunt said. "We let her run her tests, then picked her up. It was a nice try, but we upgraded our security since DIA last surveyed. Random spybeams that your telltales don't pick up. Not your fault at all. Nothing personal; we just don't like snoopers."

Which explained why the man wasn't angry. ED's new security system had been tested and found adequate. Meanwhile, the purchaser was calmly punching a number.

The DIA living-brain emblem flashed on the screen. "We have apprehended your infiltrators," Exunt said. "Take a look."

Fisk's real boss, Brown came on. "Sorry to embarrass you, ED. We had a complaint, so we had to investigate."

"We're clean," the security officer said gruffly. "To prove it, we'll run off your recordings right now. Set up your suspects."

"Done," the DIA man agreed, as though this were routine. The talk was all friendly and polite, but Fisk was sure this was mere dressing. Death Insurance and Exotic Disposals were natural enemies.

Yola brought out a mouse and flipped its broadcast switch. Nothing was audible, but its signal was bleeping out in special DIA code to be checked against DIA computer files.

"You see?" Exunt said confidently when the mouse clicked off. "If you'd come to us directly, we would have authenticated—"

"Naturally," Brown said. "And *we'd* have been accused of collusion. Shall we check the rest?"

"It's academic," Exunt said, but he gestured to Yola, who produced another mouse.

They ran through several more, and with each blank Exunt became more affable, and even the security officer began to smirk. "No point, no point at all," Exunt said.

"We've got a match," Brown said quietly.

"As I said, we're clean. We always—*what*?"

"One of our insurees is in one of your machines—alive."

Both ED officials changed color. "Impossible!" Exunt exclaimed. "We have pedigrees on every cyborg. Nothing like that could happen without my personal knowledge."

Brown merely looked at him.

Exunt changed color again, more vividly. "I tell you, it's a mistake!" he cried angrily. "We don't operate that way! We value our reputation!"

The DIA man raised a printout and read it aloud. "Nellie Lockridge. Deceased suddenly at age 57, processed for compost at your facilities four months ago." He paused. "We can locate the specific unit now, if you care to cooperate. Otherwise I regret—"

"Of *course* we'll cooperate! But it's a mistake!" Now all color had drained from both ED faces. Fisk appreciated why: possession of an illicit living brain was technically kidnapping, and if DIA even filed charges, Exotic's reputation would suffer grievously. And DIA was in business to file just such charges—when it had a case.

"We're always ready to work with a cooperative company," Brown said with the smoothness of glasslined steel. "Suppose you open your records to our representatives, and we'll ascertain the facts of the case."

The facts of the case were that if DIA nailed ED on this one, ED would very shortly be out of business. It was bargaining over a gun barrel. "Yes," Exunt said after a pained pause, glancing at his security officer for affirmation.

"All we want is the truth," Brown said, and now he was the affable one. "And our client's death." He faded out.

Exunt seemed to have aged five years in as many minutes. "Which unit?"

Yola checked the mouse against the EEG identified. "We'll have to run it through again," she said. "I didn't see where all the mice went."

They ran it through again, this time tracing the route of that one eegmouse and noting the EEG's it picked up as it sneaked through the cleaning conduits within range of a cyborg. It had a pattern-sensing program that urged it toward any mechanically mounted living brain, until the recording was made. It also avoided light and normal living brains—in short, people—as a secretive measure. This made it extremely difficult to follow.

But half an hour later they had vectored in on the suspect: the new deboner Fisk had seen in operation earlier. They checked the EEG independently. It matched that of Nellie Lockridge, the DIA insuree.

Hands shaking, the purchaser punched for his records, scanning them rapidly. "We're guilty of possession, not collusion," he said, as if fighting a rearguard action. "I want it on record that we assisted in clarifying this matter. We'll pay reparations, of course—but we don't want any publicity."

Straws. "DIA is interested in eliminating the guilty party, whoever that may be," Fisk said carefully. "If the evidence indicates that Exotic Disposals is an unwitting user, there would be no need to bring its name into the legal proceedings."

Exunt nodded gratefully. "We bought this unit complete from General Cyborg just under a month ago, and took delivery ten days later. It has given good service since. The papers are all in order, as you can see." He passed the license, tax forms and pedigree over to Fisk.

"But the EEG prints do not match," Fisk pointed out. "The papers are in order—but the wrong brain is in that unit. The brain of our client, Miss Lockridge. Don't you verify the EEG's of your cyborgs?"

Exunt's face was red. "Normally, yes. But our verification man was on vacation the week that unit arrived. We had urgent need to put it in service—business has picked up recently, owing to our successful advertising program—and General Cyborg's credentials are impeccable. There was no hint—"

"Sloppy security," Yola muttered. She had not forgiven the security man for catching *her*.

"Let's trace the brain itself," Fisk said. "Where did GC get it?"

"From Organic Computers. OC obtains brains from a variety of sources, mostly volunteer or paid. Cash in advance to needy families. We've done business with them—" He paused, realizing how it sounded. "*Not* in this case! We composted Miss Lockridge's body entire, as specified on the manifest. Brain and all!"

Fisk shook his head. "Mr. Exunt, Miss Lockridge was active in the Floral industry. Her will specified that her remains should be composted and used to fertilize flowers. Exotic Disposals handled that account—and now her brain has surfaced in an Exotic Disposals cyborg unit. You had opportunity and motive, because a cyborg reconstituted by a fresh brain is far cheaper than a new one. Your facilities are certainly capable of accomplishing this. I'm afraid DIA will have to bring suit against you for—"

"No!" Exunt cried, sweating. "We are innocent! How can we convince you?"

"Why not ask the brain, Dummy?" Yola inquired.

Both men stared at her. "Is that possible?" Fisk asked.

"Yes, certainly," Exunt said. "But the brain may not choose to communicate. I—"

"You're afraid it'll tell the truth," Yola said.

Exunt looked almost ready to kill. "I'm not afraid of the truth! Only—"

"Only *what*, kidnapper?" Yola demanded, enjoying his discomfiture.

"Well, the duty to which that particular unit has been assigned—it might be upset about—"

"Deboning," Fisk said, understanding. "That *is* a noxious job for a lady who loved flowers!"

"Exactly," Exunt said. "She might wish to hurt us—"

"Especially after you stole her brain!" Yola said.

"Face it," Fisk said briskly. "Nothing she can say can hurt you worse than a DIA suit. And she just might clear you—if you are innocent."

"Ha!" Yola exclaimed.

Exunt was now immune to her jibes. "We have no choice."

They traipsed down to Frank's lab. "Frank, this man is a DIA investigator," Exunt said. "It seems our new cyborg deboner is—ah well, we shall have to question it. Can you plug in a typer?"

"Sure," Frank said, staring at Fisk. Evidently the young man didn't like being investigated.

They plugged in the typer. "This is attuned to the impulses of a touch typist," Exunt explained. "A diminishing breed, today, since most records are voicetaped, but conservative industries like the Floral still do use them. Even if she's had no experience, she can still pick out the letters two-finger, as it were. It may be tedious, but—"

"How do we make our query?" Fisk asked, alert for some fakery. A lot was riding on this interrogation, and he had never before talked with the half-dead.

"We plug in this voicetaper," Exunt said, doing so. He handed the mike to Fisk. "Perhaps you had better—"

Fisk steeled himself. "Miss Lockridge—do you understand me? Please type your reply, if—"

The typer clattered silently—a vaguely unnerving process, but suitable to this interview. "OF COURSE."

"Hey, it really works!" Yola cried. "We're talking with a pickled—"

Fisk trod on her bare toe. "Miss Lockridge, I am Fisk Centers, of the Death Insurance Agency. You have a policy with us—"

"I CERT INLY DO! WH T TOOK YOU SO LONG?"

Alive and sane," Exunt breathed prayerfully.

"But not much of a typist," Yola said.

"It's a defective typer," Frank said. "Stuck in upper case, and the letter A's missing."

"DEFECTIVE?" the brain inquired. "T CONSOLOD TED BLOSSOMS OUR M CHINES WERE *NEVER* DEFECTIVE! WE H D L%& TYPERS, ND**"

"No problem," Frank said easily. "We can read it, so long as you stay clear of the numbers, and you can substitute another vowel for A."

"VERY WELL. THERE MUST BE MORE TH N ONE OF YOU SPE KING**I'LL TRY U. SPEUKING**IS THUS SUTISFUCTORY?"

"Yes, certainly," Fisk agreed. "There are four of us here—me, Centers, the purchaser, Mr. Exunt, my daughter Yola—"

"THUT IS FIVE ULREUDY, YOUNG MUN! YOU UND THE PURCHUSER UND YOUR DUUGHTER YOLU UND CENTERS UND**"

"Let's get *on* with it!" Exunt cried, exasperated.

"*I* am *Centers*. I'll try to identify the others when they speak! That was Exunt just now, who is the purchaser."

"CERTUINLY. BUT YOU HUVEN'T EX-PLUINED YOUR DELUY."

"We received un unonymous—I mean, *a*n *a*nonymous tup—*tip!*—that Exotic Disposals was bootlegging some of our clients to life, but lack of detailed information impeded our investigation. However, now that we—"

"You believed an anonymous tip?" Exunt demanded.

Fisk gestured him to silence. "That was an interjection by Mr. Exunt. Now that we have located you, Miss Lockridge, you may be assured that we shall honor our commitment fully. The guilty parties shall be punished, and you shall die, as is your legal right, and—

"WUIT! WUIT! I DON'T WUNT TO DIE UGUIN! I WUS MURDERED THE FIRST TIME, UND I DIDN'T WUNT THUT, EITHER!"

"Well, of course you don't *have* to—" Fisk said as Exunt brightened. "I mean, your wishes of whatever nature will of course be honored, and a full investigation will be made into your death as well as your reanimation. DIA will protect you from exploitation. That's what you paid your premiums for. But first it is necessary for us to ask you some questions. To establish the guilt in this matter. For the crimes committed against you. Because you were *supposed* to be—"

The typer was already going at a merry clip. Miss Lockridge was a touch typist, all right. "I

ENTERED THE HOSPITUL FOR U ROUTINE REJUVINUTION, MR. CENTERS. BUT U MUN ENTERED MY ROOM THE NIGHT BEFORE THE OPERUTION. I THOUGHT HE WUS U DOCTOR, SO I DIDN'T OBJECT. HE GUVE ME U SHOT**UND WHEN I WOKE I WUS IN SOME LUBOORURUTORY, *NOT* UT THE HOSPITUL. THEN I KNEW I HUD BEEN KIDNUPPED."

"But you died at the hospital!" Fisk protested. "Our records show that your body was composted by Exotic Disposals—the very same company that—"

"NO. MY BODY MUY HUVE BEEN RETURNED TO THE HOSPITUL, BUT NOT MY BRUIN. I BELIEVE U PSEUDO-BRUIN WUS IMPLUNTED IN THE SKULL OF THE CORPSE. I WUS TURNSFERRED TO THIS MUCHINE UND SHIPPED HERE."

"The brain in that client was *genuine!*" Exunt exclaimed. "I assure you we are in a position to tell the difference between—"

But Fisk was on another tack. "They must have held you in that lab for some time. Did you see—?"

"NO, THEY PERFORMED THE TRUNSFER IMMEDIUTELY, UND UFTER U FEW DUYS I URRIVED HERE."

"But that's impossible!" Fisk said. "You were in the hospital four months ago, and this unit arrived here three weeks ago. Over three months are missing—"

"Men are so dumb!" Yola said. "They must have put her in stasis, idiots!"

"Yes!" Exunt agreed. "She would not have been

aware of that! Miss Lockridge, how much time do you judge has passed since you entered the hospital?"

"CERTUINLY NOT FOUR MONTHS, YOUNG MUN. FOUR WEEKS, POSSIBLY, OR U LITTLE LESS."

"That doesn't get you off the hook," Fisk told Exunt. "Exotic Disposals could have saved her brain until—"

"But we *didn't*!" Exunt protested. "We never got her brain, by her own statement! Just her body, with a brainsponge in it—or rather, with the original cyborg deboner brain transplanted. That was dead, of course, so we couldn't take its EEG. So in good faith we composted it—"

"Maybe," Fisk said, swayed. "Miss Lockridge, do you have any clue who kidnapped you? *Someone* must have—"

"ONLY THE LUBORUTORY TECHNICIUN. YOUNG MUN NUMED FRUNK**"

Exunt wheeled on Frank, crestfallen. *"What?"*

"FRUNK MERRYWHETHER. I HEURD HIS NUME WHEN THEY THOUGHT I WUS UNCONSCIOUS UND THEN I *WUS* UNCONSCIOUS. DOES THUT HELP?"

"*This* is Frunk, er Frank Emberdinck," Exunt said, looking faint.

Frank was no less relieved. "You know I don't know brain-planting, boss. I'm strictly a shrinker. But there *is* another Frank in the mortuary business. I knew him in pre-mort, until he split for nerve surgery. Real sharp technician, but they caught him stealing from the school lab and washed him out. I don't remember his last name, but I think he got a job at Acme Elims."

"Acme Eliminations!" Exunt shouted. "Our chief competitor! Just the kind that *would* hire a dishonest tech! Those utter bleeps tried to frame us! Intercepting our delivery and substituting a bootleg brain in our unit, then tipping DIA anonymously!"

"We shall check this out, of course," Fisk said. Certainly one company trying to do the other in, whichever way it went. But by the time DIA finished, the truth would be known.

He returned to the cyborg. "Miss Lockridge, your preliminary testimony has been invaluable. But now we must see to your own comfort. We can of course keep your brain alive, but you will have to remain in a cyborg unit of some type. Perhaps you could transfer to a flower mill—"

"FLOWER *NURSERY*," she corrected him. "BUT I UM QUITE SUTISFIED HERE."

"You *are*?" Exunt asked, amazed. "I presumed a woman of your sensitivities—"

"I USED TO LIKE THE IDEU OF TURNING UGLY PEOPLE INTO BEUUTIFUL FLOWERS," she typed. "BUT IN U FEW DUYS THE FLOWERS SPOIL UND TURN UGLY TOO, SO IT BECOMES FUTILE. ON THE OTHER HUND, WHEN UN UGLY PERSON IS CHUNGED INTO U LOVELY LITTLE DOLL**"

"Yes, yes, of course!" Exunt agreed, mopping his face. "ED's philosophy exactly! Miss Lockridge, if there is anything we can do for you—"

"IF YOU WOULD PLUG IN SOME GOOD MURDER MYSTERIES FOR MY OFF HOURS,"

she typed. "IT DOES GET DULL WITH NO
LIVING BODY. . . ."

"Right away!" Exunt cried. "I'm a gothics fan
myself! I'll bring you mysteries, historicals, science
fiction—"

"NO SCIENCE FICTION! I'M U SENSIBLE
REUDER," she typed primly.

"It *was* a frame," Brown agreed, back at the DIA
office. "We are suing Acme Eliminations, and the
State is joining with us because of the murder
charge, and I rather think *Acme* will be the next
eliminated. Good job!"

"That was fun," Yola said. "What's our next
case?"

Brown put on the sorry-bad-news face. "I regret
there will be no more cases for you. Your cover
has been blown, and now every suspect will be
alert. Had you completed your mission without
exposure—"

Yola looked at Fisk speculatively. "You know, if
you were a cyborg, maybe you could hold a job
without muffing it. How about—"

"Excuse me, please," Fisk said politely to Brown.
"I have to make an exotic disposal." Then he took
off after her, lifting his spanking hand.

CHAPTER

— 6 —

"**W**e can't afford it," Fisk Centers said, sounding even to himself like a broken record.

"Oh, Fisky!" Yola cried, putting on her woebegone-waif look. "It's only a *little* one!"

"Even a *little* robot carries a *big* price tag! And we don't *need* it. Now come *on*."

He half expected a crowd-drawing tantrum of the type his pre-teen hellion specialized in when balked, but evidently she wasn't in the mood. She came along with only token drag.

The truth was Fisk would dearly have liked to own one of the displayed household robots. They *were* convenient, and Yola was consistently expert at making a mess of their apartment. But the habits of a lifetime of comfortable living had left him ill-equipped to deal with his present poverty. Particularly now that he was trying to support a daughter whose lifetime of poverty had left her well-equipped with comfortable-living appetites. So the regretful "no" loomed large in his vocabulary.

A street phone lighted. "Excuse me, Father-Daughter," a man's pleasant voice said. "Can I interest you in a respectable cash contract?"

Fisk snorted. "These shyster loaners are like prostitutes soliciting on the—"

"Daddy!" Yola stage-whispered warningly. It wasn't that she possessed even token ignorance of gutter vocabulary, but she liked to pretend, for the sake of appearances, that Fisk did.

"One moment!" the man on the phone called. "I'm not a loaner or a hawker! I'm an employer!"

Fisk and Yola halted in place. The one thing that would solve most of their problems was a well-paying job. "What type of work?" Fisk asked, turning to face the screen.

"Advertising," the man said resonantly. He was a nattily dressed rejuvenated executive with a direct stare.

"How much money?" Yola demanded, always first with the basics.

"That's hard to say, precisely, but it should be more than adequate. Why don't you step into my office and we'll discuss it?"

"Not so fast," Fisk said, intrigued but wary. He had been disappointed in sales-type positions many times before, and advertising was certainly a form of sales. "What product?"

"I can't discuss it on the *street*," the man said, and right away the very notion sounded ridiculous. *Nobody* talked business on the *street*! "Come to the

General Transport and ask for Matrans. It may be well worth your while." He faded.

"Wish *I* had an offer like that!" a stranger said. Fisk glared at him, and the man shuffled on.

Then Fisk looked at Yola. "Your antenna are sharper than mine, for this sort of thing. Is this sucker bait?"

"I thought so until the last," she said. "But General Transport—that's one of the biggest outfits in the world!"

"Maybe it's a shyster using their name."

"Uh-uh. He didn't give an address, just GT. If it's a fake, we'd know soon's we walk in and ask."

"Maybe we'd better do that, then."

She nodded thoughtfully. "Transport's got money, that's for sure. Even their robots get union scale!"

Fisk was more cautious. "It could be a rental office. The building guarantees nothing."

"Yes it does!" she said excitedly as they walked to the elevator tubes. "GT guarantees everything on its premises. It wouldn't let a shyster operate here. These big outfits are very sensitive about image."

True enough. Fisk felt a growing excitement himself. A solicitation on the street was an unpromising beginning, but not insuperable.

They stepped into the vertical shaft and whisked upward in the antigrav. The floor markers flashed by: 10, 20, 30, 50, 80, 120. They came to rest at 148 and stepped out.

The exec was there. "So glad to meet you!" he said with convincing warmth. "I'm Kirk Dunkling. Call me Kirk."

"Sure, Kirk," Yola agreed loudly.

"Fisk Centers," Fisk said, hoping she wouldn't antagonize the man before they heard the deal. "My daughter Yola."

"How much money, Kirk?" Yola asked with her normal reticence.

Dunkling showed them into his cubicle. "That depends on the contract. I think we could offer seventy-five thousand."

"A year?" she said derisively. "That's dinky!"

"For the job. Perhaps two weeks work. And there will probably be residuals amounting to more than the advance."

"Seventy-five to one hundred fifty thousand for two weeks work?" Fisk asked incredulously. "What do I have to do?"

"Nothing. The offer is for her."

"Me!" Yola cried, delighted. "You're great, Kirk!"

Now Fisk was really suspicious. "Before we go any farther—"

"It's very simple," Dunkling said quickly, sounding extremely sincere. "General Transport has developed a new product, and we need an image. Someone associated with the product, for the ad campaign. The pro actors won't do, but I think Yola here—"

"*Miss* Centers," she said primly.

" . . . is just right. She has these dramatic little ways about her, especially when she wants something."

"How do you know that?" Fisk asked, for the assessment was right on target, if euphemistic. Had the man been snooping?

"Fisk, it's my business to notice things about people. Like you being a one-time man of means, and your daughter being a new acquisition, probably adopted."

"Now just a—" Fisk started, annoyed.

"I spend several hours a day on the phone, just watching the streets. I can judge by a person's accent, by his nuances of expression, the way he carries himself. You have a genteel upbringing, but she has the state-institution manner. When I spot the person we're looking for—"

"Why not use the employment agency?" Fisk asked. "Or run an ad—since you're in the ad business."

"Not so simple!" Dunkling said, laughing with assumed naturalness. "The kind of person we want doesn't normally go to the agency, or answer ads. For one thing, he may be employed—or underage. But mainly, we require just the *right* person—and we are the only judge of the qualities we need. In this case, a pretty little mischief with expensive tastes."

"Yeah," Yola agreed.

"The product," Fisk said, not convinced. There had to be a catch.

"Right here." Dunkling gestured to a pair of screens standing upright on the floor. Each was about six feet tall by three wide, supported by a firm stand.

Dunkling picked up one screen by handles mounted on its side and carried it across the room, setting it down about a yard from the wall. "Not at all heavy, you see," he said. He returned to set the other screen near the opposite wall.

"Sure—I could carry it myself," Yola said. "So what, Kirky?"

"This." Dunkling stepped through one screen.

Fisk blinked and Yola gave a yelp of surprise. For the man had disappeared.

"Over here," Dunkling said. He was standing beside the other screen. "Catch on?"

"Matrans!" Fisk exclaimed. "Does that stand for Matter Transmission?"

"It does," Dunkling said, pleased. "The ultimate in transport."

"But it's no good for live things!" Yola objected. "Only dead things."

"It *was*," Dunkling said, stepping into the second screen. This time Fisk's head snapped about to cover the emergence across the room. There was no doubt about it: the man had jumped instantly from one to the other, alive. "It took our research lab a long time to perfect this refinement, but here it is at last. Care to try it?"

"No!" father and daughter exclaimed together. There had been so many horror stories about matter transmission that the subject had become part of the world folklore. Murders were still committed by shoving the living victim into a transmitter tuned to some distant location, where he invariably arrived whole but dead. Circus performers did their acts above horizontal transmitter planes: the world's deadliest safety nets. Transmitter technicians were insured, at phenomenal expense, against loss of life or limb through accidental transmission. If some fool poked his finger through an active screen and drew it back immediately, that finger was dead and had to be amputated. It wasn't just loss of circulation; every cell in it was devoid of life.

"That is the problem we face," Dunkling said seriously. "The average person has become thoroughly conditioned against live transmission—with good reason, until now. But we have solved the technical problems—and now we need to reeducate the market. This requires a sophisticated series of commercials."

"Not on your life!" Yola cried. "I'm not going through that thing!"

"You can't mistake it for a regular transmitter," Dunkling said. "The style is completely distinct. This has no personnel guard—because it needs none. Orientation of screens doesn't matter—see, I can go through from either side." He poked his arm into the screen from the center side, and it emerged from the center side of the opposite screen. "No line-of-sight alignment necessary; jog the screens any which way, it's still safe. Two people can use it simultaneously, crossing paths. One using the front route, the other the back. No danger of collision, no need to wait a turn, no worry about one arriving with two livers, the other with none."

"It's a fake," Yola said.

But now Fisk was intrigued. "A fake? To what purpose? *We're* no prospective market! Such a transmitter set would cost tens of thousands."

"*You* try it, then!" she cried with instant temper, pushing him.

Fisk stumbled against the near screen, throwing out his right hand to catch himself. The hand went through before he stopped.

Appalled, he stood there, looking at his severed forearm in the screen. There was no pain.

Then a hand grasped his. "Congratulations!" Dunkling said across the room. He was holding something. It was Fisk's hand and part of his arm.

"Gee, I'm sorry, Daddy," Yola said contritely. I didn't mean to kill your hand! It's your spanking hand, too."

Which meant that her grief was limited. "It's not dead," Fisk said, amazed despite what Dunkling had shown them. "It's—over there." He wiggled his fingers, and the distant hand wiggled.

"You mean it actually *works*?" Yola asked.

Cautiously, Fisk poked more of his arm through. Sensation remained. Then he nerved himself, closed his eyes, and put his head through too.

When he reopened his eyes, he was staring into Dunkling's beaming face. He looked down, and saw nothing but the floor. His legs remained on the other side of the room, a good fifteen feet distant—yet they continued to support him.

Fisk jerked back—and was in one piece at his original screen. "Yes, it works," he said.

"Your brain isn't dead?" Yola asked, chewing one fingernail nervously. "Not that it'd make any difference—"

But he couldn't spank her here in the GT office.

*   *   *

"Seventy-five thousand dollars!" Yola cried, dancing around their apartment with the credit voucher in her hand. "Now we can get that household robot!"

"Now we can live extremely conservatively until the job is done," Fisk corrected her. "No splurging. We might have to refund."

"You forget I'm the credit winner!" she said.

"*You* forget I'm your manager. You, like it or not, are a minor. Without my signature that contract is invalid."

"Pooh!" she pouted.

"Now you get your little bleep on that script and memorize it. If you want to be an actress, you've got to *act*."

But privately, Fisk was proud of her. Yola had really come through in the clutch, demonstrating that she *was* the girl GT wanted. All she had to do for the contract was repeat a few cute lines as she danced through the Matrans screens, showing by manner and demonstration that there really was no harm in it. If a sweet little imp like her had no fear of transmission, what sensible adult could retain his ridiculous prejudices against it?

Actually, it would be months before the ads were broadcast, and it might be years before significant public response developed. But in time the change in attitude would occur, and Matrans sales would accelerate. Getting it started was the big job. General Transport could afford to take the long view, and thought Yola was the best introduction.

Fisk expected trouble during the takes, but the easygoing ad director wanted naturalness above all else, and quickly discovered how to get along with Yola. He praised her constantly. The result was that in two weeks, the film sequence was complete. The job was done, General Transport was satisfied, and Fisk and Yola had seventy-five thousand dollars. Everything was fine.

Fisk resumed his fruitless search for a regular job, knowing that their windfall would not last indefinitely. Yola, bitten by the drama bug, joined the relevant actor's union: Commercial Representatives Organization, Advertising, "K" district, better known acronymically as CROAK. CROAK was dedicated to the improvement of the lot of actors who made commercials, euphemistically called "Commercial Representatives." It was active in public relations and contract review and published a weekly fax containing news and gossip of the field. CROAK was not an employment agency, and engaged in no legal transactions, but it did advise its members on an unofficial basis of their rights and best interests. The dues were nominal, and Fisk saw no harm in Yola's membership; it might keep her out of mischief. And if any problem should arise in connection with the Matrans contract, this was a ready source of advice.

Not that they anticipated any problems. The job was done, the money paid over. What could possibly go wrong?

The phone lighted. It was Dunkling. "Oh, hi, Quirk," Yola said as Fisk hastily stepped into the suiter. He wished she wouldn't tease the man so directly, but Dunkling seemed to take no notice.

"Good news," the exec said. "International Vacationer is taking a subsidiary option on the Matrans sequence. You'll have to do a few minor retakes, of course, to dub in their place names, but that's all."

"How much money?"

"Depends on the contract, which depends on how well the modifications turn out."

Yola frowned. "That's blackmail, Dunkbunk!"

Still Dunkling took no offense. "Naturally you don't have to do it, and we can write off their generous fringe . . ."

"Oh, fudge! When do I report?"

"This afternoon, studio four, 131st floor, Vacationer Building. You'll be working with International's ad director. But remember: this is an *option*. They will proffer a contract later—if they like the takes. As I'm sure they will."

The screen faded. Yola turned to Fisk. "Joker knows I've got the bug. More acting, more money—hey, how much do you figure?"

"As I understand options, the complete terms of the contract have already been fixed and spelled out," Fisk said. "IV will have to exercise it within a specified time, or the deal lapses. Funny that Dunkling didn't name the figure—but I suppose he has a conditioned reflex against talking dollars over the phone, or maybe it's company policy."

"Or maybe he isn't all *that* sure they'll take it up," Yola said. "But I still want to know, even if I have to go to his bleeping office and—"

"Why don't you dial Info and check the standard advance for this sort of thing," Fisk suggested quickly. "According to *our* contract, we get fifty percent and General Transport gets fifty percent of the net proceeds from any subcontract."

"They get half?" Yola was outraged. "What for? *I'm* doing the work!"

"Standard practice, it seems," Fisk said. "Prime contractor always takes half the income from the subsidiaries. We've got no complaint; we signed it."

"*You* signed it. It's still a gyp. You were supposed to be looking out for my interests!" she mumbled, punching the number. When Info answered, she asked: "What's the standard advance to the artist on a subsidiary contract on a filmed commercial?"

There was some back and forth, establishing the nature of the ad and the company involved. Finally the answer came: one hundred fifty thousand dollars.

"One hundred fifty thousand!" Yola exclaimed, turning to Fisk. "Twice what we got the first time!"

That made him wonder, as he had supposed a prime contract would normally be for a larger amount than a subcontract. Had General Transport taken advantage of their naivete to make an inadequate payment? But there was no point in upsetting Yola with that notion, especially when there was really no indication that the company had deceived them. Dunkling had made an offer to a pair of people off the street, and they had accepted; scale rates for hardened professionals were hardly applicable. "Remember," he cautioned, "only half of it's ours."

"Yah. That means GT gets a free ride. They get back just as much as they paid out—and they've still got the series to run! What a hoist!"

"Maybe so," Fisk said tolerantly. "But they are also investing the much larger expenses of film production, reproduction, distribution and broadcasting—all on a speculative basis, while our own risk is minimal. And we're still ahead another seventy-five thousand dollars. And we know exactly where we stand."

She agreed somewhat grudgingly. Fisk knew that next time she would balk at accepting a primary contract with this clause included—and he would support her position. The prime contractor was supposed to make its profit from sales of the advertised product, *not* from sales of the advertising itself.

Yola did the retakes, which consisted principally of her saying "Honolulu," "Moscow," "Buenos Aires," "Tokyo" and others as she stepped through the Matrans screen. International Vacationer would dub in the appropriate backgrounds from their files, and thus adapt the entire series to their purpose. It was a cooperative effort, since obviously a live-matter transmitter was useless to a person with nowhere to go, and travel was tedious unless instantaneous.

In two days, as promised, she was done. International presented her with two honorary vacations in Australia—it was the slack season for Down Under—as a goodwill bonus that was completely successful in earning her goodwill.

Fisk and Yola stepped to Sydney by Matrans, though the GT facilities were not officially in operation yet. They spent two pleasant weeks looking at the rare remaining kangaroos, exploring the ruins of the Great Barrier Reef, and touring Android sheep farms. Accommodations were first class, and they even had a moderate souvenir allowance. There was no question about it: it was fun.

Home was a letdown. Fisk still seemed to be unemployable, and Yola had no responses to her several queries to advertisers listed in the first CROAK fax. She had gotten the impression from the market report that spot-commercial character actors were in urgent demand, but the reality failed to measure up so far.

"And where the bleep's the money from the IV advance?" Yola demanded angrily when it finally dawned on her that the world was not eager to utilize her newfound talents.

"Ask Kirk Dunkling," Fisk said.

She phoned Dunkling at his office, but his robot secretary explained that he was on a business trip. Yola left her query, and the secretary promised to have Dunkling call back the moment he returned.

A month later she phoned again. After threatening a tantrum, she got through to the exec. "Why didn't you call back, Smirk? Where's my money?"

"Oh, didn't I tell you?" he asked innocently. "International Vacationer hasn't paid yet. They don't voucher their contracts until thirteen weeks after the commercials are aired. But we'll relay your share the moment we receive their payment." He faded.

Yola turned indignantly to Fisk, as though he were to blame. "Thirteen weeks after they use it! And they call that an *advance*?"

"Maybe CROAK can explain it," Fisk said, surprised himself. Contract terminology was not to be taken literally, it seemed.

She headed for the fooder, as she always did when under stress. "No—I don't want to bother them with a stupid question. Vacationer treated us okay."

"That's what CROAK's there for, Yola." But he knew what she meant. International Vacationer had given them an excellent two weeks, and Yola would seem both naive and ungrateful if she inquired too quickly about their policies as though they were suspect. Her new pride as an actress wouldn't allow that.

Actually, that pride was not a bad thing, Fisk thought. Yola was less like a brat than she had been before, and easier to tolerate around the apartment.

Time passed. Fisk found a job selling fruit-flavored foamer soap, but it didn't last. His jobs never did, though he always tried his best. Their family funds diminished. Yola finally got a bit part in a spot mailfax house ad, but it paid only twenty-five hundred dollars, with no subsidiary shares available, and was never actually run. "Microdinks!" she said: the superlative of "dinky."

"When the bleep is that Vacationer loot coming?"

"Don't swear," Fisk muttered, but he wondered too. It was now four months since International Vacationer had accepted the retakes for the subcontract—and still those ads had not been aired.

Yola dialed two triple decker licorice-mushroom foamwiches from the fooder, handed one to Fisk, and turned on the evening play. This was one of the expensive receivers their assets had been frittered on. Fisk had fought against it and lost, as it *was* relevant to Yola's income-producing propensities. Meanwhile, he had to gird himself to digest the foamwich without gagging.

A vision coalesced in the center of the room, expanding outward like an uncorked genie, until its limits coincided with the walls behind the two watchers. Fisk and Yola were in the scene, but not *of* it. The four dimensional image converted their doorway into a large fireplace inhabited by a smudge-faced but pretty girl.

"Oh, not Cinderella again!" Yola expostulated. She reached to change the station, but paused as the commercial came on.

Yola stepped through the tall screen prominently labeled MATRANS. "Paris," she said pertly—and emerged before the Eiffel Tower.

"The IV ad!" Fisk and Yola cried together.

The image-Yola smiled impishly. "I said I'd drop dead before I'd go through a matter transmitter." She poked a finger through gingerly, and it wiggled back in the New York setting. "I lied." She faded out, and the Cinderella set resumed.

Yola skipped to the fireplace and mimicked the ash-strewn girl there. "Fisk, they're *running* it! Wasn't I cute? Count off thirteen bleeping weeks for the money! Maybe now I'll be famous and'll get oodleumpteen offers! Do you think it'll sell Matrans screens? They cut my bestest line, where I say if I didn't drop dead *before*, I'd sure be dead *after*! Can we replay tapes so I can watch the series anytime? I sure am a cute brown tyke, aren't I! Why aren't you saying anything?"

Fisk didn't need to comment. It was Yola's moment.

Yola's business did pick up. Several enterprising companies liked her style and made inquiries. But she balked at accepting the 50% subcontract split clause, and they balked at its exclusion. It was standard in the field. Fisk sided with her; to him it seemed like an industry-wide conspiracy against actors. But there did not seem to be much any one or two persons could do about it. He wondered whether CROAK would be interested in undertaking a class-action suit against the practice, since it smacked of monopolistic collusion—but surely CROAK had long since looked into the matter, and would have acted had there been a substantial case.

If Yola wanted to act in commercials, she had to accept the terms proffered. She wrestled with the problem for a month, and finally decided she had no choice. Half a subcontract was better than none.

Then Dunkling called. "We're gearing down for a new project," he said warmly. "You did so well on Matrans—"

"How much, Jirk?"

"One hundred thousand."

Yola didn't ask about the subcontract split.
Dunkling went on to describe the product: a
mass-capacity elevated conveyer belt for industrial
commuters. Because it was fast for a belt—135
MPH cruising speed—and high—1,000 feet—a
certain initial popular resistance was anticipated.
Dunkling would put Yola's name and record into
the Hibelt publicity office, which was a different
department. He thought it almost certain they
would accept his recommendation, however, as it
was all in the company. "All GT," he put it, in the
firm's slang for "perfect."

"We're in business again," Yola said as the man
faded. "I clucked out on the sub. At least Shirk
named the figure, this time!"

Fisk nodded. He was glad she wasn't
rationalizing about her capitulation to standard
practice. She had grown.

In the ensuing months, the Matrans/Vacationer
ads appeared profusely. Whether they were
accomplishing the primary purpose it was
impossible to tell, because there was such
pervasive conditioning against live transmission.
Normal reaction to the very notion should have
been derisive laughter—which was how the ads
were playing it, while planting the seeds of doubt.
An intensive campaign of years would be required
to show measurably positive results.

But International Vacationer's business seemed
to be suffering an upturn, and Yola's reputation
as a child actress developed nicely. She no longer

had to solicit employment; employers contacted her
with offers. Fisk signed her up for an option with
Consolidated Construction—$125,000 with a 70-30
split in her favor on subcontracts—and for another
with Ace Atomic: $100,000 with a 90-10 split. It
seemed that the 50-50 split was not so standard,
when the employers really wanted the account.
Things were definitely looking up.

But Fisk discovered that there were personal
liabilities of success, too. He had appreciated Yola's
increasing maturity as she wrestled with the hard
contractual decisions; but now those decisions were
past. Never exactly shy, she was rapidly developing
into a pint-sized prima donna. She would fly into
an object-throwing tantrum whenever balked—and
she felt balked when Fisk refused to let her watch
the late evening show, that ran until one AM and
was rated triple-X-negative for under age 35. She
also affected obnoxious little mannerisms, such as
answering the phone "*The* Yola Centers speaking,
lout!"

Then the General Transport statement of account
arrived by mailfax. It was a formal document listing
the commercial, the artist (Yola), the advance paid,
and the earnings due the artist based on a royalty
of four and a half percent of the net profit realized
after taxes on each set of Matrans screens judged
by the GT sales board to have been sold on the
open market owing to primary influence of her
commercials.

Fisk looked over her shoulder, frowning. "Well,
we knew they didn't expect many early sales," he
said. "That's why they give a big advance—not that

they *did*, as these things go. So it takes a decade to earn it out—that's advertising!"

"What about Vacationer?" she demanded. "Aren't they supposed to be listed here too?"

Fisk looked again. "Their payment must be listed on a separate sheet."

She shook the fax. There was no other sheet. And the space reserved for the listing of subsidiary contracts was blank.

"They goofed it up!" she cried indignantly. "That subsale was made six months ago!"

"Call GT's accounting department and get a corrected statement," Fisk said. "There isn't any actual money involved right now, since only two months have elapsed since the ads started airing. But we might as well keep the record straight."

Yola called. In the course of fifteen minutes of ungracious haggling the computer's corrected fax appeared.

It was identical to the first.

Yola swelled dangerously. "Why you blathering fat-eared stink—"

Fisk dived for the phone and cut the connection before she warmed up. "Wait! Wait!" he cried. "Let's recheck the contract first! If GT's wrong, we can nail it in polite language." No use trying to convince her to restrain her own language; he would just have to make sure he did the talking next time.

He brought out the contract and skimmed its provisions. "See?" Yola cried, pointing. "It says Artist gets fifty percent of payments from major subcontract by another established company!"

"So it does," Fisk agreed patiently. "But that is not the present question. We need to know how soon GT relays such payments—and when they have to report on the subcontracts."

"Gobbledegooky!" she muttered.

They read on. "At the next annual statement after receipt of cash," Fisk said.

"But the cash isn't coming for another month, and we've just *had* the first annual statement. You mean we won't get our money for a whole 'nother *year?*"

"That's what the small print seems to say."

"But we need that money to *live* on! Anyway, the print's the same size as the rest of it!"

Fisk shook his head. "Do you think General Transport gives a plugged slug how we survive? We signed the contract. And 'small print' is just an expression meaning that there are reservations in the contract that tend to ensnare the unwary party. It isn't literally small, anymore."

"It *ought* to be small!" she exclaimed. "It ought to be so ashamed, acting like that, it'd shrink right out of sight! Then why did Bunkling say we'd get the loot right away?"

Dunkling *had* said that! Fisk went on through the contract, reading every clause carefully. "Here it is! They'll pay on receipt if the artist puts in a request!"

"Goody!" She reached for the phone. Fisk moved to stop her, then decided this was positive enough to trust to her discretion.

"By all means," the robot secretary said. "Your share will be vouchered at the moment of receipt."

Yola, relieved, became silent. Perhaps she had learned the advantage of caution and reconsideration before acting. "Thank you," Fisk said for her. "We appreciate it."

And they celebrated by setting up the richest supper their fooder could deliver, sparing *almost* no expense. Fisk barely stopped Yola in time: she had been dialing peppermint flavored caviar.

"Sometimes I just screen about town," the image-Yola said brightly. "It's not as much fun as using the highway. . . ." Her image faded into a mélange of traffic-jammed vehicles, swearing drivers, sagging pedestrian belts and lifts bursting with sick-looking commuters. Then back to Yola, emerging unruffled in a fetching little-girl dress at a plush restaurant. "But it *is* faster!" She looked out the window at the ravening throng. "If only I had time to mix in. . ." she finished wistfully, shoving her elbows out as though forcing her way through a crowd.

The Yola Centers shook her head. "They cut that one, too, bleep it! I got to tromp toes in the takes!" She put on the next replay.

The thirteen-week post-airing subcontract date arrived, but no voucher from General Transport. "Hold on!" Fisk said, restraining Yola at the phone. "Give them a chance! It takes a few days to process such things!"

She turned on him a look of withering skepticism that would have done credit to the initial sequence of a before-after commercial. "This is the computer age, Fisky! They can handle any paperwork in six minutes." But she waited.

Days passed, then a week. No money. "All right," Fisk said, becoming concerned himself, and unable to withstand her vehement pestering longer. *"I'll* call."

He did. "Data insufficient," the robot secretary said.

"The artist's share of the International Vacationer advance on the Yola Centers Matrans prime contract," Fisk said evenly. "Do you need the contract number? I believe that payment is overdue."

The robot took the number and clicked, checking. "There is no payment owing on that contract," it said.

"What?"

"Please turn up your sound if you are having undue difficulty hearing," the robot said impersonally. "There is no payment owing on that contract. Thank you." It faded.

"I told you it was fishy," Yola cried, gratified. "But you wanted to be bleeping *reasonable!* The bleeps are stealing our money!"

"Let me look into this," Fisk said, shaken. "I can't believe a company like General Transport would renege on a contract."

"What's to look, gook? You can't argue with a robot, and robot's don't make mistakes. GT's grabbing all the loot! And they cut the best lines out of my takes, too!"

Fisk got out the contract again. The fax sheets were becoming worn at the creases. "Give me a couple hours to analyze this thing all the way," he said. "I'm going to get to the root of this."

She looked at him appraisingly and saw his determination. "Okay, Daddy. I'll go joyriding."

He gave her the programming key for the Fusion, and she departed. She was too young to drive, but the programmer would keep the machine on course and safely moving even without human occupation. Fisk never had to worry about parking his car; if space were not available, he merely sent it home alone, and summoned it when he needed it again.

Fisk reread the entire contract, making notes. He was surprised to discover a number of minor clauses he had forgotten. They were not good, bad, or particularly significant—just reasonable, neutral guarantees against special situations.

Then he hit pay dirt: "ALL PAYMENTS MADE TO ARTIST UNDER THIS CONTRACT SHALL BE RECOVERABLE FROM ALL MONIES ACCRUING TO ARTIST UNDER SAME."

That one had not seemed remarkable to him before. He had presumed it was necessary in order for the prime contractor to obtain its legal share of subcontract income, buttressing the 50-50 clause. Now he saw that this could be interpreted as a device to reserve *all* monies to GT, depending on how much of the original advance had been earned back by royalties at the time of the statement. Read this way, it obliterated the schedule of contract/artist division of spoils.

The Matrans advance had been seventy-five thousand dollars. Only fifteen thousand dollars had been earned back, according to the first statement. That left a sixty thousand dollar deficit. All they could expect to receive at this time from the subcontract share was $15,000—a poor fraction of their expectations. Theoretically they would eventually have the full amount—but that would be a long wait. Fisk knew when any novel product first hit the market there was a rush of early sales, to collectors and the curious, but that this burst soon petered out into the regular pattern. Even the infamous Edsel car of history had sold well, the first few days. So it was with Matrans screens—but now that the opening-day novelty was off, they would be lucky to earn a thousand dollars a year in royalties. Until the attitude of the world changed.

So the trap had two prongs: a very slow royalty pattern, and GT's right to keep all subsidiary money until that pattern was complete. He was reminded of the classic test paper legend: ninety-nine difficult questions, with number one hundred saying "Ignore questions 1-99." He had fallen into a variant of that trap—and it wasn't going to be easy to explain it to Yola.

But still, there should have been *some* payment! And why hadn't the IV subcontract been listed on the statement of account? The prime contract plainly said: PRIME CONTRACTOR SHALL RENDER ANNUAL STATEMENTS OF ACCOUNT OF THE NET ROYALTIES EARNED TO DATE, AND SUBSIDIARY SALES, LEASES AND OPTIONS.

Fisk went at it again and again. They had been distracted from this matter before by Dunkling's assurance that they would be paid promptly. But there was no way around it: that omission of the

Vacationer subcontract was a direct violation of the contract.

So it boiled down to two questions: why no subcontract listing, and why no money, however little? Both of these had been challenged, and neither resolved. Which suggested deliberate abuse on the part of General Transport.

Yola reappeared. "You mad now, Fishy?"

That was one takeoff on his name he didn't appreciate, particularly at this moment, but he refused to let her know. "Let's just say that some questions need further exploration."

"Yep. You're mad." She liked that. Yola lost what little temper she had ten times a day, and recovered it ten times. Fisk was exceedingly slow to anger— but he could take weeks to cool, as she had learned the hard way. She obviously felt much better having him mad on *her* side.

Fisk punched for Dunkling. "This is a personal matter," he said sharply to the robot. "I want Dunkling himself, and I want him now."

"Mr. Dunkling is in conference," the secretary said. "The first available appointment—"

"This concerns contract violations on your part," Fisk said precisely. "I shall either speak to Dunkling now, or I shall call the Illicit Practices Commission. Do you understand?"

Yola clapped her hands with glee. "You're a terror, Daddy!"

Dunkling's face appeared, and for once it wasn't smiling. "Centers, I'm not accustomed to—"

"One," Fisk said. "You made no listing of International Vacationer subcontract on your annual statement. Two: you failed to pay over any part of the artist's share of the subcontract advance. I want a corrected statement and I want the money—while I wait."

Dunkling turned red. "You've got a nerve—and a lot to learn!" he snapped. "That Vacationer sub was not listed because it was not completed within the fiscal year for which the statement was issued—as you would have known had you given even cursory attention to your contract. And you received no payment because you have none coming. The prime advance has not been earned out. Clear now?"

"No it isn't!" Fisk snapped back. "As I read the contract—"

"And our option with you on Hibelt is herewith declined," Dunkling said. "You have no need to contact General Transport further, as none of its divisions will be doing business with you in future." This time he didn't fade, he crackled off.

"Come back here, you bastard!" Fisk shouted, but of course it was too late.

"Brother, is he asking for it!" Yola said with fierce anticipation. "What do we do now, Daddy?"

"What we should have done in the first place: query CROAK for advice."

"What about the Illicit Practices Commission?"

"IPC? Let's hold that in abeyance. Dunkling was too sure of himself. We'd better find out *why*, before we get any deeper. The first thing we need is information; then we'll know how to prosecute our case."

Yola called the CROAK contract-review office, but learned that their expert was traveling, and would not be available for several days.

"Very well," Fisk said. "We'll print up an itemized summary and query and leave it for his consideration when he gets back. Meanwhile, we'd better get a lawyer."

"A lawyer!" Yola cried, thrilled. "You're gunning for elephant!"

"There are no elephant," Fisk said. "This is merely smart procedure. If we had had a lawyer go over our contract before we signed—"

"There's a pseudoelephant at the zoo," Yola said. "But you know lawyers are expensive—"

"A pseudo is a fake, by definition. We'll rent a small lawbot. This is all preliminary, anyway."

"What happened to the real elephants?" Yola asked, but Fisk didn't answer.

Lawyers *were* expensive. Fisk had to settle for an elementary yes-no model that would be tedious to use. He paid a week's rental and went to work.

First he had to type the entire contract on its alphabet-board—an interminable chore. Then he had to program his questions. The machine was equipped with a standard catalogue of relevant law, but alignment with their particular situation was a problem he had to work out by himself.

"Ask it how much money they owe us," Yola said impatiently.

"Money is not the object, now," Fisk said, but he tried.

"DATA INSUFFICIENT" the machine typed.

"That's what happens," Fisk said. "We don't have the data on the International Vacationer subcontract, so the lawbot can't answer."

"Sure we do!" she said. "Seventy-five thousand, our share—and it should have been one hundred fifty!"

"That's not official," he said, looking for an appropriate opening to tell her the real figure was more likely fifteen thousand. "We need the actual contract or statement of account—and we have neither."

"But that's why we're fighting! That lying statement—"

"We can't get a meaningful answer from the lawbot when the data itself is at issue," Fisk said.

"Well, how about the other?" she demanded. "The sale they didn't list.

"I'll try." Fisk typed the question. "Is the International Vacationer subcontract required to be listed on the prime contract annual statement of account?"

"DATA INSUFFICIENT."

"That machine's lost a bleeping cog!" Yola cried. "*Why* is it insufficient?"

"For that we'll have to play 'twenty questions,' " Fisk said. Yola obviously didn't comprehend the allusion, and he was reminded again of the span between their ages. She was eleven, he fifty. In the intervening thirty-nine years, the world had changed mightily. Not that that was relevant to the current problem. "We have to phrase questions subject to yes-no answers. That's the hard part."

"The *hard* part is getting old 'Data Insufficient' to answer a stupidly simple question!"

"That too." Fisk mulled it over, made some notes, and commenced: "Is a subcontract normally required to be listed on the annual statement of account as defined by this contract?"

"YES."

"Hey!" Yola cried. "Junkbox answered!"

"Merely the first step in what may be a long staircase."

"What?"

Oops! Another image taken from a foreign generation. "First aperture in a megalevel chute."

"Oh. Why didn't you *say* so, Frisky?"

Back to work: "Should prior referenced subcontract normally appear on the referenced statement?"

"You already asked that one," Yola said.

"No. This is one stage nearer the present case. We'll keep going until we discover the balk-point, then rephrase and try again."

Meanwhile the machine had printed its answer: "YES."

"Ask it what happened to the elephants," Yola said.

"Is absence of prior ref. subct. on ref. statement necessarily indicative of prime ctr. malfeasance?"

Yola shook her head. "I sure hope *you* know what you're saying!"

"I do—and the lawbot understands, too. I think we're zeroing in on the loophole."

Then he read the answer: "NO."

"Loophole?" Yola asked.

"Yola, I can't translate every dated expression I use! Just let me work."

She bristled, but decided it was better to keep

him mad at General Transport instead of at her.

After a tedious back-and-forth, Fisk narrowed it down to the essence: the legality of the missing listing hinged on the applicable definition of "sale." The standard definition provided by the library was: "A contract made for the transfer of property from one legal entity to another for a valuable consideration."

"If the standard definition holds," Fisk said, "then we have a specific violation of contract, regardless of the money involved. 'Valuable consideration' includes the agreement to pay at some later date; it's all the same, legally, and execution of the contract constitutes the sale. But it is possible they aren't using the standard definition, and don't consider the sale complete until the money is actually received. That's why the lawbot balked the first time."

"Can they get away with that?" Yola asked.

"I doubt it. Normal presumption is that they are following the standard; otherwise they'd have to announce their basis for divergence, and print that in the prime contract, which they haven't done. But it means we'll have to take them to court to get a specific ruling for our case—and we just don't have the money to push our suit properly."

"We don't have the money because they bilked us out of our share!" Yola exclaimed furiously.

"That's one way of looking at it. But we're not dealing with pure legalities now, but with reality, and it seems might makes right."

"Clout wins the bout," she echoed in her own terminology. "Money gets the honey. But bleep it, Fisk—"

"Let's wait to see what CROAK says," he suggested. "We're obviously sandlot players in a major league park."

"Toddlecart in the Hurdle," she agreed. "But—"

"General Transport isn't the only company in the world, fortunately. And maybe we've learned a lesson that will save us a lot more money in the long run than we lost this time. Now we know we have to be constantly alert for company idiosyncrasies—like paying thirteen weeks late— and unscrupulous policies. Public reputation means nothing. If CROAK suggests a feasible procedure, we'll take it; otherwise—"

"You mean give up?" she demanded, horrified.

"Sometimes it is necessary to forfeit the battle in order to win the—"

She shook her head sadly. "I guess you're right, coward."

The image-Yola winked at the audience. "My Daddy says next time I do this—" pouring instant purple cement-foam into the disposal hopper—"he'll ship me to—" a horrendous grinding and breaking sound as the cement-foam hardened, ruining the machine. Yola stepped hastily through the Matrans screen. "Siberia!" she finished, shivering in snow.

The phone lighted, and Yola switched off the replay. "The Yola Cen—"

"I am Maxima Bubonik of CROAK," a suave young woman said, obviously uninterested in

Yola's credentials. Fisk had seen her a number of times in assorted commercials, but never heard her stage name before. "Contract-Review relayed your complaint to me—"

"It wasn't a complaint," Fisk said over Yola's shoulder. "It was a query."

Bubonik continued as if she hadn't heard, her fine eye on Yola. "Because I have done many commercials for General Transport, and am more familiar with their mode of operation—"

"Isn't that conflict of interest?" Fisk asked, annoyed. "We wanted an *objective* review of—"

"Now I have taken your complaint directly to Mr. Dunkling of Transport and Mr. Shooper of Vacationer, and am satisfied from what they tell me that this entire confusion stems from nothing more than your own inexcusable ignorance of standard practice—"

"You took our query to *Dunkling*?" Fisk cried. "And involved Vacationer too? That was a confidential note—"

Bubonik's gaze remained fixed on Yola. "And may I say, as one girl to another, in the most rational and gentle fashion imaginable, that you have acted precipitously and foolishly in this matter, and done yourself incalculable harm. One simple query to Mr. Dunkling or to CROAK could have resolved your misunderstanding amicably, and—"

"We queried *both*!" Fisk snapped. Yola kept her mouth shut, since he was obviously working up to another thoroughgoing mad. "Dunkling responded by cutting off our Hibelt option, and CROAK—how the bleep do you think you *got* this info, if not from our—"

"But instead," Bubonik told Yola, "you have taken your fraudulent hysteria to a *lawbot*, of all things, and libelously maligned one of the very finest advertisers in the business and given a bad name to CROAK in the process. Naturally you will issue a formal apology—"

Fisk opened his mouth, but his internal pressure had jumped to such a level that he could not make a sound. Yola made a squeak that sounded like stifled laughter. That had to do for their response.

Bubonik paused meaningfully. She was an experienced commercial actress, and her pause was timed to perfection. Her attitude suggested that she was dealing with unruly children who had to be restrained for their own good.

"However," she said softly, "since you are obviously in difficult straits, and perhaps guilty more of blunder than of intentional mischief, Mr. Dunkling has agreed to waive Transport's contractual prerogatives and relay the full scheduled subcontract share to the artist. To you, Yola. This is a remarkably generous attitude on his part, considering the affront! His only—and, I might add, quite reasonable— request is that you desist in your efforts to undermine Transport's well-deserved reputation for complete integrity and fair dealing, and that you let the entire matter drop as of this moment. Your CROAK complaint has already been destroyed, so that it will not embarrass you further."

"They're going to pay!" Yola cried, and Fisk realized that Bubonik's concentration on her had been a skillful and effective ploy. "How much is Dirk slicing off for us?"

"The full advance paid by International Vacationer was fifty thousand dollars. Your share will be twenty-five thousand. And since your commercials are doing very well for them, there should be additional payments when that advance is earned out, in about a year. Quite possibly you will receive another twenty-five thousand."

Fisk reached across Yola to break the connection, and Bubonik faded.

"Hey!" Yola protested. "They're *paying*! What are you trying to—"

"They're *bribing*," Fisk said. "Twenty-five thousand dollars for us to shut up. The offer made through an unofficial intermediary, the query responsible for it destroyed, so GT can't be called to account at law. And a pittance, at that—only a third of what a standard contract should have brought. They must think we really *are* fools!"

"But the money—!"

"Money? *Garbage!*"

"Fisky, we need that loot! Our credit balance—"

"*Need* has nothing to do with it. We are not going to become accessories to graft! When CROAK and Big Advertising are in collusion at the expense of the individual artist—"

"Oh, phooey! They're just paying us what they owed us all along. Why complain, when we've got ours?"

Fisk looked at her, disgusted. He had thought she was maturing. "Your values are in tune with the times, it seems. But they're selfish, short-sighted, eleven-year-old values. When you outgrow them and learn the meaning of integrity and true personal pride, then you'll be an adult. And I mean to see that you do get there."

"You're just not living in this century!" Yola said. "Why don't you ask the lawbot, even?"

Sensible suggestion! If she would accept the verdict of the machine, that was a start in the right direction. Fisk typed in the offer with its silence proviso, then asked: "Should artist accept?"

"YES," the lawbot replied.

Fisk stared. "There's a mistake!"

"No mistake, Daddy," Yola said reasonably. "You just won't admit you're wrong."

"I'm *not* wrong! There's a fundamental ethic involved—"

She shrugged in the tasteful, rehearsed way fashionable in commercial acting. She had certainly picked up the phoniness of the trade quickly. "Fisky, I was mad too, and I still think the money's way too little. But it's the best we can get, and we can't afford to sue anyway, so we've just got to be practical."

Fisk rephrased the question to the lawbot, got another wrong answer, then cleared the entire temporary data bank and fed in all the relevant information from scratch. The answer was unchanged: make the deal.

It seemed that what was not specifically illegal, by the logic of the machine, was acceptable. There was no ethic beyond the literal law.

"This junk's going back to the shop!" Fisk said, disgruntled.

Yola shook her locks in the manner of one acquiescing to a lunatic. "God is dead; about time you learned."

Fisk got busy. He had not been this angry in a decade. He returned the defective lawbot to its shop, made some notes to organize his thinking, and set out to strike back at General Transport in a manner that would make it take notice.

He punched the number of the Illicit Practices Commission, District K. "I wish to make a complaint of illicit practice against General Transport, Matrans Division, Promotion, specifically relating to Kirk Dunkling and the artist's contract for Yola Centers," he said.

"Bleep, Fisk," Yola said. "You scare me when you get like this!" For once she was not being facetious. "All for such a little thing, when Maxima went to so much trouble to help—"

"Please identify yourself and itemize your particulars," the human IPC secretary said. This was obviously routine to her.

"Fisk Centers, father and manager of Yola Centers, child commercial actress. Item One: Subject company by both verbal and contractual statements deliberately misled artist to believe that a larger payment for her services would be made than was actually contemplated." He documented this by quoting from memory Dunkling's promise that "their share" would be relayed promptly upon receipt, and his earlier statement that "residuals" would probably amount to as much or more than the initial advance. "When in fact," Fisk continued, "the subcontract advance was set at an artificially low level, far below standard practice, so that no share would be relayed." He also read from the prime contract itself, which specified that "royalties" were to be chargeable against the advance, while making a separate listing for subcontract division. "This implies that said subcontracts are therefore not chargeable against that advance, but are instead portioned as specified in that listing," he said.

"Hey, you're right!" Yola murmured, surprised. "I never thought of that."

"Item One noted," the secretary said coolly.

"Item Two: Subject company issued a deliberately inaccurate annual statement of account that omitted listing of a major subsidiary contract already executed." He documented this also, giving the approximate dates of Vacationer's option and contract, the standard definition of "sale," and establishing Transport's specific refusal to correct the statement when challenged on the omission. "In the face of Item One," he concluded, "Item Two can only be construed as a further attempt to mislead and defraud the artist."

"Item Two noted," the secretary said with a bored air.

"Item Three: Subject company, by way of collusive intermediary, proffered a payment of from twenty-five to fifty thousand dollars to the artist, providing that she desist from the complaint on Items One and Two."

"Oh, they *did*!" the secretary said, coming to life.

"Very well, Mr. Centers. IPC will process this complaint, and will notify you of developments." She faded away.

Fisk sat back. "Now we'll wait for the bleep to hit the transmitter."

"Aw, they'll just stall it to death," Yola muttered. "All that money we could've had—"

"Yola, if our complaint proves out, we'll have the money as well as self-respect."

"We *will*?" she said, brightening. "Why didn't you *say* so?"

"And I daresay it will not be long before we have a response," he said, stepping into the foamer for a cleanup. "They called it a complaint when we queried CROAK; now they've got the real thing, thanks to Maxima Bubonik."

"What do you think GT'll do?" she asked, worried.

"Well, this IPC complaint will show them that they can't muzzle us. They may just apologize, claim it was all a mistake, pay up and reinstate the Hibelt option. That would be much better for them than the ugly publicity of a contested complaint—especially when they know they're wrong."

Yola shook her head dubiously.

In just six minutes a form emerged from the mailfax. Yola snatched it up and began reading: "Notice of Suit against Fisk Centers."

Fisk leaped as if the foamer had goosed him. *"What?"*

"I think something went wrong," Yola murmured, handing him the sheet.

It was the preliminary notice of a libel suit filed

against him by General Transport, based on his
IPC complaint.

"LIBEL: a false publication tending to injure
the reputation or damage the business. . . ." Fisk
looked up from the book. "This is ridiculous! I didn't
libel them, I made a complaint about their unfair
practices!"

"*Any* complaint is libelous to General Transport,"
Yola said. "When you queried, they called it a
complaint; when you complained, they called it
libel. I wonder what they'd call it if you announced
they were bleep eaters?"

"Murder," he said. "Maybe even genocide! I need
a lawyer, and a good one."

"We've been through that," she pointed out. "You
wouldn't listen, and now we pine in brine—"

"The lawbot was inadequate to the need. A human
lawyer would have—"

"You know what a live lawyer *costs*?" she asked
incredulously.

"Yes. We are left with no alternative but to make
application for state assistance."

"Why not play roulette for life-stakes while you're
at it? Listen, Daddy, I was a Ward of the State, and
I know—"

"It is a gamble of desperation," he admitted. "But
sometimes their help is valuable."

"Sometimes their help gets their clients
brainvacked, too!"

Fisk sighed. He punched the State Assistance
number.

"Fool," Yola said.

But luck was with him. He was issued a permit for one hour's time on the District F Legal Aid Computer (FLAC), the only qualified machine available at this time for State Assistance on a civil suit. That was it. He would stand or fall on that hour's legal advice.

"I have a bright idea," Yola said. "Why don't we put ashes on our heads and crawl down to General Transport and—"

"That's what they expect. Their hand isn't any stronger than it was before; they've just raised the ante to a level they figure we can't match. In other words—"

"Don't bother. I *know* that particular obscurity. We played poker all the time in the dorm. Once I took one hundred and fifty dollars off three boys. Good thing I didn't lose!"

"Those were coed dorms?" Fisk asked, shocked. "What happened when you *lost*?"

She made a face. "Same thing't'll happen to you when you lose *this* one! Why don't you quit when you're ahead?"

"Yola, that would be playing right into their hands. There's no guessing the number of other artists they have browbeaten into submission by just such tactics. Artists who thought they were protected by associations like CROAK. It is high time someone stood his ground."

"You'll be standing your ground horizontally in a Perpetual Laser Memorial Plot, and I'll be a waifless home—"

"Homeless waif." She really was upset! "But don't be unduly concerned. That education fund I set up from the Hurdle winnings will see you through to adulthood."

"Fat consolation! Fisk, this libel suit can wipe us out!"

"It *could*—if their own grounds weren't spurious. I have told IPC nothing but the truth, and the truth will redeem my position."

"Do you really *believe* that?"

Fisk didn't answer, because his belief was much less firm than his statement.

The hour on FLAC was more important than it looked to Yola. Fisk was permitted to take it in installments of as little as one minute at a time, and FLAC was a major computer. It could dish out an extraordinary amount of legal strategy in one minute. Fisk's problem was one of management: how to make good enough use of his time to win his case. He needed to program carefully.

He ordered more texts from the library and perused their faxes avidly, seeking a reasonable line of defense. Then, one by one, he tested them on FLAC.

First he tried to establish the defense of "Truth." He had made three specific charges, and they were as far as he knew true. But he discovered that he could not merely affirm his IPC statement, for that would be just a repetition of the supposed libel. He had to set forth particulars, and document the particular aspects of his statement that established accuracy.

He reassembled his evidence for the first of his three charges: that of Transport's deceptions about the payment owing to the artist. The phone company, for a fee, provided a dated tape of Dunkling telling Yola " . . . we'll relay your share the moment we receive their (Vacationer's) payment." That was a clear statement of intent, hardly suggesting the later "There is no payment owing" of the robot secretary. Dunkling's original estimate that residuals might exceed the original advance was not available, as that had been made verbally in his office. That necessary omission weakened Fisk's case. But he re-quoted from the prime contract itself, where it implied separation of payments, and from the library's standard-practice manual.

He fed this package into FLAC, using up a good ten minutes of his allocated computer time. Now for the payoff: "Is this a valid defense against a charge of libel based on this portion of this complaint?" If so, and if he disposed of the other portions as readily, the suit would be thrown out before ever coming to trial.

There was no delay. "No," the resonant FLAC voice said.

Fisk was stunned. Fortunately he didn't have to pry for the complete answer when dealing with a computer of this level. FLAC provided it automatically: the term "deliberately" was not in order, as it did not admit the possibility of clerical error, always possible where humans were involved. Dunkling could have promised the money in good faith, being unaware that the balance would be too small to earn out the prime advance. In order to prove his charge, Fisk would have to establish that Dunkling knew *at the time he promised payment* that none was owing. Further, even that was dubious, because Dunkling had not promised a specific amount, but only the artist's *share*—which turned out to be nothing. Of course the implication was the full fifty percent of the Vacationer advance had been meant, but such implication did not in itself constitute grounds for the charge Fisk had made.

Fisk shook his head slowly, as though stones were sloshing in brine inside it. He knew he had no chance to establish Dunkling's specific knowledge and intent at times in the past. He might *be* right— but his defense of Truth had washed out, and his certainties were slipping. Why had he had to say "deliberately" in the complaint?

He checked into other available defenses against the libel charge. One was "Qualified Privilege," but it turned out to be inapplicable. Another was "Right of Reply"—but GT had not accused him of anything prior to the suit itself, so he had no legal reply in kind. The actress Maxima Bubonik had accused him of plenty, by implication—but she was not the one suing. Once more the network of Big Industry and its camp followers had given him very little avenue for redress. They were indeed professionals.

He considered "Reliance Testimony"—for he had relied on his information that the standard subcontract applicable to his situation was one hundred fifty thousand dollars, and had been misled into believing that GT had made such a contract with Vacationer. But the mistake had been in his own assumption; no one had

promised him standard terms or provided any
of the relevant figures. GT had been very canny
about omitting such details—but again, he could
not prove prejudicial motive.

Fisk went on down the list, his eyes becoming
bleary. "Justification?" Not if "Truth" was defunct.
Who could have imagined that it would be so
difficult to defend against the preposterous charge
of libel, when *he* was the injured party!

Of course the onus to prosecute was on GT—but
he had to be certain of his responses when their
lawyers pressed their case.

"Fisk, this is ridiculous!" Yola said. "You're just
grinding through all those stupid defenses when
you know none of them will work!"

He didn't answer. He was pondering the defense
of "Fair Comment!" This required that he prove
that his facts had been truly stated, as they had;
that his comment was an honest expression of
his real opinion, as it was; and that no corrupt
or dishonorable motives had been ascribed to the
party criticized. "But that's the whole point of it!"
he cried aloud. "If Transport's motives had been
honorable this never would have happened! How
can I be sued for *telling the truth*?"

"Truth, schmooth!" Yola retorted. "Who cares
about that? The truth is that you're fat, but
you'd spank me if I told you that. They have the
clout to put us away no matter what the truth,
and *that's* what counts in this world! You're just
committing suicide, oinkheaded suicide, and taking
me down with you—*when we could have had the
money*!"

"Not another word!" Fisk roared, cowing her momentarily. "This world is *not* like that, and *we* aren't going to act like that!"

There was silence for a full fifteen seconds. When Yola spoke again, she was unusually subdued. "Daddy, I've been patient with you. Very patient, for me. But I can't stand by and watch you throw your fool life away for nothing. "It's my fault some, 'cause I wanted you mad—but that was when I figured you were right. Now you're not *right*-mad, you're *wrong*-mad. And you don't know when to quit."

Fisk stared at her, impressed and discomfited. This was a facet of her personality he had not seen before. Perhaps it had not existed before this crisis. A serious, concerned Yola, who was trying to work out what was right. Yet still limited by her conception of *might* as *right*, however she phrased it. To her, there *was* no right in the face of one's inability to defend it. Thus, by her definition, Fisk had become "wrong" when his case became a loser.

"A man must act in accordance with his philosophy," he said quietly.

"Yes." She thought for a moment, and he could see that she was working up to something extraordinary. "So maybe you'll understand why I've got to do it."

"Do what?" He didn't like the look of this. Was she going to throw a furniture-breaking tantrum?

"Leave you."

Completely surprised, Fisk stuttered for a moment before he could speak. "Y-you can't leave me! You have nowhere to go!"

"Yes I do, Daddy. I'll use that stupid educational fund. I can go to school far away, and you can't stop me. I can stay there *forever*!" Now she was crying, and Fisk was deeply touched, because he had never seen her do it honestly before. Yola had always been ready with a smile or a tantrum, both being pure artifice; seldom did her real feelings emerge directly. It was an almost impenetrable emotional defense she had developed in the course of her years as an institutionalized orphan. He had been assured she liked staying with him largely because she had never run away.

Now she wanted to leave—but not secretly. Openly. Which meant she did not really want to go. And that put him in a nasty position, for if he didn't try to stop her she would take it as proof that he wanted to be rid of her, even though this particular subcrisis was of her own genesis. He understood enough of the processes of her mind to be certain of that.

Yola went to the phone and punched a number she must have looked up beforehand. A woman appeared, speaking in a foreign language.

"Hook in a translator," Yola said, mopping her eyes without affection. "I can't speak Swiss."

Swiss! Fisk was startled again. Of course she didn't speak Swiss; nobody did, as there was no such language. But she really meant it, about going far away. That was a school in Switzerland.

He had to stop her, and not just to play her game. It was the last thing Yola would admit, even to herself, but she needed him. She needed to be part of a family, however small;

to be somebody's daughter. She had called him "Daddy" consistently during this dialogue, instead of her usual impolite variants of his name; that was another signal. Another institution, however elaborate, was absolutely no good for her.

"Yola Centers, age eleven," she said in answer to the translated query. She also gave her current address.

Fisk stood, about to haul her away from the phone by brute force. She would throw a doozy of a tantrum, but this was what she really wanted. To be kept at home. Otherwise she would have waited until she was alone to make the call.

But he paused. If he stopped her, he would have to pacify her with some compromise—such as capitulating on the libel defense. That he couldn't do. And—if he managed to keep her in line, and continued the libel defense, and then lost the case—he would no longer be able to afford to maintain her, and might in fact be legally stripped of the right. General Transport would see that punitive damages wiped him out beyond hope of recovery.

So perhaps it was better that she make the break now, of her own volition. She would never go if he tried to *send* her! No one could touch her at the Swiss school; the scholastic fund was inviolate. She would have care and education until maturity. There was a lot to recommend that. After she graduated, there would be opportunity for a happier life.

"We shall dispatch a taxi," the school-voice said. "Be ready in fifteen minutes."

Yola looked at Fisk—but he was back at his references, ignoring her. He had made a decision she was bound to misunderstand, but he didn't see any better way. It was the lesser of evils.

She saw that he could not be moved, and her mind went through the channels it had to and finished in the slough awaiting. She smiled, tentatively, as though commencing the defense of "I don't care; see, I'm laughing!" but she couldn't make that stand up. So she went into the alternate defense of "Righteous Fury," and banged around noisily as she packed her scant belongings.

Fisk sat through it all, wishing she would drop the case entirely—and knowing it could mean disaster if she did. If only she could comprehend that his position with respect to GT was very similar. What had to be done, had to be done— no matter what the cost.

The taxi arrived and hovered urgently at the landing, and there was nothing Yola could do except go out to it. "Oh *Daddy!*" she cried at the door, for the moment entirely naked in her hurt. But Fisk, steeled, did not even look up from his papers.

Fisk worked and slept for three days, taking pills to accomplish each. He had been single for fifty years, and a father for less than one—but it was not easy to revert to his old habits. He had grown accustomed . . .

Finally he called the court having jurisdiction over this case. "I am ready for the initial hearing,"

he said. Complex matters such as a libel suit did not
jump right into a full-scale court trial; there would
be a series of hearings and much legal maneuvering
preceding the public manifestations.

"Very well, Mr. Centers," the human clerk said.
"The prosecution is also ready. We shall connect
you for the hearing at noon today."

Fisk shook his head as the screen faded. He had
been under the impression that it was afternoon,
but his clock agreed with the clerk: it was morning.
At any rate, he would be present; an appointment
of this nature carried an automatic warning of
"Fail Not in This Appearance, under Penalty of
Contempt," whether voiced or unvoiced.

His confusion was unsurprising, he realized.
Time had become unstructured since Yola had
gone. He missed the AM argument about what
to punch for breakfast (oyster stew or marijuana-
flavored cupcakes), and the PM fracas about
what program to watch (Murder Killfest or Porno
Geography), and the thousand lesser frictions
between. There was nothing like an incorrigible
brat to make every moment a stress situation. He
had lived more life in the past few hectic months
with her than he had in the preceding few placid
decades, it seemed.

He dialed and punched the fooder randomly and
ate the result without appetite. He soaked in
the foamer and emerged unrefreshed. He stepped
into the suiter for the first time since Yola's
departure, not even checking the setting—and
emerged wearing a fetching dress several sizes
too small.

He laughed, appreciating the feel of old times. Then his eyes burned, and he reset the machine for a masculine outfit.

At noon the phone lighted. "All stand," a voice said peremptorily. Fisk stood, watching the curtain on the screen. "Its Honor, Judge Computer KaDist," the voice announced as the curtain parted.

The BE SEATED light flashed on the computer's imposing front panel, and Fisk sat. He was not playing any game; he was at this moment legally before the judge of "K" district, and the last thing he needed was a contempt citation.

Judge KaDist wasted no time. "Present Defense," it told Fisk, fixing him with a disconcerting stare from one intake beamer. No doubt it was simultaneously receiving the specifications of the libel charge, on another circuit.

"The Defense of Provocation," Fisk said.

"That is a partial defense," KaDist responded as though advising a child. "Not sufficient."

"May it please Your Honor," Fisk said hastily, "I know it is a partial defense. I wish to apply it to just one word in the specification. Two words, I mean. Three. I—"

A red light glimmered momentarily on KaDist's panel. "How many words?" it inquired heavily.

"Three, Your Honor. One in each item."

Now all lights were calmly white. "Proceed."

"The word 'deliberately' in Item One. The same word in Item Two. And the word 'collusive' in Item Three."

"Make your plea."

"Your Honor, we—my daughter Yola and I—received an insulting and provocative call from the actress Maxima Bubonik offering—"

"One moment, Centers," the judge said, blinking orange. "Are you prepared to put this call on record?"

"Yes, Your Honor. Her complete call and my responses. It is obviously relevant to the case, though—"

"Clerk will mark the transcript of that call 'Exhibit A' and enter it in the record," Judge KaDist said.

There was a delay of perhaps two minutes while the clerk commandeered the transcript and entered it. Fisk was sweating. FLAC had given this line of defense a 75% probability of acceptance by the court, and it was the most promising of the alternatives. But Fisk had to make the proper presentation, or he would throw away even that uncertain chance.

"Proceed," KaDist said, its beam winking at Fisk in a decidedly uncomical way.

"Your Honor, this call infuriated me. This whole affair had been angering me increasingly, and the sheer arrogance—" He paused, as the red light was beginning to glow. The judge had little patience with extraneous detail. "I terminated the call abruptly, as the record shows, and had immediate words with my daughter. Thereafter I made my complaint to IPC. Had I not been freshly provoked by that call, I would have phrased my complaint more moderately, and omitted those three words."

"The record shows that your call to the Illicit Practices Commission followed the termination of the Bubonik call by three hours and thirty-six minutes. This is normally sufficient time for the human system to abate temporary anger."

"Yes, Your Honor. But I am not a normal man! I'm fifty years old—"

"Irrelevant."

"And very slow to cool. I stay mad for hours. So—"

"This is inconclusive," KaDist said, and Fisk's heart seemed to gain a pound. "Are you prepared to document?"

KaDist was giving him a chance after all! "I would need character witnesses, Your Honor. I—"

"Provide names of your recent acquaintances, excluding relatives. We shall select from that number randomly. You will be confined to quarters and your phone blanked until their testimony is available, to prevent prejudicial contact."

The computer certainly was thorough! "Uh, I didn't anticipate this, so I have not said anything to—"

The red warner flashed, so Fisk dropped his attempted explanation and spouted names. "Mr. Brown of the Death Insurance Agency, and Mrs. Pontimer, and Mr. Black of the Deep Space Memorial Chapel, and Dr. Bickel, and Bill—I don't know his last name—he's a racer at Fusion Motors. And—"

"Sufficient. Have you any Defense for the remainder of the charge, exclusive of these three words?" KaDist asked.

"The Defense of Truth, Your Honor. Without those words attributing motive, the three items are accurate, so far as I know."

The full panel of lights came on, green predominating. "Court recessed," the bailiff announced. "The hearing will resume at fourteen hundred."

The screen faded and Fisk collapsed into a more comfortable chair. He was incommunicado now, with his set locked off and his door inoperative, but his combined defenses were on the way to being accepted—maybe!

Promptly at two the phone relighted. The brief court ceremonies were honored. Then: "Mrs. Pontimer to the witness stand."

Mrs. Pontimer's story was soon on record. The widow of an erstwhile client. Fisk, as a representative of Perpetual Laser Memorial Gardens, had sold her and her husband an attractive plot within the sixty story mausoleum. Mr. Pontimer had died shortly thereafter, and Fisk had helped with the funeral arrangements.

"Do you consider this man Fisk Centers to be short of temper?" KaDist asked her then. Fisk was a little amazed at the versatility of modern computers; the judge was filling a lawyer's shoes now.

"Mr. Centers?" the old woman asked, amazed. "No, no! He is a wonderful person, never gets angry!"

Little did she know! Fisk thought ruefully. Naturally he tried not to show temper before a client.

"But assume for the moment that something did make him angry. How long would you say it might take him to regain equilibrium?"

"Your Honor, I don't believe Mr. Centers ever would be angry," she said firmly. "He's such a nice, kind, decent, sensible man. . . ."

Fisk bit his tongue. Her loyalty was touching, but she was unwittingly destroying his defense.

After further inconclusive questioning, KaDist excused her and the next witness was called.

"William Ribboner to the witness stand."

The man Fisk had known only as Bill appeared on the screen. "Look, I'm preparing my machine for a race—" he protested as the bailiff hustled him forward.

"Are you declining to serve as a character witness for the defendant Fisk Centers?" Judge KaDist asked, glimmering orange.

"Fisk Centers? Hey, I remember him! What's this about 'defendant'? He wouldn't—"

"I'm being sued for libel, Bill," Fisk said. If he spoke out of turn, the judge would cut off his phone, but this clarification should be in order.

Bill looked around, spying him in the screen. "Sure, I'll testify for *you*, friend! I know you didn't do it!"

"The witness will face the court," KaDist said, lights dancing warningly. "Mr. Ribboner, have you had prior discussion with the defendant concerning this matter?"

Bill looked embarrassed. "Uh, no, Your Honor. I just know Fisk wouldn't do anything wrong, ever. He—"

"In what connection did you know the defendant?"

"Racing, Your Honor. Fisk and I were in the Hurdle together, and he saved my life. What a driver! Did you know he cracked the—"

"Do you feel that you know him well?"

"As well as one man can know another," Bill said grandly. "That driving he did—"

"Approximately how long were you in contact with Mr. Centers?"

"Well, Judge, the race was only half an hour, counting the—"

The clerk and bailiff were smiling. The red light flickered warningly on Judge KaDist's face. "You knew him for just half an hour?"

Fisk quailed, knowing what was coming. Of all the witnesses to have selected—!

Bill turned a shade darker. "Sir, for most of that I was unconscious."

This time the entire bank of warners came on, bright and fierce. "Unconscious!"

"Your Honor, you can learn an awful lot about a man—a lot of what counts—in a crisis situation," Bill said earnestly. "I know every section of that race, so I know exactly what he went through, just as if I'd watched direct. If you only knew what the Hurdle's like—"

"One moment," KaDist said, cooling to a dim glow. "Clerk will obtain a transcript of the relevant Hurdle car race, mark it Exhibit B, and enter it in the record."

It was done. The film was run for the human participants at the same time, and Fisk saw

the tremendous vehicles charging along at five
hundred miles per hour, slowing for the Narrows
and Hairpin, and saw his own car spin out. His
hands sweated coldly. He should have died ten
times over even before making that supersonic
leap through the raging flames of the pileup at
the end! This was hardly a fit recommendation for
his contested equilibrium.

"That was a remarkable race," KaDist said after
assimilating it. "Very fine machine, that Fusion.
Witness definition of the crisis situation is accepted.
Mr. Ribboner—"

"Call me Bill," Bill said, as Fisk mopped his brow
with relief that this definitional hurdle had been
negotiated. "Everyone does."

"Very well, Bill," the judge said. There was
evidently some small humor within its voluminous
windings. "Please confine yourself in the future to
the questions. Would you consider Mr. Centers to
be of an even disposition?"

"Sure! Never gets shaken, never gets mad. Cool
all the way."

Fisk shook his head. It was happening again!
His friends thought they were helping him, but
his Defense of Provocation was disintegrating.

"Could you conceive of this man becoming
angry?"

Bill fidgeted. "Well, sir, I couldn't swear to every
possible circumstance, you know."

"Assume he is provoked."

"Well, if he ever did get mad—" Bill hesitated,
then turned to Fisk. "I'm awful sorry, friend, but
this is on oath and I just have to say it. You saved

my life, but you're awful stubborn in the clinch or
you'd never've gotten through that race, and if you
ever *did* get mad—"

"Address the court!" the bailiff yelled angrily.

Bill turned back. "Fisk's just not the kind to cool
off fast. Like the Hurdle—he just wouldn't let go
for anything, even if it killed us all! He'd probably
stay mad for days, and I just don't know what he'd
do—"

Victory! Poor Bill looked so woebegone, believing
that he was harming his friend, but that was the
very testimony that would save the defense.

"What might make him angry?" the judge asked
without inflection.

"Not the usual. I guess you could sock him—
not that I *would!*—and he wouldn't worry much.
But he's got some kind of funny ethical discipline,
especially about money—"

"Hypothetical case," KaDist said. "If a party
offered Fisk Centers money to alter his set position
on a financial matter—"

That computer was pretty sharp, Fisk realized.
KaDist wasn't just presiding and interrogating, it
was genuinely trying to bring out the facts.

"Fisk just doesn't *take* money on that basis," Bill
said. "I tried to make him take half the Hurdle
winnings, and he—"

"Please answer the question."

Bill looked miserable again. Actually, the man
was overestimating Fisk's reservations about
money; he preferred to follow his own standards
in *any* endeavor. He had tried to make a financial
killing by investing in Marsland, and gotten killed

himself; now he went after only what was due.
No more—and no less. General Transport had
attempted to take him for a sucker: that was the
fundamental source of his ire, he realized now, not
the specific machinations.

"Well, Your Honor," Bill said slowly, "I'm afraid
he might do something he'd be sorry for."

That was inaccurate, too. Fisk *wasn't* sorry;
he had gotten entangled in the technicalities of
wording, but he regretted his stance not at all.
Somebody had to stand and cry "Enough!" and
make it stick, so he was standing. . . .

"Witness is excused."

Bill left, not looking at Fisk, who was reminded
painfully of Yola's departure. Conscience was a
stern master—but God bless those few who had
it!

"Mr. Centers," Judge KaDist said, and Fisk
jumped to attention. All this theorizing could come
to nothing if this court lacked sympathy. "Your
partial defense of Provocation is sustained, but this
is not sufficient to dismiss the suit. The case will
proceed to trial with your Defense of Truth entered
against the modified charges. Hearing adjourned."

"Thank you, Judge!" Fisk cried, but the screen
was already blank. The worst hurdle had been
overcome.

"It's absolutely safe," Image-Yola said, tripping
from New York to London to Istanbul to Bombay
to Tokyo to Los Angeles to Rio de Janeiro and back
to New York. "But after I've circled the world a few
times, it sure is great to get home!" Her isolated

hand waved good-bye as she vanished for the last time.

Fisk felt a clutch in his gut as of a heart seizure, and had to turn the replays off. "I wish you *were* home . . ." he said.

He was in the foamer washing off the sweat of his legal endeavors when the phone signaled for attention. "Take a message!" he yelled at it.

Then abruptly curious, he climbed out of the foamer in mid-cycle, dripping bubbles, and went to read the message.

"NOTICE OF CANCELLATION OF SUIT—"

General Transport had dropped the libel suit! "But why?" he demanded aloud as more foam slid to the rug. "They might have won—"

"They might have won a technical decision over a nonentity who has no future in the business anyway," a voice said. "Then again, they might have *lost*—which would have set a precedent for a countersuit by you—and thirteen thousand *other* nonentities they've browbeaten the same way over the years."

"Yes, that makes sense," Fisk agreed. "A trial would expose their actual way of doing business, and win or lose their reputation would suffer." Then he did a double take. The phone was off—and that was Yola's voice.

He turned to the door. There she was, as impish as any commercial. "I didn't recognize you in all that educated vocabulary!" he said.

She looked at him defiantly. "I figured if you could outbluff *me*, you sure could outbluff *them!*" Then her eyes dropped demurely. "You *were* bluffing?"

About wanting to be rid of her? Yes! But she had to be told the proper way. Fisk huffed a big breath. "You bundle of trouble! I'm going to set a precedent on your impertinent fanny! Running out on me—"

She skipped into the hall, and he was clothed only in foam and not much of that. He had to stop until he could get rinsed and suited.

"Stay your vile hand, hangman!" she cried happily through the open door. In a moment he knew everyone on the floor would be paying avid attention. "Black and blue innocent waifs don't make such cute commercials—and *then* who would earn your living, Fisk Centers?"

He was rinsed and dried. He dived for the suiter, dropping the act. "Why did you return, Yola? You couldn't have known about the suit being dropped."

"I had a dream," she said, coming in again. "There was this long, long, long line of white woolly sheep, all bleating naively and following one after the other to be sheared. I never saw a real sheep in my life, but that's what I dreamed. And in this line was just one fat ornery old goat, with crooked horns and hardly any decent wool. But when the shearer started, that goat—well, I just had to come back, Daddy. I sort of like goats."

Fisk stepped out, fully clothed at last, and hugged her. "I missed you, Mischief!"

"C'mon!" she said, wriggling away, pleased and embarrassed. "I have to fetch us some loot."

"I don't think—"

But she was already punching a number. "Supervolt Electronics," a secretary answered.

"Give me your advertising office," Yola said briskly. Then: "I'm Yola Centers. You know—the Matrans series? You expressed interest in an option, but there was some fuss about the subsidiaries. Well, I'm ready to—"

There was a momentary consultation at the other end. "We're sorry," the Supervolt office said. "We are not engaging in advertising appropriate to your talents at the present time."

"Bleep!" Yola swore, and called another. "Mannequin Androids? I'm Yola Centers, and last time we talked—"

The android looked pained. "We regret—"

Three more calls brought similar results. Yola snapped her fingers as the screen faded on the last. "Bleep! I should have known! It's the blacklist!"

"You can't ever really win against Big Industry," Fisk agreed. "General Transport was stupid to offer us something to fight and refute. As soon as the libel suit got sticky, they dropped that tactic—but that hardly means they are really sorry or that they have any intention of changing their ways. The other companies are no different. They all reflect the contemporary mores, and improvement will be excruciatingly slow in coming. None of these outfits appreciate goats in the sheepfold. So they will never give the true reason, because there are stringent regulations against blacklisting—as there are against libel, monopolistic collusion, and all the rest—but your career as an actress is finished. I'm sorry."

"We oughta sue!" she muttered, going to the fooder.

"We can't. Not on the blacklisting, because it's impossible to prove even though everyone in commercial advertising knows the score. No artist will dare testify, either, because he would be blacklisted too. But my complaint remains at IPC—and by and by that will have its effect. Some year better policing will come, and the practices of commercial advertising will improve—and we will know we helped it happen."

"Come off it, Frisky," she said, taking out her entree. "You're just relieved to get me out of acting."

"Well, a daughter *is* better than a prima donna," he agreed. "Unless you grew up to be like Maxima Bubonik. . . ."

Then he ducked, but she had anticipated him. The double-decker chocolate-nut whipped-custard sandwich hit him cornerwise on the nose.

One of America's most popular storytellers,
Piers Anthony presents
his most brilliantly imaginative adventure . . .

KILLOBYTE

When a policeman is critically injured in the
line of duty, he takes refuge in a virtual
reality computer game. But the game becomes
as deadly as real life . . .

*Here is a thrilling excerpt
from this exciting new novel—
available in hardcover
from G. P. Putnam's Sons . . .*

CHAPTER
1

NOVICE

"**D**raw, tenderfoot, or I'll plug you where you stand!"

Walter Toland blinked. There before him stood a gunslinger straight out of false western American history: broad cowboy hat, leg chaps, low-slung holster and all. The man's right hand hovered near his six-shooter. Could he be serious?

"Look, mister," Walter started. "I don't know what you think you're—"

The man's hand dived for his weapon. He *was* serious! Walter threw himself to the side, behind a barrel of nails.

The gun fired. Glass shattered behind Walter. He scrambled on hands and knees, trying to get away from the vicinity without exposing himself.

"You lily-livered coward!" the gunslinger shouted. "I'll rout you out and lay you away! Stand up and fight like a man!" The gun boomed again, and there was the thunk of a bullet hitting the barrel.

Walter cowered behind the barrels. But there were only three of them, and nothing beyond. They hid him, but he was trapped. What could he do?

"So you want it in the ass!" the gunslinger said, his voice rich with contempt. There was the sound of his footsteps crunching the dirt as he approached the barrels.

And that was just about where he'd get it, too, Walter realized, because the man was coming toward his rear. Frantically he cast about.

Then he discovered that he too was in cowboy dress—and there was a gun at his hip!

"All right, you sniveling snake!" the gunslinger said as his shadow fell beside the barrels. "You're done for."

Walter yanked his gun out of his holster and pointed it at the shadow. Then the body of the man appeared.

Walter pulled the trigger. The gun fired. It bucked in his hand, and smoke puffed from its muzzle.

The gunslinger stiffened. Daylight showed through a hole in his belly. He fell forward.

Walter scrambled out of the way, so as not to be pinned under the man. He didn't quite make it; the gunslinger's head struck his foot. It was curiously light.

In fact it wasn't a head at all. It was cardboard, flat and blank on back. The whole man was cardboard!

A sign appeared in the air about six feet away. Walter stared at it for the moment not comprehending its nature or message.

```
PLAYER: Walter Toland

LEVEL: Novice

SCORE: 1      OPTIONS
```

Then it registered. He was a player in a game! A computer game. He had finally gotten the equipment to enter the most sophisticated class of games, the ones that put the whole person in, in effect. The helmet, the gloves, the special connections—it had happened so suddenly and completely and compellingly that for the moment he had forgotten the reality and just lived the scene.

And what a scene it had been! It had seemed completely real, as if he had been physically dumped in this little western set and made to fend for himself. Sink or swim.

What would have happened if the gunslinger had plugged him? Then he would have been out of the scene, with a score of 0. A real humiliation for one who had once been pretty sharp on the primitive computer games, the kind where things danced on the screen and had to be shot down before they got too close. Or where things had to be collected to use to penetrate to the finish. But that had been before the accident.

He shut that out and studied the sign. It identified him as the player. Fine. His level was Novice. Okay, fair enough; this was a new game to him, and he was just starting. And his score was 1.

That must be one kill. But what were the options? How did he invoke them?

Then the sign faded out, leaving only the scene. Walter got up, dusted himself off, holstered his gun, then lifted the cardboard. It was a mock figure, painted on the front with the clothing, gun, and menacing face. There was a hole in the right side of its abdomen, where his bullet had torn through.

Walter shook his head. How could he have been fooled by that? A cardboard cutout! Yet it had spoken to him, challenged him, and advanced on him. It had shot at him, too! There was the broken glass of the store window, and there was the slug in the side of the keg of nails. Those had been real bullets, not cardboard ones.

That reminded him of his own weapon. The gunslinger's gun was now cardboard, but his own was not. He drew it again and looked at it. It was a solid six-shooter, probably of authentic design; he knew modern guns, but was no expert in ancient ones. Whoever had crafted this game could readily have done the necessary research. So this much, at least, was probably real. Within the framework of the game.

Something else bothered him. Since when did a bullet in the gut kill instantly? If that man had been alive, he would not have died; he would have staggered back in agony. So this was a game thing too: any score on the torso was fatal, by definition. It didn't have to be through the heart. Novice-level marksmanship.

He reholstered the gun, set the cardboard figure down, and walked across the street. The far side turned out to be a painted backdrop: tavern, horse hitches, and scenery. Even the sun: a bright yellow disk against the blue background. He touched it, and it was room temperature. Absolutely unreal.

Then what had cast the shadow, when the gunslinger had approached the barrels?

He walked back to where he had started. Behind the broken window was a dark wall; there was no chamber there. Now he saw that directly behind his original location was a door. The store was a façade of wood and glass, but the door was real. It was in a sturdy frame, and it had a brass knob. He must have stepped through it to enter this scene, though he didn't remember doing it.

So was this also the way to leave the scene? In which case, would he be out of the game with a low score? He wasn't ready to quit, yet. It was obvious that he had a lot to learn about this game, and already he was feeling the fascination of it. It was a lot more intriguing than his outside reality.

So if he didn't use the door, how should he move on? There had to be a way to encounter new challenges and rack up higher scores. But he couldn't do it against cardboard figures.

He walked down the street to the left of his original stance. It ended twenty feet along, in another painted backdrop: a picture of a street continuing through the town.

He tried the other direction, which he thought of as south. This ended similarly, twenty feet away, in a painting of a few more houses and then the open country beyond town.

He was in a chamber about forty feet long and twenty feet across. He was unable to touch the top, but ten feet seemed reasonable. Wait, he could check it. He took a nail from the keg and threw it up into the sky. It struck almost immediately, scratching the paint of a white cloud. Ten feet had been a good guess.

So it seemed that there was nothing more to do here. Unless he wanted to smash down the scenery, he would have to use the door. He had made his score, and this scene was done.

Still, he did not quite trust that door. It might be a decoy, or the exit for a quitter. Like the escape key on a computer keyboard: hit it when you're in over your head and just want to get out. The challenge was to figure out how to control his destiny within the game. How to get into the next scene.

He walked across the street again and put his hands on the painting of the tavern. He tried to shove it to one side or the other, but it didn't give.

He went to the kegs of nails and tried to lift one. It was either too heavy to budge, or bolted to the ground. He tried to twist it, as if it were a big knob, but that didn't work either. So he started taking out the nails, in case there could be something useful hiding among them. But the nails turned out to be only an inch deep; they were another kind of façade. Below was just a panel, painted with more nails.

This was curious. Why hadn't the kegs become cardboard too? Since this was all a game set, it should have been easy to do that. The nails must have been left in their "real" state deliberately. So that a novice like him could use them to throw at the ceiling and scratch the cloud? That didn't seem sufficient.

What else offered? There had to be something. Some devious key to the next step. If he could only find it. He cursed himself for being rusty on games. It was probably obvious; he just didn't have the right mind-set. He didn't see the simple way out of the locked chamber.

Then he heard something. The ground was shuddering. He looked around—and there in the distance, where the street left the town and wandered into the prairie, were shapes. Big ones. Many of them.

In fact those were cattle—and they were stampeding. Already they were funneling into the town and thundering down the street, directly toward him. A cloud of dust was roiling up behind them. He had to get out of the way or he would be trampled in seconds.

Trampled? By animals in a picture?

But the gunslinger had fired real bullets at him.

Those cattle looked excruciatingly real. So did the setting, at the moment. In fact the cutout of the gunslinger now looked like a body—and there was a pool of blood beside it. He heard music from the tavern across the street.

He took another nail and threw it at the sky. It flew high, arcing well below the cloud, and landed in the street. The bright sun cast shadows.

The set had come alive again.

The first steer outdistanced his companions and
bore down on Walter. The thing looked dangerously
real. The hide was flecked with dust and foam, and
gouts of dust leaped from the striking hooves.

Walter drew his gun and aimed at the animal. But
he hesitated. That was merely the first of dozens of
steers, and he had only five bullets left. Or so he
hoped; he hadn't checked the remaining chambers
of his six-gun. Even if any hit on the body instantly
felled the animal, five was all he could take out
before he got trampled. The gun could not save
him, this time.

Meanwhile the creature was looming frightening-
ly close and large. It was a juggernaut. A picture?
No way! This was real.

Walter dived for the door. He felt the wind stirred
by the first animal as he grabbed the knob and
turned. He yanked; the door opened; he threw
himself through.

As he left the scene, he thought of something,
too late. He could have taken those loose nails and
scattered them across the street. Or maybe driven
them through boards and set them out with their
points projecting upward. That well might have
stopped the stampede. Maybe such a ploy wouldn't
work well in real life, but he suspected that by game
rules it would. It explained why the nails had been
left solid in an otherwise painted scene: to allow
the player to prepare for the next challenge.

He was in the next scene. It was a jungle. Literally. The air was dark and steamy, and the
trunks of tall trees were shrouded by clinging
vines.

There was a growl. Walter looked—and there was a tiger crouching as it oriented on him.

He whirled, lurching back through the doorway. But there was no doorway there. Only a solid tree. He could not retreat. Once he had used the door, he had committed himself irrevocably, it seemed. Unless he had thought to do something like jamming a nail into the crack to stop the door from closing behind him.

The tiger pounced. Walter hurled himself to the side, as he had before when attacked by the gunman. The tiger landed where he had been, snarled, and turned, reorienting. The thing was massive, and certainly capable of killing him.

Walter grabbed for his six-shooter. But now it was a snub-nosed rifle. He wrenched up the muzzle as the tiger sprang again, and fired.

The tiger screamed with pain and dropped to the ground. The landing was light: it was a paper tiger, literally. With a hole through one shoulder.

The sign appeared:

```
PLAYER: Walter Toland

LEVEL: Novice

SCORE: 2      OPTIONS
```

No big surprise there; he had scored again. He was still a novice, and still didn't know how to invoke the options. He had ascertained that the door did not lead out of the game, but to the next setting. And that the scene turned unreal when the action was done. And real again when more action came. He had had about ten minutes between actions, so wasn't unduly rushed, but when an action did start, he had to act within seconds. The rules were coming clear. It seemed like a well-designed game.

He got up and inspected the new setting. The trees turned out to be cardboard mockups, the vines painted on them. The tree behind him was painted on a wall—and there was now a door in it. Yet all of it had seemed real before the kill. Surely it had been real, in the context of the game. For the game could do that. It could animate its settings and creatures, making them almost as tangible as reality. That was the appeal of this class of game. Its realism. What was known as virtual reality.

Walter's living body was sitting in a wheelchair, with a sophisticated helmet on its head. Goggles and earphones connected to it, providing three-dimensional sight and sound, and wires were attached to skin patches at strategic locations. There was even limited odor emitted from a noseplug. Gloves and boots picked up the attempted motions of the extremities, so that his game body moved as he willed it to. It was, literally, like stepping into another world.

It had taken him a long time to arrange this, because this class of equipment was expensive. In the interim whole new classes of computer games had evolved, prospered, and faded back into relative oblivion. It didn't matter; they remained the most popular genre available. Because they represented vicarious experience which was so close to direct experience that the distinction blurred. He had heard that there were sex programs that some claimed were better than the real thing.

But sex was not his object, here. Sex was gone from his life. He wanted diversion. So his first game was a hard-hitting adventure. He hadn't even bothered to read the instruction manual; those things were always way too big and obscure to make much sense. It was more fun just to wade in and learn by doing.

So he had ten minutes before another challenge came for him, in this jungle setting. He intended to use it, because he didn't want to take the easy route, door to door. He wanted to discover the more devious aspects of the program. Because this was the one game he had for rental, this week, and he wanted to make the most of it.

He lifted the paper tiger and used it to prod the ceiling. Still ten feet. He felt the walls on all sides. Still a twenty-by-forty-foot chamber, though the painted walls made it look larger. It would have been nice to check it while the full animation was on, to see whether then he could really travel miles through it. It seemed impossible, yet this was not reality, but an emulation that approximated a chosen situation. So the game could make a jungle seem to extend for miles, if it was programmed to— and perhaps it was. He wanted to find out how to explore the parts of the jungle that the makers of the game didn't intend players to reach. Maybe he could do that, if he could just find the way to extend the setting while it was in its "real" phase.

He found a number of sticks on the ground, and realized that these must have been fallen branches when it was animate. Was there a reason for them to be here? Just as those loose nails in the top of the keg, in the western scene, might have been used to stop the stampeding cattle? Maybe these sticks had something to do with the next challenge.

He picked one up and hefted it. It was actually a fairly solid length, possibly serviceable as an aid to hiking, about six feet long. Others were shorter, but thicker. He also saw several lengths of cord strewn across the mock trees; probably those were vines during animation. Not much use at the moment, though.

Something changed. The trees became real, and the cord did indeed become vine. The set was coming alive again! Sooner than the other one had, unless his perception of time was distorted.

There was a rustle. He looked, and saw a snake. A big one. A python, slithering toward him. No doubt of it: the next challenge was starting.

He backed away from the creature—only to realize that one of the cords had become a serpent in a tree, now lifting its head to strike at him. He ducked, avoiding it, but more were appearing on the ground. He recognized rattlesnakes, water moccasins, and what were probably exotic pit vipers. If any of them bit him, he would be dead, and out of the game.

Walter still held the stick, which was now a black staff. He used it to fend off an advancing cobra.

He had to get out of here. But he had foolishly allowed himself to be caught away from the door.

The space between him and it was filling almost solidly with a river of snakes. All of them surely poisonous.

A tiny snake tried to score on his toe. Walter knocked it on the head, and it hissed and fell back. What had it been, during the null period? A piece of string? If he had gathered up that string and tied it in a knot, could he have stopped the snakes before they got started? He had foolishly frittered away his time, and now was in trouble.

Three more snakes slithered purposefully toward him. He knocked them back with the staff. But there were too many; soon they would overwhelm him. He was sure that just one bite would wipe him out, by the rules of the game. But how could he reach the door without stepping on the myriads of snakes which now blocked the way?

There was rustling behind him, and to the sides. Then Walter got a notion. He pointed the staff ahead, took two running steps, and jammed the staff into the ground, heedless of what it might land on. He heaved himself up in a crude pole vault, passing over the massed snakes. He crashed into the door, scrambled to wrench it open, and fell through to whatever lay beyond.

He found himself in a car, speeding at about a hundred miles an hour. He had no idea where it was going.

Then a brick wall loomed ahead. He was on a dead-end drive. He stepped on the brakes—and his foot plunged to the floor. The brakes were gone!

But the wall did not extend beyond the pavement. He could veer off the road, crash through the wooden barriers, and roll to a stop. He turned the wheel.

The wheel spun in his hand. The steering was also out. This car had really been pied.

But Walter had been in trouble before on the highway, and his reflexes were fast. He used the clutch and jammed the gearshift into low. Thank God racing cars didn't use automatic shift! The low gear made the motor drag on the wheels, and the car slowed. But not enough; he would still hit the wall. So he grabbed for the handbrake, and that slowed the vehicle further. He did reach the wall, but only nudged it.

The seat collapsed under him. The cardboard could not sustain his weight. Then the sign appeared: SCORE: 3. He had gotten through another challenge.

He pushed aside the cardboard side of the car as the sign faded, and climbed to his feet outside. The wall was the only solid part of this set, and now he saw the door in it: his entry to the next scene. But again he didn't take it; he wanted to explore while he could, to see what other avenues offered.

He was in another chamber, of course, with the scenery all around painted on, including the blue sky above. There was no way out except the door. Maybe this was a straight-line game, with no real choices along the way. If so, it wasn't much. The effects were marvelous, and he loved having the full use of his body, instead of being confined to his wheelchair. But largely mindless adventure would not entertain him long. He remembered the three or four types of conflict, from a long-ago class on literature: man against nature, man against man, man against society. And maybe man against himself. This was really man against nature, even when it was against a man, because the gunslinger had been programmed for attack, not interaction. The car had been much the same as a beast; riding a tiger would have been similar. So this was pretty simple stuff, and pretty readily handled. The right reflexes were all that was required.

So what would the next challenge be here? Not a speeding car, because the only way it could threaten him was to try to squish him against the wall, and it would smash itself in the process. Even if it tried, he could simply step off the road to the side, avoiding it. In any event, he still had several minutes to prepare.

He checked the painted chamber, but it was tight. If there were secret buttons to push, he didn't find them. He went through the cardboard car, but there was nothing special there either. That was an interesting device, turning things to cardboard once the challenge was done. But the novelty of it was already wearing thin. The computer could do whatever it wanted, and realism was as easy to program as artificiality, with the equipment available. Which suggested indifferent programming. He hoped that this wasn't the limit of what the game had to offer.

Because Walter was looking for high-powered diversion. He had what amounted to no life at all, in the real world. His legs had dwindled to ugly sticks; he kept them constantly covered not for warmth but for shame. Once he had been athletic. Now he couldn't walk at all, and even sitting up would have been a pain except for his intricate harness. The doctor, with an attempt at humor that hadn't been effective, had informed him that they had patched up the lower half of his body so that it worked, but not to put any weight on it. So a game like this was the only place he could move normally. He could walk, here, because the boots picked up the feeble efforts of his legs to move, and translated them to directions for the game-figure legs. Obviously his game figure didn't have to do much balancing, because it remained erect without his effort. That was nice.

But what was the point of poking around a closed painted chamber? As virtual reality went, this was a virtual prison.

There was a honk in the distance. Walter looked, and saw that his own car was now alive again: metal instead of cardboard. The next threat was coming already! It had hardly been five minutes.

In the distance a shape loomed, growing rapidly larger. It was a semitrailer truck. It was so massive, and coming with such velocity, that it was evident it would not be able to stop if it wanted to. It would smash him and his car and the wall, and hurtle on through regardless. So much for his notion of safety.

He ran to the side, and banged into the painted wall. He had forgotten that the scenery wasn't real. He couldn't step off the road—and now he saw that the truck filled the entire space. He could not avoid it. The damned set was coming only partly alive:

the part that would kill him.

He dived for the door. As he wrenched it open, he realized that he had missed a bet: he could have thrown himself to the pavement in the center, and let the truck pass over him. There had to be enough clearance, in a vehicle that size. He could have bested it.

But he was already passing through the door. He saw the grille of the truck looming close.

Then he was in a square roped enclosure. He was wearing sneakers and white shorts. Big soft padded gloves were on his hands. Boxing gloves.

Uh-oh. He caught his balance and peered ahead. Just in time to see the other boxer closing in on him. The one in black shorts.

The other threw a roundhouse-right punch. Walter wanted to duck, but didn't have the time. He wanted to draw back, but his inertia was wrong. So he did the only thing he could: he threw himself forward, into the other boxer. A clinch was the first refuge of the incompetent. He wrapped his arms around the man and hung on.

"Get off me, jerk!" the man sputtered. "Stand up and fight like a man."

But Walter knew that if he did that, he would get knocked down or out. Because he had discovered in the course of his job training that he was not cut out to be a boxer. He had learned how to duck a punch, and that was his most effective ploy. What he didn't know about this sport would fill an encyclopedia.

"One. Two. Three. Four." There was no visible referee, but Walter heard the count, and knew that he had better stop clinching in a hurry, or be penalized. So he broke and staggered back, holding his arms up to try to protect his head and upper torso.

It wasn't much good. The other boxer was boring in, battering his shoulders and sides. Walter didn't feel pain, exactly, but he did feel the impacts, and knew he couldn't protect himself long. Each time the other scored on his arm, the arm dropped a bit lower, and Walter couldn't bring it up again. It seemed that the game had ways of forcing the issue. His face would soon be open to attack.

So defense was no proper ploy. He had to take the offense. Even if he wasn't any good at it.

He aimed a right at the other man's face. But the man simply moved aside, then caught him on the ribs with a solid counterpunch. Walter realized that he had laid himself open, and it had been an elementary matter to capitalize on it.

But maybe he could use his brain. The other man was a figment of the game program. He would probably react the same way to the same situation.

So Walter set himself and aimed the same punch again. But this time he was planning on counterpunching the counterpunch. He swung, the other countered and scored on the ribs again—and Walter let fly at the man's face with all the power his left fist could muster.

He scored. His white glove flattened the man's nose and rocked his head back. The man fell—and it was a cardboard cutout that landed on the floor.

In life a single punch would have been unlikely to end the fight, but this was the game.

The sign appeared: SCORE: 4. OPTIONS.

Suddenly Walter got a notion. He poked a finger at the sign, the cardboard glove sloughing off. He touched OPTIONS.

The sign changed. Now it read:

```
NOVICE OPTIONS:

HELP

FORMAT

REPLAY

QUIT
```

Walter feared that the sign would disappear in five seconds, as before, so he quickly touched the FORMAT option.

The screen changed again. Now it offered him three of what it considered to be formatting options: VELOCITY, SUBSTANCE, and BOX. What did those mean? Again, he was afraid to wait, so he touched BOX.

New words appeared: SIZE LOCATION DURATION ITEMS.

Aha! It was referring to the information box. Since he wanted time to consider, he touched DURATION.

The new words were what he wanted. DURATION: SECONDS 0-60 MINUTES 1-10

PERMANENT DEFAULT 5 SECONDS.

So he had noted. He touched PERMANENT.

The prior information appeared. This time he touched SIZE. This enabled him to make the box smaller, so it wouldn't obscure his view of the action. LOCATION let him move it to a corner of the chamber. ITEMS let him specify what he wanted it to cover, of the choices he had already seen. He decided to leave that alone for the time being.

But now the next challenge was upon him, only about two minutes after the boxer. The game was squeezing him harder, and it seemed that postponement was not one of his options. Unless VELOCITY covered it. But right now he had to focus on the threat.

This turned out to be a martial artist in a white jacket and trousers, tied with a black belt. Karate, probably. Walter knew just enough about it to know that black was the master level. He didn't want to mess with this man!

The man faced him and made a little bow with his head, not taking his eyes off Walter. Walter turned around and found the door he knew would be there. He turned the handle and stepped through.

He was high up on a chilly mountain. He was in mountain-climbing gear, with spiked boots and heavy gloves. A rope was anchored to a heavy harness around his body, the other end connected to a piton just above him. His fingers were clinging to a tiny ledge. Below him the mountain sloped steeply, until it converted into a vertical drop-off. He was evidently making his laborious way across

one of the bad spots, inching toward a larger ledge
that would allow him to walk, carefully.

A stiff gust of wind tugged at his body. The
fingerhold ledge gave way, and that jogged his
boots loose. Walter slid abruptly down the face of
the mountain, his horror making the slide seem
slower than it was.

Then the safety rope went taut. He hung there,
just above the drop-off, scrambling for purchase.
His heart was thudding in his ears. This was almost
too much realism!

He felt a vibration in the rope. He looked up—
and saw that the anchor piton was starting to give
way. It wasn't quite tight, and was nudging down.
In a moment his weight would pull it out of the
rock, and that would be all.

Walter looked wildly around. There was no other
person near. The rock within reach was a flat face,
offering no purchase at all. All he could do was
watch the piton slowly change position.

Maybe he could hammer in another piton! He
felt around his body, but found only a hammer. If
he had any other pitons, he couldn't find them in
the few seconds he had.

Then he had a better notion. He braced his feet
against the steeply slanting rock, closed his gloved
hands about the rope, and walked himself up the
face. The effort was easier than it would have been
in life, as the game responded to the muscular
twitches of his real body. In a moment he was up
within reach of the piton.

He drew his hammer, set himself, and pounded
the piton back into the rock. In a moment it was

firm again, and he was in no danger of falling. Now he had only to find new handholds, so that he could complete his traverse and put his feet on the ledge ahead.

But there turned out to be no need. The mountain became cardboard, and the box in the corner said SCORE: 5.

It now appeared that the drop-off was only the painted floor. It had certainly looked realistic a moment ago! And where had that wind come from?

Walter made his way to the ledge and sat on it. He couldn't follow it on around the mountain, because that too was a painted scene. So he reached for the score box and touched OPTIONS. He might as well make use of his time to learn anything that might improve his chances in the next challenge.

He didn't want to quit yet, and he certainly didn't want to replay that wild swing above the abyss. That left HELP and FORMAT. He didn't want to ask for help yet either; that seemed too much like cheating. So he touched FORMAT, and then VELOCITY.

It turned out that he could indeed adjust the time between challenges. He could make the second challenge in a setting come immediately, or he could delay it the maximum: ten minutes. The default was ten minutes for the first challenge, eight for the second, and so on down to two for the fifth. So he hadn't been imagining the shortened time!

Then the mountain shuddered. The abyss below took on the semblance of reality. The second threat was upon him.

Walter looked up. Something was stirring up there. An avalanche was starting! Already the first small stones were plunging past, bouncing off the slope and disappearing beyond the drop-off.

He didn't hesitate. He grabbed for the door in the mountain and wedged himself through before the main part of the avalanche passed.

This time he was in a comfortable waiting room. He looked nervously around, alert for the next threat, but saw none. Instead the opposite wall became a screen.

CONGRATULATIONS, NOVICE! YOU HAVE COMPLETED THE CHALLENGES AND ARE NOW A JOURNEYMAN PLAYER. YOUR NAME HAS BEEN ADDED TO THE ROSTER OF PLAYERS ELIGIBLE FOR THIS LEVEL.

A list of names appeared. There was a considerable number, filling several columns of the screen.

Walter hadn't anticipated this. He had thought this was a stand-alone game, but evidently it was multiple-player, with each computer serving as a separate input. He should have realized that before, because it required a modem: a phone connection to the central game authority. Well, that was all right, though it did seem to make for some crowding.

He looked at the list. He recognized none of the names. His was the last. The next to last was BAAL CURRAN. Funny name! Walter wondered what the man looked like. Not that it mattered, since the player would probably appear in the game in the image the computer dictated, rather than the real one.

WHEN YOU ARE READY TO PLAY, TOUCH YOUR NAME.

Good enough. Walter touched his name.

*   *   *

Note: Call 1-800 HI PIERS as a source for all Piers Anthony's books.